NO REFUGE

NO REFUGE

GREG ELSWOOD

NO REFUGE
ISBN: 9781798859346

Copyright © Greg Elswood 2019

Greg Elswood has asserted his right under the Copyright,
Designs and Patents Act, 1988 to be identified as the author of
this work.

For Elaine and our girls

Inception

The train growled into Euston as Paddy roused himself from his disagreeable slumber. Like the yawning commuters around him, he stretched, then wiped his aching eyes, knowing full well that it would do nothing to ease his extreme exhaustion. He'd endured a long, rough, overnight trip, punctuated by numerous train changes designed to shake off any potential pursuers. Not that Paddy thought he was being followed, it was simply a habit he had developed from years of covert operations. An easy but tiring precaution.

He took out his phone and looked at the message from Donovan, the Brethren's leader and a person of few words:

Get to London Mon morning. Meet Michael @lockup. Delivery Tues.

Michael, his comrade-in-arms, had been lying low for months, awaiting orders, and would be refreshed and ready for the challenge. Lucky man. Paddy picked up his bag and sank to the platform behind the other passengers. He trudged towards the London Underground and joined the teeming mass of humanity, the very people he was sworn to kill in just a few days' time.

1

This was without doubt the best time of the morning. The air was clean, the hordes hadn't yet arrived, and everything was silent.

From his vantage point high above the City, Jacob could see clearly in every direction. The first shafts of light were breaking out over the eastern horizon, creating a kaleidoscope of colour that would lift the spirits of even the most despairing soul, and he breathed in powerfully, eagerly, seeking intoxication. Cold air flooded his lungs, heightening his senses and magnifying every detail of the view. This was it, the best thing in his life, right here in front of him.

Little else moved Jacob so deeply and nothing gave him such a sense of freedom and ascendency as standing here, high above everyone else, beholding in silence a dazzling display he was convinced few others appreciated. But Jacob knew that if he turned, he would lose the euphoria of this moment, as to the west all was in darkness, with brooding clouds settling over London like a shroud. In place of the bright colours of daybreak were the dreary shadows of yesterday, where millions of people slept, oblivious to the spectacle Jacob witnessed. The early morning sunrise and the dawn chorus weren't for them. They would wake to the muted half-light of morning, the drone of traffic and the contemplation of another day's grind, grey suits and sombre skies.

So, Jacob didn't turn. He instead looked down at the decaying photo in his hands, as vivid reds and violets dissolved into the pastel pinks and blues of the morning sky, criss-crossed by pale jet-trails slowly melting away. The fading colours of the two smiling faces in the picture mirrored the waning sunrise, and Jacob supposed that was why he was so drawn to it. Everything was so fragile. He couldn't explain why he had risen so far, so fast, and then suddenly found himself at the bottom of the heap, and he often wondered whether he would make the same choices if he had his time again. Deep down, he suspected he would still end up as he was, standing alone over forty floors up on the roof of Shakespeare Tower.

Just a few minutes more. He tore his gaze away from the snapshot of his wife and daughter and looked back at the eastern sky. He would stay until either the last wisps of colour had disappeared or he was spotted by the tower warden and ordered to leave. It didn't matter which, it was time to move on anyway. Within an hour, the City would be overflowing with people, hungry for power and success, or at least what they considered to be success: money. These weren't Jacob's people, and he wouldn't be sharing in their fortune. Not today, not anymore.

'Time to go,' he murmured.

***

Brandon had always been a bit of a loner, so it was no surprise to find him at the end of a deserted platform at Stratford railway station, leaning against the railing with his laptop open, staring into the distance. Shabby, in old, faded jeans and a baggy hoodie, and facing down the tracks, to the casual observer he looked just like any other trainspotter, waiting to log serial numbers and arrival times into a spreadsheet. A pointless exercise and an anonymous existence, and no one would look twice at the figure at the end of platform eight.

Which was exactly how he wanted it.

But Brandon needn't have worried. At this ungodly hour there were no casual observers, unless you counted the foxes and rodents that he'd watched wander across the tracks since he'd been standing there. He felt a strange kinship with the animals, lurking in the shadows, scavenging for scraps and avoiding the company of others as they carried out their mundane activity. He felt their desolation, their loneliness. Outcasts.

Yet Brandon wasn't your average trainspotter, and his work was anything but mundane. Supremely confident in his abilities, Brandon saw himself on the verge of greatness, rising above the pathetic mediocrity he saw all around him. He had no interest in timetables, freight schedules or the digits printed on the side of the carriages, only the people that rode within them, the early morning commuters on their way into the City. Although they didn't know it, these passengers were part of his dark plan.

For the third time that morning, he checked his laptop for power and saw that it was fully charged. Brandon knew that he was on edge, but he wasn't taking any chances; where technology was concerned, he never did. For today's trial it was particularly important, as his *Proximity* program consumed an inordinate amount of power, and he'd probably need several test-runs to get it right.

This was it. History beckoned, it was his time and he was ready. All it would take was a simple act, then everything would change. He lowered his gaze and looked at the *Proximity* icon, its glowing skull daring him to go on, taunting him, and despite the chill of the early morning air, he felt clammy, sweaty, as he contemplated his first time, the maiden outing of his program. Brandon touched the screen, no more than a gentle caress, and a wave of nausea washed over him. This was the moment of truth and he knew that, if it worked, there would be no turning back.

Immediately two windows appeared on his screen, the first a simple list of drop-down boxes and the second a series of graphs and charts, currently devoid of any data. Brandon moved his fingers over the touchscreen with practised ease, selecting various inputs from the first window for *Proximity's* debut.

First, he chose a low power setting, corresponding to a transmission range of about twenty metres, sufficient to reach the passengers in the final carriage of each train from his position at the end of the platform. That would be fine for this first test, and only when he was ready for the real thing would he extend the range to its maximum setting.

In the next box Brandon selected 'Android' as the target operating system, and in the third he highlighted a pre-prepared short message:

IF YOU FEEL ALONE, CLICK HERE => ⊙

In Brandon's opinion, this was the cleverest part of his program, as it made no difference whether the message's recipient selected the radio button or closed the pop-up box by hitting 'X close' in its top right-hand corner. Either action would result in a viral download, and the virus would be saved in less than a second without interrupting any other applications. The only way to avoid it was to ignore the message completely, which Brandon knew would rarely happen if the device was being used. It would remain on screen for as long as the train stood at the station or in range of his laptop, typically about thirty seconds, but in today's impatient, always-connected world, it was almost unheard of for someone to allow a message like this to sit on screen for half a minute, rather than close it and go back to playing a game or scrolling Facebook messages.

He clicked on the final drop-down box. The virus itself, or as Brandon preferred to call it, the 'bug'. On this occasion he selected the smallest one, designed specifically for today's test, whose sole purpose was to confirm that a gadget had been infected. Compared to most viruses, it was benign. All it did was emit a single message back to *Proximity* to confirm it had been installed, including details of the infected device. Thereafter it snoozed in the background, without interacting with any other applications or software, and Brandon had therefore named it *Sleeper*. Brandon always christened his programs and bugs, as a child would give names to toys or imaginary friends, giving them character, imagining them alive, talking to them and nurturing them as he honed their capabilities. At this stage of its development, Brandon merely wanted to be sure that *Proximity* worked, and he had no intention of risking his project by installing a malicious or larger file that might be detected or arouse suspicion. That would come later.

The East London breeze pulled at the frayed hem of his hood, and Brandon shivered. He was all set, and it was time to select his first prey.

He looked up from his screen and focused on the headlights of a train making its way through Maryland station, less than a mile away. Before he could hear the engine itself, the rails hummed and then whined under the weight of the approaching carriages, and seconds later the train rattled through the points. The front coach rumbled into the station, and the driver in his cab flickered with each passing platform light. The red stop signal reflected in his otherwise blank eyes and he didn't even glance towards Brandon, apparently blind to anything beyond his vacant stare.

Even this early in the day, the first couple of carriages were at least half-full with commuters, many of whom were slumped in their seats catching a few minutes of fitful sleep before the final leg of their journey to Liverpool Street in the City. But as the train slowed, each coach became progressively emptier, and Brandon regretted placing himself at this end of the platform, rather than at the far end where he would have caught the busier front ones.

However, as the train came to a standstill, he was relieved to see that the last carriage was almost fully occupied, with a handful of people standing up at the doors ready to leave the train at Stratford. The perfect target. With a sense of excitement bordering on delirium, he pressed the command button on his laptop.

Unleashed, *Proximity* instantly sprang into life.

Brandon glanced back at the carriage. Many of the disembarking passengers carried smartphones in their hands, some of them hardly looking up from their screens as they stepped off the train and headed towards the Underground. Several of the remaining passengers dozed, but Brandon saw with delight that others held phones up to their faces or looked down at their laps intently, presumably reading, studying their tablets or playing games.

It didn't matter that Brandon couldn't see what they were doing below the window. *Proximity* wasn't limited by line of sight and was capable of infecting any device within scanning range, inside or out. He smiled to himself at this thought and, with the rapt anticipation of a hunter, looked down at his screen to survey the results of his first attack.

The graphs and charts in the second window, his dashboard, recorded the progress of *Proximity*. On the first chart, the bar plotting the number of hits was rising, but its progress was excruciating to Brandon, who had always imagined *Proximity* infecting its targets as a plague of locusts might devour a field of ripe crops; easy pickings for such a virulent and voracious predator. Disappointed, desperate for success, he willed it to speed up.

He then screwed up his face at the sound of alarms that heralded the closing doors and, when the train pulled out of the station to continue its onward journey to Liverpool Street, Brandon was sure that he hadn't given the program enough time.

With trepidation, he gazed back down at his screen, but his anxiety quickly turned to joy when he saw that *Proximity* had made nineteen hits and, of those, a dozen people had dismissed the pop-up message that had appeared on their gadget. He touched the glowing figure twelve on his screen. A new window opened, listing the devices, their serial numbers and confirmation that each was now infected with the *Sleeper* bug.

Brandon was elated; he could barely contain himself. Despite being a naturally shy and reserved person, he would have pumped his fist in the air if it wouldn't have attracted unwanted attention. This outcome far exceeded his expectations, especially for a first attempt. Imagine how successful it would be after a little fine-tuning.

Brandon noted that none of the passengers had selected the button within the pop-up window, the one they were invited to click if they felt alone. He wasn't surprised. It was hardly the sort of thing most people would admit, especially via an unknown and unsolicited link. Brandon thought it ironic that the sad-looking commuters staring longingly at their phones and craving social media contact had decided not to acknowledge their loneliness. Not that he cared. The message itself was irrelevant, other than it should be one that people wanted to remove from their screens as soon as they saw it. As far as he was concerned, the result was the same: his trial had been a success and that was all that mattered.

Flushed with the ecstasy of his first time, he craved more, urgently. Seeing that his battery still had plenty of charge, he decided to stay where he was, to test *Proximity* on a few more trains, challenging its limits and gathering data to feed his programming skills and ingenuity, determined to make his program the best it could be.

He squinted down the tracks in search of his next fix.

Trainspotting? Maybe it's not such a pointless exercise after all.

2

With no fear of heights, Jacob grabbed the cold, hard steel, leaned over the barrier, and looked down over four hundred feet to the terraces and gardens of the Barbican complex below, savouring the simple pleasure of the wind on his face. Yes, it was cold, as it often was up here at this time of day. But feeling cold was a way of life to Jacob, and it didn't dampen his enthusiasm for these trips.

As always when he ventured to the roof of Shakespeare Tower during one of his occasional early-morning excursions, Jacob had climbed the steel ladder to the upper tier. Unlike the lower level, which was enclosed by a concrete wall, the smaller upper deck was surrounded only by railings. With so little separating him from the precipitous edge, he felt free. Alive. Yet in the exhilaration of his precarious perch, he also imagined the thrill of the ground surging towards him, the finality of such a rush, and he sometimes wondered if true freedom lay that way. It seemed so easy, so tempting. But he knew he'd never do it. If he had faith that he'd be reunited with his wife, maybe then. Just maybe...

Jacob roused himself from his reverie and gazed straight ahead. After a final lingering look at the last vestiges of the majestic sunrise, he turned his back on the view and retraced his earlier steps across the roof and down the ladder to the lower tier. He paused at the emergency exit, which he had left an inch ajar on his way onto the roof, and peered through the opening. The corridor was clear, so he widened the gap just enough to sidle through, taking care to step over the wires he had attached to the alarm contacts about six inches above the floor, and ducked to avoid a similar set near the top of the door.

Jacob was well versed in the difficulties of reaching the roof undetected, having previously been discovered several times in nearby Cromwell Tower. He could still remember the warden's nose wrinkling in distaste at his tattered clothes and pungent aroma as he escorted him off the roof. Jacob knew that he'd always be considered an imposter in this wealthy City residence, and it was clear that the building manager in the neighbouring tower was now watching out for him.

But for some reason, Shakespeare Tower was different. The staff were easier to evade and he hadn't been stopped once, and it had crossed Jacob's mind that they knew of his occasional visits but viewed them as harmless and not of any risk to the tower's residents. More likely, though, Jacob had simply become better at avoiding them, learning from his previous escapades and calling on his experiences from past times, memories never far below the surface.

On his way to the rooftop, Jacob had noted the alarm points in the door frame, and had inserted wires, attached to small contacts made of foil, into the tiny gap so expertly that the electric current was maintained when the door opened. Stealth was vital to the success of this mission, and something as simple as a door alarm could easily catch him out, leading to a slow, painful death at the hands of the enemy.

After stepping across the threshold on his way off the roof, Jacob closed the door behind him, muffling the sound by holding his fingers in the gap until the last moment. With the same delicate touch, he removed his improvised electrical circuits and placed them into his trouser pocket. So far so good, although further dangers may still lie ahead. Leaving the building was arguably more difficult than entering, as the later hour meant that more inhabitants would be up and about when he exited. Fortunately for Jacob, people seldom used the stairs, even when going only one floor, which he put down to general laziness and an increasing reliance on technology to do everything. He found it amusing that soldiers and civilians alike would even go to the gym, with the explicit purpose of taking some exercise, yet still use the lifts in their accommodation blocks to travel one or two floors. But he wasn't complaining; it reduced the chances of someone disturbing his escape.

Jacob entered the stairwell and crept down the stairs. He slowed as he approached the first floor, not solely from his breathlessness at the descent, but also because he knew that the building's odd design of having two external entrances, one on each of the first and ground floors, increased the footfall on these few flights. He paused at the door to listen out for approaching footsteps, heard

14

none, and then continued down to the ground floor, his senses highly tuned. This was dangerous territory, where anyone could enter from above or below while he stole between the two busiest levels.

At the ground floor Jacob again paused to listen. Just as he was about to proceed, he heard footsteps hurrying across the tiles towards him. Had he been discovered? Did they know about the mission? Jacob instinctively jumped across to the hinged side of the door, knowing that as it opened into the stairwell it would shield him for a second or two. His grip tightened on his gun and he braced himself. The door flew open.

Jacob caught hold of the handle, preventing the door from springing back immediately, concealing himself from view for a vital few moments, but not before he had seen the tell-tale fatigues of an enemy fighter, bounding up the staircase, two stairs at a time, clearly in a rush. Seconds later, the door to the first floor banged open and the sound of footsteps receded. Jacob closed his eyes briefly and took a deep breath. That had been close. He released the door and let it close naturally, before resuming his descent.

Jacob slipped unnoticed out of the building's lower level door and into the chill of the early morning air. He hastened away before he was discovered and, more importantly, to avoid the blast that would rock the building to its core within minutes.

Mission accomplished.

At basement level, Jacob considered his choice of exits. The quietest route would be through the restricted area, home to storage rooms, generators and other building infrastructure. Even though he thought of the Barbican as an architectural carbuncle, Jacob liked its warren-like structure below ground, a maze of passages and tunnels that at times resembled a gothic horror movie with sinister shadows, forbidding corners and cold, austere brickwork. What it lacked in gargoyles and vampires, it made up for with its ugly countenance and its collection of homeless people that sheltered from London's harsh streets, especially during cold winter nights. Jacob knew all too well about those.

His other option was to leave via the resident exit that provided access to underground car parks, terraces and gardens. Jacob knew that it would be quicker and was probably the safer choice, and following his earlier close shave with discovery he didn't want to take any more chances. The car park it would be.

He peered around the corner and was relieved to see that the parking attendant this morning was Whoopi, so-called because of her striking resemblance to the American actress, and he knew that he'd have no trouble from her. As he turned the corner, she looked up and greeted him in her usual effusive manner, which Jacob assumed she put on to imitate her nickname.

'Oh, my good sweet Jesus. How many times have I told you not to come through here?' She lifted her hands to her wide-open mouth in mock fear. 'You gave me quite a fright!'

Her vibrant smile revealed her true feelings, and Jacob couldn't help but grin back.

'Morning Whoopi. Good to see you too, beautiful.'

He put his grimy fingers to his lips and blew her a kiss, and Whoopi's laugh echoed around the walls and low ceiling.

'Oh, get on with you, Jacob. Next time I'm calling security, see if I don't!'

Once out into the tunnel-like structure of Beech Street, Jacob pondered what to do. Should he seek food at the Refuge or try his luck elsewhere? He was in good spirits after his trip to the top of the tower and Whoopi's infectious gaiety. He didn't feel like dampening his mood just yet by joining his fellow destitutes at the Refuge. The weather was fine and he felt his luck was in, so he turned east, towards the light, to see what he could find.

***

Now that Paddy had arrived, it was time to wake Michael. Short as it was, he could hardly keep his eyes open as he concentrated on his message, and Paddy had to re-read it three times through the fog of his exhaustion before he was happy to hit the send button. But it had to be done now, before he fell asleep standing up.

And so began the road to slaughter, with one simple message:

In London now. Meet this pm. Goods arrive tomorrow.

Paddy took a long, last drag from his cigarette. The smoke filled his lungs, caught in his throat, and he coughed hard. He doubled up, wheezing between each rasping hack, and pain shot through his chest. He ground the cigarette into the ashtray, put his hand to his heart and waited for the episode to pass. Bloody things. He should have packed them up years ago, although it was too damned late for that now.

He slumped back against his pillow. Why had he volunteered for this mission, when there were far younger and fitter men ready to risk everything for the Brethren? But he knew the answer to that question and, despite his discomfort and the hideous, murderous thoughts in his mind, he was asleep in moments, shattered by his overnight journey.

It was not the sleep of the righteous.

***

Jacob often wandered in the direction of Liverpool Street station at this time of day, searching for some of the free food and drink that was regularly handed out to early morning commuters. Promotional chocolate bars, soft drinks or new types of snack were irresistible to anyone living on the streets. Yet they were surprisingly difficult to get hold of. For the homeless.

Jacob's stomach growled at the prospect and he hurried past the gates of the Honourable Artillery Company, a grand building fronted by a large parade ground. Despite his own career in the British Army, Jacob never lingered by the gates or admired the view; it brought back too many painful memories of his darkest times. In any case, as far as Jacob was aware, nowadays it was used for corporate entertainment in the City rather than for any real military purpose, so why would he bother? He had other things on his mind, and right now he needed to keep moving to get to Liverpool Street in time.

It was still well before rush hour, but workers were already arriving at their offices. Up ahead, a suited man held a phone in one hand, a cup of coffee in the other, and didn't look up once as he wandered towards Jacob. An everyday sight, almost everyone seemed to do it. One of the homeless men at the Refuge had nicknamed them 'zombeciles', which Jacob thought an apt description of the imbecilic, almost trance-like vegetative state of their addiction to their screens. *These people are asking to be shoulder-charged.* But, avoiding the confrontation, Jacob dodged the man with a frosty stare as he lurched towards him.

Wilson Street had a tatty, run-down feel that was now largely absent from the rest of the City, and he walked past a shivering girl in the recess of a fire exit. Homeless people regularly camped in doorways along here, wrapped up in their cardboard and newspapers away from the main thoroughfare, or they rummaged through the bins behind the Broadgate complex looking for scraps from the locality's plentiful restaurants and bars. He looked at the girl's frayed gloves and hat, scant protection from the elements, and felt like stopping to help. But he didn't. The chances were that she would shrink away from him or lash out, suspecting he was attacking her for what little she had in her pockets. Anyway, what did he have to offer her? Maybe he would drop her a snack on the way back.

Jacob knew that the young people handing out promotional freebies might see him coming and not give him anything, even though he was clearly in greater need than the well-fed commuters passing through the station, some of whom would grab handfuls of free snacks. He could tell from their apologies that they genuinely felt sorry, and Jacob couldn't blame them for not risking their jobs if they had been told not to serve the homeless, although he didn't understand their justification for refusing him.

But his greater concern was the security guards. They were definitely not apologetic; ill-tempered or hostile would be more accurate descriptions. However, Jacob had learnt that, if he timed it right, he could dash in whilst the promotional stalls were being set up, then walk away with a couple of items in his pockets. That was the plan. A quick in-and-out.

He turned into Eldon Street and was spurred on by the sight of a group of young women, dressed in bright blue tops and black leggings, unloading a van at the station. This was exactly the time when they would be distracted and not paying attention to people walking past their boxes. His mouth watered.

He moved towards them, the covered walkway helping to conceal him from the security guards, while also avoiding the oncoming zombeciles drifting out of the station. He was just yards away when the driver pulled down the shutter at the back of the van and walked round to the cab to drive away, leaving the women to carry the boxes into the station itself. Jacob knew that a few would be left unguarded. This was going to be his lucky day.

However, when he reached the boxes and saw what they contained, his lips cracked dry. There were two sizes, the larger boxes full of bright blue rubber stress balls emblazoned with the words 'Blue Fits Gym', which Jacob found oddly distasteful, if not disturbing. The smaller ones contained flyers printed with details of a new fitness and leisure centre opening around the corner, including an early-bird discount voucher or, as the flyer put it alongside a cartoon of a blue bird, 'Blue Fits Blue Tits'. Jacob imagined what other tawdry comments the rest of the promotional material might contain, and he pitied the young women who were being paid next-to-nothing to hand out this rubbish, probably having to put up with lewd comments and leering stares from some of the commuters arriving at Liverpool Street.

As he shook his head in disgust, Jacob heard loud, coarse laughter close behind him, and he turned to find himself looking down at the hateful smirk of Bill Conran, the most spiteful of the security guards at Broadgate.

'Ha, ha, you old beggar, you should see the look on your face.' Bill edged closer to Jacob, the joy of seeing him squirm clear in his wild eyes. 'You can't eat those balls, although no doubt you've tasted worse!'

Jacob had given up trying to work out Bill's comments or rising to his provocation, so he stepped to one side to walk away without a word.

'Not so fast you low-life, I haven't finished with you yet,' Bill said with a sneer, and moved to block Jacob's escape.

'You think you're so clever coming down here, stealing food intended for hardworking City folk, not layabouts like you. But I saw you coming a mile off. What, did you think I wouldn't spot you? And I smelled you way before that, as you stink today, even more than usual.' He held his nose and glanced at his two cronies lurking a few yards away with a snigger.

Jacob stood several inches taller than Bill and, despite living on the streets, was still a strong man. It would be so easy to push him away. But for all the satisfaction it would give him, Jacob knew that it wasn't worth ending up in a fight he couldn't win, not with Bill's fellow security guards for company. They would take great pleasure in roughing him up with some well-placed kicks and punches, while manhandling him to the estate office. Eventually they'd let him go, but only after further verbal and physical abuse. It just wasn't worth it. Jacob decided to take Bill's insults, right here and now, as the lesser of two evils.

'I'm getting sick and tired of seeing your ugly face around here, and if I see you again there really will be trouble. Do you hear me?' he asked, jabbing Jacob in the chest with a finger. 'Why don't you crawl back under that stone you came from, eh?'

Bill's attention was then drawn to the lycra-clad women from Blue Fits Gym, who had returned to take the remaining boxes to the station concourse. He watched them bending down to pick up the boxes and a lecherous grin crossed his face, but his expression changed to anger when Jacob followed his gaze to see what had distracted him.

'Hey, stop looking at those girls. They're not interested in a filthy, old beggar like you.' He spoke in a low, menacing growl, then suddenly spat on the floor between them.

'You leave them to real men like us.' He swept his hand towards his two colleagues. 'Understood?'

Then, raising his voice so that everyone in the immediate vicinity could hear, he said, 'Now get out of here, and don't let me see you around here again, pestering decent people.' Bill shoved Jacob as hard as he could, and kicked out at him venomously when he stumbled, catching him squarely on the calf and sending him sprawling to the pavement.

It took all of Jacob's willpower not to jump up and punch the odious little man. *Don't do it, he's not worth it.* He seethed quietly on the ground and glared up at his adversary.

Bill looked down at Jacob with smug satisfaction, daring him to retaliate. When Jacob didn't move, he laughed and turned away.

His humiliation complete, Jacob picked himself up, his head bowed in shame that he hadn't fought back. He retreated from the battlefield, comforted only by the fact that he lived to fight another day, but not before overhearing Bill boasting to the young women that he had stopped a tramp from stealing their boxes, no doubt expecting to impress them with his courage in the face of such mortal peril.

However, after a short pause, one of the women responded in a puzzled voice. 'What on earth would he want with our stress balls? Surely that's the last thing a tramp needs.'

Bill had no answer to that.

3

Orla hummed to herself as she cleared up after breakfast, a cheerful melody while she worked, and she looked around the Refuge's small dining area. A few of the usual suspects were still at their tables, dragging out their last spoonful of porridge or sip of tea, but the room was otherwise deserted. Most of the crockery and cutlery had been put on trays and left in the racks against the wall, there was little waste in the scrap bowl, and the people leaving had seemed in good spirits. All the tell-tale signs of a successful meal.

Orla enjoyed working at the Refuge, despite the constant reminders of how miserable life was for some people, as she felt she was helping people in genuine need. She most liked the evening shift, welcoming the homeless as guests to a special place of safety, warmth and kindness, and she never doubted that her volunteering was truly worthwhile. It was etched on the faces of the people who crossed the Refuge's threshold. When she worked the morning shift, she served the same hungry people hot, nourishing food, and who wouldn't find that rewarding?

Orla stopped humming and sighed. But now for the hard part, the inevitable chore that followed breakfast. Soon it would be time to move many of the men and women housed in the Refuge the previous night back onto the streets. She dreaded this part of her work, telling many of their guests that they had to leave the shelter and go back to the streets, whatever the weather. It felt wrong.

Orla knew how the system worked, that it wasn't as heartless as it appeared, and over time she had become used to it. She reminded herself that many of them would go to a safe place for the day or would find accommodation elsewhere. But this didn't dispel all of her doubts. She knew that some of the people they ejected would wander the streets and then seek shelter again tonight, either back at the Refuge itself or another similar haven. But a few might end up in hospital or a street gutter. She shook her head. Surely there must be a better way.

Orla wheeled the full trolley into the kitchen, then picked up a clean pile of trays to carry back into the dining room. Deep in thought, she turned—

Her heart lurched and she reeled back from the figure blocking the doorway. She immediately recognised the woman standing there, but it still took Orla a second or two to catch her breath again.

'My God Maria, what are you doing? You made me jump.' Orla composed herself before continuing. 'I almost dropped these trays.'

Maria looked down at her feet and stepped aside to let Orla through the door with her load.

'I was only coming to say thanks for breakfast,' she said, with a slight tremor in her voice. 'I'm sorry if I startled you.'

'That's OK, Maria, you just surprised me, that's all. I didn't hear you coming.'

Orla put down her trays and touched Maria on the arm. 'I'm glad you had a good breakfast. What are you doing for the rest of the day?'

'I think I'll head down to the Job Centre this morning,' she replied. 'I know they haven't had anything for the past few weeks, but I've got to keep trying. I'm beginning to wonder if I'll ever get a job, or if I'll ever have enough money to move out of here.'

Maria fidgeted with a lock of hair as she searched for the right words. 'I mean, it's nice to stay at the Refuge while I find my feet again, but I don't want to stay here forever. No offence, but you know how it is.'

'Oh, don't worry, I'd think the same in your position. I also hope you'll be able to leave here soon. No offence!' Both women laughed.

'If there's nothing at the Job Centre, I'll try the shops and offices along Commercial Street. They sometimes have signs in the windows for casual work, so I may get lucky.' Maria's smile brightened. 'It's worth a try.'

'Sounds like a good idea, Maria, but mind how you go. Some of those businesses are a bit dodgy and you don't want to get in with the wrong people. Some of them won't pay you much, or even pay you at all.' When Maria's smile faltered, Orla said, 'Just be careful is all I mean.'

'Thanks, I'll be fine. See you again tomorrow.'

Orla watched Maria leave and wondered if she'd been too negative with her. She knew that Maria had had a tough time and that her anxiety sometimes got the better of her, but at least she was being positive about looking for a job. *She'll be fine, stop worrying, she's not a child.*

But Orla soon forgot about Maria. She finished wiping the tables and her mind returned to her final job before going home. Oh, joy of joys.

As it turned out, most of the guests shepherded out of the Refuge by Orla and the other volunteers were in reasonable spirits. Everyone could see that it was bright and dry outside, so very few provided any resistance to being coaxed gently out of the doors.

Another volunteer closed the door behind the last guest. 'Hey Orla, that wasn't too bad this morning, was it?'

'No, it seems to be getting a bit easier.' Orla knew that Kasia found it easier to be firm with the Refuge's residents and was a fan of the system. 'But maybe it's just the weather.'

Kasia stopped to look through the door panes at the people dispersing. 'I think it helps that we know everyone that stays now, and that the council approves all of our overnighters. There's rarely any trouble anymore, at least not compared to what it used to be like.'

'I guess you're right,' Orla said, although she was reluctant to concede the point. 'But don't you think that more people are now staying here who should be housed elsewhere?'

It was hard for the volunteers and staff, who wanted to help the most vulnerable in society, as the vetting process seemed to leave more people on the streets. Orla knew that it made the Refuge a safer place, by reducing the amount of violence, drugs and other abuses in the shelter, so it helped protect people like Maria. But it didn't work for everyone.

'I suppose so,' Kasia said. 'But don't forget Refuge-Eat. Anyone can eat here, even those who aren't allowed to stay overnight.'

Orla nodded. Funded solely through charitable donations, the shelter's management had named the food service 'Refuge-Eat' because they didn't like it being called a soup kitchen. But why pretend? That's what it was, a Dickensian facility of last resort, within a stone's throw of one of the richest places imaginable, the City of London. It fed people like Jacob, who had fallen into homelessness through no apparent fault of his own, but who wasn't able to stay in the shelter overnight because someone had decided that he'd chosen to make himself homeless. But as Orla frequently told people, including other volunteers like Kasia, choice was purely a question of personal perspective.

Orla remembered that she hadn't seen Jacob this morning. She had a soft spot for him and his dignified, intelligent and considerate ways, as did most of the volunteers at the Refuge. Perhaps he had been here but she'd just missed him.

'Kasia, talking of food, did you see Jacob at breakfast this morning? I haven't seen him for a few days.'

'No, sorry, but then he doesn't come every day.'

'That's true, but it just seems to have been a while.'

'I wouldn't worry too much about him, he's used to handling himself.' Kasia stopped and saw the look of concern in Orla's face. 'We'd probably be the first to hear if he was in trouble.'

'Yes, I guess you're right. I was just thinking about him.'

'Ha, don't tell Michael. Isn't he the jealous type?' she said, laughing at her joke.

Orla grinned back and they turned together to the locker room, both relieved to have finished their shifts.

But after she'd said her brief goodbyes to the other volunteers, and stepped through the doors of the Refuge onto the Shoreditch streets, Orla's thoughts returned to Jacob. All of the volunteers had tried to help him over the years, as they did with each of their guests, but even though he faced dangers every day, had been attacked numerous times and had been in plenty of scrapes, he always went back to the streets. Orla knew that Kasia was right, he could look after himself. But she also knew that Jacob was haunted by his past and that he wasn't just homeless, he was restless too, as if running away from something. She thought he'd keep it that way, even if he had somewhere else to stay.

Orla worried that Jacob would eventually die on the cold, harsh, City streets.

***

Brandon was buzzing. He had spent a further hour at Stratford station, pushing *Proximity* to its limits, and it had passed each examination with top marks. He had infiltrated countless devices, from mobiles to tablets, and had increased his range to way beyond the length of one carriage. By sending the program's signal as a train was pulling into the platform, a couple of seconds before it came to a halt, *Sleeper* had infected the mobile phones of people leaving the train, not only those who remained on it. On one occasion, he even saw the screen of a woman's phone turn bright purple right in front of him, the unmistakable sign that his pop-up message had arrived. Within a few steps, she had glanced at her screen and closed the message, and then carried on studying her phone as she walked down the platform, apparently oblivious to what she had just done.

Brandon left the station when his laptop ran out of power, deciding against recharging it and staying longer. That would have taken him into the daylight hours, risking unnecessary enquiry from station staff or prying eyes of interfering commuters. In any case, he had proved that *Proximity* worked, and he was confident that he had devised an instrument capable of inflicting cyber carnage on an unsuspecting public. Next time he would use a much more virulent bug than *Sleeper*, and Brandon shivered at the thought of what that would do.

He jumped onto a City-bound Central Line train, like one of the thousands of commuters who pass through Stratford each morning on their way to work. Lonely and anonymous like many others maybe, but when the train plunged underground and the famous landmarks of the former Olympic Park disappeared from view, Brandon looked around the carriage at the glum faces surrounding him and basked in the triumph of his work, satisfied that he had already completed his day's primary objective.

At Liverpool Street, Brandon bounced along the Underground platform, in stark contrast to the lethargic shuffles and dragging footsteps of others around him. During his short train ride, he had considered rewarding himself by taking the rest of the day off, but the closer he came to the City, the keener he was to get home before the stock market opened. He knew he was addicted to trading, or more accurately, he was hooked on making money from it. What better reward could there be for baptising *Proximity,* than indulging his addiction?

He didn't really need to be at home to trade. He could access everything from his laptop or tablet, but he preferred to do it from his flat where he could display charts, market data and news feeds across several monitors. It still gave him a thrill to sit down in front of his screens each morning, surveying the markets from Sydney to Hong Kong ahead of the open in London and Frankfurt, working out where the best opportunities lay.

Brandon jogged up the steps two at a time. He emerged onto the main station concourse a few yards from where a stall had been set up to announce the opening of a new gym, Blue Fits. He didn't take a second look at the girls in blue tops and black leggings, but headed down the passage that skirted the side of the station towards Exchange Square. From there it was a short walk to his apartment in a converted warehouse north of the station.

But first he needed breakfast, and there was only one place for that: Il Miglior Caffè, his favourite coffee shop.

'Buongiorno, Brandon, my friend,' Gianluca called from behind the counter with a broad grin. 'Good to see you, and of course you are still taking your coffee black? And don't tell me, your usual cookie to take away?'

'Hi Gianluca,' Brandon said. 'Yes, the usual, thanks. But watch out, one of these days I will spoil myself with one of your apple crumbles.'

'That will be the day. When you win the lottery, eh?'

Gianluca had been running the shop ever since Brandon had lived in the area, and probably for a long time before that. But, although they had spoken almost every morning for the past few years and were virtually neighbours, their brief conversations rarely went any further than the weather or the contents of Brandon's orders. Brandon wondered if Gianluca was actually a little shy beneath his typically Italian animation, or perhaps he felt intimidated by Brandon, possibly finding him unusual, even in this modern and enlightened age.

As a reserved person himself, that suited Brandon just fine. The last thing he needed was intrusion into his personal affairs, especially now that he was so close to perfecting *Proximity*. He picked up the paper bag containing his coffee and cookie and stepped back out onto Worship Street.

Brandon had identified the potential of this district a few years ago, at a time when the City seemed to end abruptly in the streets just behind Liverpool Street station. It had always struck him as odd that wealth or value were defined by an artificial line on a map, and he had agreed a bargain price for the leasehold of the whole top floor of what was at the time a ramshackle building, yet just a short walk from the modern, sparkling towers of the City.

Following his shrewd investment, he spent the majority of his spare cash renovating and improving what he now called his 'loft'. He'd believed it was just a matter of time before prices would rocket and he'd make a killing. However, even Brandon wouldn't claim to have forecast the speed at which the area would become a magnet for technology start-ups, venture capitalists and wannabe entrepreneurs, who swarmed into Shoreditch with the aim of making it a leading centre for financial services technology, or 'fintech' as they liked to call it.

Brandon marvelled at how the area had changed. Whole streets had been redeveloped, and he couldn't think of a single building that hadn't been either renovated, remodelled or, in some cases, flattened. What was previously derelict was now inhabited and in demand, and property prices had raced higher, putting them out of reach for all but the richest in society. But, more importantly to Brandon, he now had access to some of the latest and most advanced telecommunications, installed and maintained by people who shared his passion, of making money through technology.

The thought made Brandon smile. It was a world away from his former life and he was determined to make the most of his change in fortunes. *Proximity* was the means.

***

'Hey, wait up Orla.'

Surprised, Orla turned and saw Maria hurrying along the pavement after her.

'Thanks for waiting. I hope I didn't startle you again, but I had to shout. I thought I'd never catch you, you walk so fast,' Maria said, stopping to catch her breath. 'I didn't know you lived up this way.'

'Yes, I've lived in Shoreditch for years. It's really handy for working at the Refuge, as it only takes about ten minutes to walk.' Orla didn't add that she couldn't afford to travel far to a job that didn't pay anything. 'It also helps to be close to the crèche during these horrid Underground strikes.'

Orla shook her head, remembering that the next strike would start this afternoon, this time lasting two days. Several of her colleagues would struggle to get in or out, so she might be a little busier than normal, but at least she could walk to work herself. Everything considered, this district suited her well and she felt a strong affinity with it.

At least she used to think that way, but she wasn't so sure anymore. Things had changed.

They crossed Great Eastern Street and Maria looked into a coffee shop. 'Maybe this place will have some vacancies, as it's only been open a few days hasn't it? Mind you, I'm not sure if I'll fit in here, it's not at all like the café that was here before. I used to pop in sometimes and they'd give me a free cup of tea, but I'm not sure this place would do that.'

She looked at Orla, who gave her an encouraging smile. Maria took a deep breath. 'But I'll see if they need any help, you never know. No need to wait for me, Orla, I know you have to get to work.'

'OK, thanks, if you're sure. Good luck with the job hunting. See you tomorrow.'

Orla watched Maria join the queue of customers, who gazed up at a handwritten chalkboard behind the counter, choosing from a myriad of different teas and coffees at inflated prices. Other customers sat at wooden benches staring at their tablets or laptops. In their uniform of pristine jeans and T-shirts, Maria was right, this was a very different crowd.

Orla walked along what had been poorer, neglected streets barely a few years ago, but which had now been redeveloped after the previous occupants had moved further away from the centre of town. The district had become trendier, almost like an offshoot of the City, and along the way it had lost its original identity. She glanced up at the buildings. In some ways little had changed, as many of them looked the same, other than being cleaned and repaired. But during her daily walks along the same streets, she'd witnessed interiors being completely gutted and rebuilt, kitted out with the conveniences of modern life. Better wiring, plumbing, kitchens and technology, so that behind the facades, everything had changed.

There's nothing wrong with that is there? Isn't it just progress? But Orla wasn't convinced. She couldn't dispel the odd sensations of superficiality that had crept into her walks, and she missed the hubbub and life of the streets that she had known when she first arrived. Where were the people from all those years ago, the genuine, hardworking, salt-of-the-earth types, and the ones like her and Maria, just looking to make ends meet? They were nowhere to be seen.

However, as Orla approached home, the streets became more like the old ones she knew and she relaxed in her familiar neighbourhood. She didn't need to be at the crèche until eleven o'clock and she was looking forward to a long, hot shower. Hopefully Michael had already left for work, because it always took so much longer to do things when he was around.

Orla reached into her bag for her door key, but then through the frosted glass she saw someone else approach from the other side. Her neighbour from across the landing stepped out onto the street.

'Oh, hi Orla, excuse me, sorry, I'm running a bit late,' Jenny said. She was out of breath and sounded a little flustered. 'You're back a little early today, aren't you?'

'Yes, we managed to turf out the inmates quite quickly,' Orla answered, frowning at her own use of the word 'inmates' to describe the Refuge's residents, knowing that's what Jenny usually called them.

Jenny smiled over her shoulder and then hurried away with a cursory wave.

Orla climbed the stairs to the first floor where she shared a flat with Michael. The light was on when she opened the door. Michael must still be home. She pushed the bedroom door open and saw him sitting up bare-chested in bed, hurriedly stubbing out a cigarette, and he looked guiltily in Orla's direction when she stopped in the doorway.

'Michael, what are you doing? You know how much I hate it when you smoke in bed.' She let out an exasperated sigh. 'Shouldn't you be at work by now?'

'No, I thought I'd told you. The job today doesn't start until eleven, so I won't be leaving for another hour or so.'

Michael was relieved that Orla had asked a second question, as it meant he didn't have to explain his smoking. Encouraged, he changed tack.

'But since you're home early, perhaps you could come back to bed for a little while.' He pulled the duvet down over his bare midriff, then patted the creased sheet next to him.

'Oh Michael, you know I don't have time. I need to take a shower, wash my hair and get ready for work. As I'm early I was going to stop by Edna downstairs to see if she needed me to bring anything home for her tonight. She's still not getting out much after her operation. Sorry.'

'Oh, come on Orla, just a few minutes,' Michael pleaded. 'You know you want to really. I can't believe you'd turn me down for Edna—'

'No Michael, I've told you, I don't have time!' Orla turned away, missing the look of surprise on Michael's face, and strode to the bathroom.

She undressed swiftly, threw her clothes into the linen bin and turned on the shower. As it warmed up, she gripped the sides of the basin and studied herself in the mirror. Why was she so angry with Michael? Was it the smoking, his insistence that she should have gone back to bed, or something else? But none of these things were new, and it wasn't like her to get so upset by them.

She did wonder about his work, as she didn't understand what he did, other than it was something to do with computers, apparently some sort of freelance help-desk that he ran with a couple of his friends. She'd never met them, as Michael insisted on keeping his working and personal lives separate. He always had enough money to pay the bills, and Orla knew that she wouldn't have managed as easily on her own, but recently it didn't seem like he was working regular hours. She'd have to ask him about it. But not now. He was probably in a bad mood as she'd turned him down, and no doubt she'd have to be the one to apologise.

Orla stepped into the hot shower. She let the water soak her hair and then stood with her eyes closed, face turned up towards the shower head. Despite the power of the water drumming into her face, she instantly felt more relaxed and stood motionless as she savoured the intimate pleasure of the moment, lost in her thoughts.

'That's so good.' She purred at the caress of the warm water running over her shoulders and down her back.

Suddenly she gasped, then shrieked as a hand slapped her naked stomach. Another cupped her right breast.

'I knew you wanted to really, and this way you won't lose any time,' a familiar voice whispered into her ear, and he pressed himself against her back. 'And you may still have time to see Edna before you leave.'

Orla's eyes were wide with shock and she shivered, despite the heat of the water. How dare he? She wanted to turn around and push Michael out of the shower, kick him and scream in his face that she'd already said 'no' and that she meant it. She was overwhelmed with anger, at Michael's smoking, his lazing in bed and his forcing himself upon her. But that wasn't all. She was suddenly angry with everything else too, with the Refuge, the techies of Shoreditch, Maria, Jacob, everyone, with her life. She didn't know why, she just wanted to yell at them all, starting with Michael.

But Orla was scared. She had heard the scorn in that voice, and had sensed something menacing in his taunt; she wasn't sure what, but it was there, deep down, dark and sinister. She shivered again. Orla didn't know how it would end if she refused Michael, and she wasn't ready to find out.

The water cascaded down her back, no longer a sweet caress but a screaming torrent endured inside and out. Wordlessly, she gave in and let Michael have what he wanted. But she hadn't said 'yes' and she suspected that he didn't know the difference.

4

When Jacob returned to Wilson Street, the young girl beneath the newspapers held a cup of tea, presumably given to her by a passing stranger. She sat hunched in the corner and, despite the steam rising from the drink, the girl shivered hard. It would take more than that to warm her up, but it was better than nothing and, in Jacob's experience, an uncommon occurrence.

Most people walked by homeless people without making eye contact or would shake their heads at the sight of them. If they were lucky. It was not unusual for passers-by to mutter insults, scold or even spit, although the worst was usually reserved for after dark, when there were no witnesses or after the accusers had had a drink. Being ignored was often the best that Jacob experienced, and a cup of tea or a little loose change was a bonus, in a City of big bonuses.

Jacob didn't stop. The early hope of the day standing at the top of Shakespeare Tower had evaporated, and he didn't know which was worse; the emptiness in his stomach, the frigid morning air, or the desolation he felt after his miserable experience with Bill. He sighed and shook his head. Why couldn't he fend for himself better on the streets of London, given his background? He'd suffered far more inhospitable environments during his

Army days, and it saddened him to think how much he had let himself down.

After walking for a few minutes, Jacob suddenly felt exhausted, something that never would have happened before, not even a couple of months ago. He slumped down on the pavement to catch his breath and put his head in his hands. It might just be the lack of food and shelter that made him feel weaker, but he didn't think his apathy was all down to hunger or the cold. He felt low, constantly rejected and despised, almost as though he was a stranger in his own country. How could he have fallen into such a desperate state?

Jacob had been born with many advantages in life: a middle-class upbringing, supportive parents, intelligence and good health. At school he had been one of the popular kids, not because he was the life and soul of every party, but because he was approachable, reliable and always mucked in. He had been good at sport, owing to his natural athleticism, and his classmates seemed to follow him both on and off the playing field. So where did he go wrong?

After passing his exams with some of the best grades in his school, he didn't want to go to university like many of his friends, and he could still remember the words of the school careers adviser.

'Have you considered joining the Army? It will give you valuable training, and you'll learn far more than you would at university; real skills you can use anywhere afterwards. But even better than that, it will be a life full of travel, adventure and unimaginable experiences.'

They had been so right, but not in the way they had meant.

Jacob thought he'd be sent to Iraq after his initial training, coinciding as it did with the invasion of Kuwait, but instead received his orders for Northern Ireland. Ulster was a tough baptism to active duty, and even today Jacob found it hard to describe the atmosphere of fear and raw tension to anyone who hadn't lived through it. But he progressed rapidly and soon took charge of his own section. His fellow soldiers liked him, he commanded respect and he was unquestionably loyal to everyone who served with him. At the time, that had seemed so important. However, when he looked back now, Jacob would have swapped his progression and the admiration of his colleagues for the life of any one of the men he had lost, their names and faces indelibly carved in his memory.

But no matter how difficult Northern Ireland had been, he was ill-prepared for what followed during his subsequent postings in Bosnia, Kosovo and Iraq. Unimaginable horrors and unspeakable atrocities. In contrast to his time in Northern Ireland, Jacob remembered little about his time in Pristina or Basra, but whenever he closed his eyes the terror deep inside him stirred, and when he slept the demons clawed at his tortured soul. The word 'nightmare' cannot do it justice.

It was time to move on. Jacob rolled onto all fours, took a couple of deep breaths, then pushed himself upright with a little stagger. Suddenly, seemingly out of nowhere, a cyclist moving at pace swerved to avoid him. He pulled up sharply a few yards away and swivelled in his saddle.

'Watch where you're going, arsehole.' He glared wide-eyed at Jacob. 'Go and get yourself a job and do something worthwhile. Bloody layabout.'

Jacob knew better than to provoke him further, so he simply watched him bridle. Sure enough, when Jacob didn't respond, the cyclist dismissed Jacob with an aggressive wave of his hand. 'Waster!' he said, and cycled off.

Roused from his malaise by the brief confrontation, Jacob turned and continued his walk beyond the edge of the City. A couple of years ago, he would have found an empty building on these streets where he could pass some of the day. Countless places had afforded shelter to homeless people over the years, but they had now been converted into apartments, offices or shops. Jacob didn't resent the change; it just meant that he had to walk further to find shelter.

The exception was the Refuge, where the owners had so far resisted the temptation to sell up. Jacob wondered why. Maybe it was their social conscience, or perhaps they were just holding out for more money later. Whatever the reason, he was relieved to have a familiar place to visit when in desperate need, staffed by good people. Jacob knew that he was visiting the shelter more frequently of late and, as much as he hated himself for taking its charity, he was resigned to the fact that the Refuge was now part of his life.

Once beyond Old Street, Jacob made his way along back lanes and alleys that he had come to know well over the years and headed for one of the small gardens between the housing blocks, where he could stop to rest for a short while. He wouldn't stay anywhere in the open for long, as even in this neighbourhood he would be a sitting duck for locals wanting to have a go at someone. Abuse was waiting for him everywhere, not only in the City.

He stopped on a bench next to a public tennis court, partially hidden from the street by trees and bushes. The bench was covered in graffiti, some of it etched into the wood, and one of the rails was broken. Amongst the debris underneath, Jacob could see needles, condoms and other detritus of local life, but he didn't care. It was somewhere to rest for a while. The morning sun was strengthening, and now shone brightly between the trees and warmed his skin. He sat back and looked up into the sky.

A few people wandered past without saying a word or even looking at Jacob, on their way to work, nursery or school. He felt their disgust, suspicion and fear, even if they didn't look straight at him, and he closed his eyes. It wasn't just tiredness, or the comforting glow of the dappled sunlight on his eyelids. He had learned that closing his eyes helped block out thoughts of the passers-by, and it probably helped them too, to think that he hadn't seen them.

Peace and quiet, if only for a few minutes.

***

Brandon entered his code into the key pad by the door. Other than a fresh coat of paint, the front of the building looked almost the same as the day he had moved in, but inside it was unrecognisable. For one thing, all of the floors were now occupied.

The ground and first floors were let to a private investment fund, recently established by a well-known dotcom tycoon who was using her personal wealth to incubate start-up companies, particularly those developing unique or highly specialised technology. The redesigned space included large, open-plan rooms of whitewashed walls, benches and break-out areas, alive with people either intensely studying screens or huddled in small groups on bean bags and low sofas. It was the type of building where pipes and air-conditioning units hung from the ceilings, promoting a feeling of relaxed indifference to the office environment, despite the high-tech nature of the discussions that took place beneath them.

However, below ground, the feigned informality gave way to a state-of-the-art conference auditorium and presentation suite. When Brandon had first seen it, he thought he'd walked into a science fiction movie set. Modern lines, smooth, charcoal walls and soft corners replaced the exposed pipes and white glare of the upper floors, and the quiet hum of the hidden technology created an atmosphere of perpetual hushed tones and whispers.

The second and third floors housed smart, modern apartments, rented to the well-heeled of the City. Brandon hardly ever saw the occupants other than the occasional chance encounter in the lift, and he didn't think the apartments were used as anything other than an occasional weekday bolt-hole, by people who spent most of their time in business hotels or at their other homes. It seemed a bit of a waste, but who was he to tell others how to spend their money, given some of his own choices?

At the fourth floor, the lift doors slid open and Brandon stepped out into the small vestibule. He placed his key fob to the reader and typed a four-digit pass code, and the apartment door opened to the sound of a short, soft beep. He closed it behind him, took three strides forward and then stepped down the single stair into the apartment. He was home.

The entire fourth floor of the building was Brandon's and, following his extensive renovations since buying it, he loved the place. The first change he had made after moving in was to replace the former set of steel-framed windows with enormous floor-to-ceiling panes, so that light flooded into the large, modern, open-plan living area. It had been a wonderful decision, and Brandon always congratulated himself on it when arriving home.

Through habit, he dropped his hoodie over the back of one of his sofas, and then continued past the neat, minimalist kitchen. Brandon had designed the second half of the loft as a distinct area from the airy living space, with softer furnishings and muted light. It consisted of his den, where he spent most of his waking time, and two bedrooms with en suite bathrooms. In retrospect, Brandon wondered why he had bothered with the second bedroom and bathroom. They had never been used, and there was little immediate prospect of that changing.

Brandon went straight to his den, where he docked his laptop into its cradle to recharge. He then woke up his desktop, grabbed his coffee and cookie and relaxed in his seat in front of his array of six screens, from where he would watch the London markets open.

This was his usual morning ritual, sipping black coffee, catching up on the news and watching the symbols and numbers on his screens change colour. When the markets were quiet, or if he got bored, he would cross to the other side of the den, his gaming area, and immerse himself in one of PlayStation's surreal worlds. He found it easy to stay alert to events happening in the markets, even in the middle of a game, which he put down to the fact that the activities were so similar. He believed that he had a natural gift for reading the market, almost a sixth sense of how prices were going to move, and was that any different from a computer game? Some people are better than others at manipulating the console and second-guessing where the next danger is coming from, and Brandon was exceptional at video games.

In reality, his stock market success owed almost everything to the computer-driven mathematical models he had developed that tracked prices, volumes and trends, and then generated lightning-fast trades to exploit small price variations. Brandon knew that his algorithms and technology were why he consistently beat the market, but he still fancied himself as a bit of a player, and he settled down to watch.

***

Orla hurried along Appold Street, almost jogging in places, and arrived on the stroke of eleven o'clock. Her face was flushed and she could feel beads of perspiration on her brow.

This was not how she wanted to start her day at the office. She hated cutting it so fine, as she felt she was letting down the children and her colleagues if she was late or flustered on arrival. She always tried to get there a few minutes early, which gave her time to chat with her workmates and then be calm and professional with the children. But that hadn't been possible this morning.

Orla wiped her forehead with a tissue, and took several deep breaths to compose herself. Throughout her walk to work, she hadn't been able to stop thinking about this morning's events. The day had started well and she had left the Refuge early, and should have had plenty of time to get to work. But Michael had set her back and ruined her schedule, not to mention her mood, and in the end she hadn't even had time to call in on Edna. She thought about her elderly neighbour, unable to get out of her flat and with no one to talk to, and Orla shook her head slowly. Why couldn't Michael take no for an answer?

But that wasn't what was really bothering Orla. She was beginning to wonder if there was something she didn't know. Michael had become more temperamental over the past few weeks, almost as if he didn't care about anything anymore, and his working hours seemed haphazard and irregular. Did he have problems at work? He still pulled in the money, so things couldn't be that bad, but Orla couldn't shake the feeling that everything was not as it seemed. Maybe he was under pressure because of the recent spate of hacking and data scandals, which must have increased his workload. But, if anything, Michael was working fewer hours rather than more. It didn't add up.

More disturbing, though, was the memory of him whispering in her ear in the shower. Just thinking about it made her shiver again, and the same wave of cold dread washed over her. He had always been insistent about sex, but until today she had never felt that side of Michael, never felt scared or unsafe with him. Was she overplaying it, and had she imagined something in his tone that wasn't really there? She wasn't sure, and the sudden uncertainty in their relationship troubled her.

But she didn't have time to dwell on it now. She was at work and she couldn't let the children see her distress. They were the only important thing right now.

Orla stepped through the front doors into the grand lobby of Chalmers & Mason Asset Management, one of the City's oldest and best-known fund managers. She went straight to the second floor, to the children's crèche where she worked. The firm had been one of the first City institutions to provide a full time, on-site crèche, and Orla felt privileged to work here. She loved her job. It was a perfect match for her skills, ambitions and personal circumstances, and she couldn't think of a better way to spend her time.

Orla hung her jacket on the hook and placed her bag into her locker, just as her colleague Martina walked over.

'Hi Orla, I was wondering where you were,' she said. 'Everything OK?'

'Yes, all fine thanks. I just got a bit distracted on the way here, that's all. Nothing to worry about.'

'Oh, that's good. Just to let you know, I'm on the early shift today, so I'm about to take my break. Also, it's Josh's birthday today, so his dad brought in some cakes for everyone. Not only the kids, but the adults too, they're in the kitchen. Better hurry, though, as they're going like hot cakes!' Martina giggled at her joke.

'Thanks, I'll pop up there now before they all go. I'll also find Josh to wish him a happy birthday. Catch you later.'

Orla turned and walked towards the nearest group of toddlers. They rushed forward and surrounded her, all chattering and laughing, each child clamouring for her attention. Orla laughed with them and tried to answer all of their questions at once. This is what she worked for, the opportunity to share time with the children, their pure, blissful innocence a world away from Michael, or the people she helped at the Refuge. *They can look after themselves.*

Her day at the crèche had begun, and all thoughts of Michael, Maria and Jacob melted away.

***

A smug, self-satisfied smile on his face, Michael sat up in bed and smoked another cigarette and contemplated his morning so far. He still couldn't believe his luck.

First there had been Jenny, who had joined him within minutes of Orla leaving for the Refuge, and that had been fun. Jenny knew what she wanted and Michael was more than happy to oblige. Her morning visits were becoming more frequent, and it was almost as if she waited behind her door for sounds of Orla leaving, so that she could dash across the landing immediately afterwards. He knew that Jenny was taking a bit of a risk, as Orla might forget something one day and return, and that would spell the end of their secret liaisons, but wasn't that part of the thrill? He certainly didn't want to put Jenny off by warning her, he was enjoying her far too much for that.

Orla coming home early had been a satisfying bonus. She had denied wanting sex and had snapped at him, but Michael supposed she was just angry about his smoking. It had only been a bit of banter and she hadn't refused him in the shower, so she must have forgiven him. She wouldn't have if she'd known what he'd been doing with Jenny earlier, but what she didn't know wouldn't harm her. He chuckled. Now that she had gone to work again, he had time for a snooze and another smoke, and it wasn't as though he had much else to do. The perfect morning.

However, this afternoon would be a different matter. He looked again at the message he'd received from Paddy a few hours earlier. What did he have planned for him this time and what were the goods he was expecting? He'd known this day was coming, but he didn't know what the mission was; the Brethren's leaders were far too cautious to share anything before they needed to.

Michael had enjoyed the last few months hiding away in this part of London, awaiting orders. It was anonymous, he could come and go as he pleased, he had two women on the go and he had plenty of time for beers and fun. The retainer paid by the Brethren had been generous too. But now it was time to earn his money.

Michael grinned as he remembered a few of the old times and he took another drag of his cigarette. He was excited by the prospect of becoming active again, it felt long overdue, and even though it might be dangerous, he was sure that Paddy would have prepared everything meticulously. After all, if anything went wrong, Paddy would be the one to take the flak back home. *And he won't want to be on the wrong side of the Brethren.*

Michael turned on the TV and flicked through a dozen channels, but there was nothing worth watching. He switched on the bedside radio instead and turned up the volume so that he could hear it throughout the flat. No doubt even Edna downstairs could hear it, but so what, at least it would be some company for her. Michael stubbed out his cigarette, then wandered naked to the bathroom for his second shower of the day. Only this time alone.

5

It was stifling, the sun beat down on scorched metal and the air was thick with dust rising from the road. The men closed their eyes as the steady drone of the convoy laboured on, all conversation long since exhausted in the confined space of the armoured personnel carriers.

They made their way through the devastation and ruins of what used to be a bustling street, where the colourful everyday pageant of market stalls and drying clothes had been replaced by funereal mounds of sandy rubble and limp rags hanging from holes in the building walls. People no longer sat on their steps drinking coffee, watching their children play; they were long since gone or had retreated to the depths of the town or into shadowy recesses along the convoy's route.

Jacob never saw the explosion, the blinding flash of light that erupted from the lead vehicle three ahead, but the blast battered his ears and he felt his own vehicle lift at the shockwave before it slew to a halt on the dusty road. Yells and orders rang out from all around and his machine-gunner swivelled the mounting suddenly to the right, and his ears reverberated with the sound of their returning fire.

Gunfire rained down on the group. Jacob's vehicle resonated to the sound of bullets and ricochets as it sat isolated and exposed in the middle of the street. The whine of the carrier's tracks started up again, the engine revved and they lurched away from the road, the ferocity of the assault reducing as they narrowed the angle from their attackers and prepared to disembark. None of the men wanted to be fried inside the carrier if it took a direct RPG hit or overturned, although the thought of leaving its armoured protection equally filled them with dread.

The stench of cordite and acrid smoke charged the air. The men launched themselves out of the carrier and into the dark confines of a burned-out building, and took cover as mayhem raged in the streets and grenades exploded all around. Static blurted out of the radios and commands were given, and the unit hunkered down to wait for the reply. It had better be soon.

Prayers answered, after a couple of minutes that felt like hours, helicopter-launched rockets streaked blazing into the buildings from which the ambush had first erupted, creating plumes of dust and debris that burst upwards, then returned to earth as showers of rubble. The dark smoking holes briefly exposed the ruined interior of the building before it was engulfed in flame as grenades exploded from within. More rockets arrowed into the building, the bombardment silencing the flurry of grenades and the cracking of snipers' guns.

The attack was all over in a matter of minutes. Securing the buildings afterwards would take longer, as one by one the rooms would be inspected and declared safe, not for habitation but from snipers or insurgents.

After ordering a few of his men to manage the recovery of the unit's casualties, Jacob joined the rest as they made the sweeps.

In the first building, they slowly ascended the gutted staircase to the second floor. Suddenly, a blood-curdling scream cut through Jacob and his men as an enemy fighter threw himself towards them, his arm raised as he clung onto a grenade, the pin pulled out. The explosion ripped apart the suffocating air in a blinding, searing assault on their senses.

Jacob awoke with a jolt. He gasped for breath, his heart pounded and he fought to bring his shaking under control. He scanned all around him, years of training taking over, until he realised he was back in London. He was safe. Almost.

Jacob looked around again, this time more slowly. Two young girls hurried away from him, although one peered over her shoulder with a frightened expression, and across the road an elderly man stared at him. There was nothing else out of the ordinary.

Jacob felt clammy, but otherwise he had almost regained his composure. The shivering subsided after a minute or so, despite his skin feeling even colder than before, damp under his clothes. The morning sun wasn't going to help that very much. But it was time to get going again, before any trouble arrived. Sooner or later it always did. He looked around warily, rose from the bench and headed down the side of the tennis court and then between the neighbouring blocks of flats.

He tried to recall his dream, but the images had vanished as soon as he opened his eyes and he struggled to remember any of the detail. He thought it related to Basra, and that whatever incident he had recalled had traumatised him enough for his waking mind to have blocked out the worst of his mental scars. It was all gone. Until the next time he fell into one of his nightmares.

A loud horn sounded from a passing car and a boy stuck his head out and yelled something at Jacob, the words obscured by passing traffic. He stopped, dazed and confused, unsure which way to go. *I need a drink.* It was a thought that he couldn't dispel, that always lurked somewhere just below the surface. But since his dream it had become urgent, insistent, and it was getting louder.

Jacob looked up from his trance and discovered that on autopilot he had wandered to the district immediately north of Silicon Roundabout, home to hotels, pubs and student accommodation, where if he was lucky he might get hold of some alcohol. A chance to escape his horrors for a while.

Jacob navigated the backstreets to a side road flanking the City Road Inn, which seemed a promising target. The main reception and the entrance to the car park were both at the front of the hotel, although the car park was on the corner of the plot, separated from the street by a corrugated fence. Jacob saw cameras and a security barrier at the front, but the dilapidated fence had several gaps and holes near the back, a couple of which appeared large enough for Jacob to pass through, near to a pair of closed gates used by trade vehicles.

Jacob shuffled past the holes. He glanced through them when he paused, as he pretended to catch his breath and straighten his stiff back, and then looked both ways down the street. Heartened by what he'd seen, and happy that the coast was clear, he squeezed through the largest opening and ducked behind a large wheelie bin.

From his hiding place, Jacob saw half a dozen bins of various sizes and colours, lined up against the fence directly across the tarmac from an exit at the end of the hotel. Two further bins stood outside another door, ten yards down the building to Jacob's right, alongside several crates half-filled with empty bottles. Cigarette butts littered the floor outside both doors.

It looked almost perfect and Jacob hoped that his luck was in. He felt that he was due some. Now it was just a matter of waiting, and he had all the time in the world.

***

Watching, waiting for something to happen. Anything. Every so often, Brandon leaned forward, looked up a particular news story or price, or made a series of calculations. But he struggled to concentrate on his screens, and by mid-morning he decided that it was no use, he was too distracted by *Proximity*. The markets weren't going to fill him with excitement today, so he would concentrate on his new project instead.

Brandon was excited about the capability he had developed. He knew that he was on the threshold of a major breakthrough that would be the envy of the hacking world and would send shockwaves along the digital spines of governments, security services and technology companies around the globe. Yet all he was doing was taking advantage of systems that had been developed to support people's desire to be connected to the internet, and to each other, all the time.

The principles were simple. Almost everyone owned a gadget with Wi-Fi capability, and most of these devices searched for the best signal available whenever they were turned on. Smartphones and tablets incessantly scanned for networks, and Brandon's program used a modified version of a Mi-Fi hotspot, established on his own laptop, to interact with any device that came within transmission range. These everyday mobile networks and hand-held devices were the basic building blocks for Brandon's scheme, but what turned them into weapons of cyber-crime was the way they were used. Because, just like the principles, people were also simple.

It never ceased to amaze Brandon how much private, sensitive information the average person was prepared to give complete strangers; not face-to-face, of course, but behind the security blanket of social media or their phones' applications, as if this somehow made it more secure. As well as being free with their personal details, many gadget users were hooked on location-tracking applications. Brandon understood the usefulness of finding the nearest restaurant, public toilet or Underground station when needed. But why did the device need to reveal your location all the time, even when asleep? The result was that their gadgets could be tracked anywhere, anytime, and then snared. For someone with Brandon's programming skills and technical ability, it was a simple matter to intercept the signals and interact with applications on their phones, hijacking the permissions they had granted.

The combination of constant location tracking, the ease with which personal data could be accessed or manipulated, and the public's carefree attitude to mobile security, made a lethal cocktail when in Brandon's hands. He had tested it at Stratford, and it worked. *Proximity* could locate a device, put a message onto its screen, and then tempt the user to press a button that gave permission to download a virus. Behind it all there was some clever digital subterfuge and programming, but Brandon was amazed at how easy it had been.

But it wasn't perfect yet. He now had to work out how to generate a critical mass of compromised devices. That was the challenge he set himself and, if he could do that, he would be ready to commit the greatest financial crime ever known.

***

He pushed open the door and cast his eyes around the pub. There were only two other souls in the place: James the barman, stacking glasses behind the bar, and Gerry, who sat in his usual place in the corner, his first pint of the day already in front of him.   Michael nodded at Gerry, who answered with a slight dip of his chin and then resumed staring at the bottom of his glass.

'Hi James, the usual, and one for yourself too.'

'Wow, someone's in a good mood this morning.' James opened his eyes wide in mock surprise.   'What happened, did you win the lottery or something?'

'Oh, bloody funny I'm sure. But as you asked, yes, I'm having a good day. Very good. But if you don't want a drink on me, that's fine, I'm sure old Gerry will have it,' Michael said, and he nodded towards the corner.

'Much obliged Michael, thanks, I'll have one with you. I don't think I'll be run off my feet this morning, and Gerry looks happy enough with what he has.'

James poured a Guinness and left it to settle while he pulled himself an ale, before he topped off Michael's glass.

'There you go, and thanks for the drink. Cheers! Or should that be Sláinte?'

'Sláinte indeed.'

Michael took a long swallow of the Guinness and wiped his top lip with the back of his hand. 'That's good, well, as good as it gets in London anyway.'

'I'll take that as a compliment. So, what was so great about this morning?'

'Oh, this and that, just a nice laze in bed.' Michael cast his mind back, and smirked. He looked at James, saw his raised eyebrows and realized that he had been expecting more. 'I also have a business meeting this afternoon that I hope will bring me some good news.'

'Oh right,' James said. 'Hope it goes well. Could there be anything in it for me?'

'Oh, I don't suppose so. It's a former associate of mine who's in town and looking for some help. It may just break up my days a little for the next week or so, and I'm not sure how much help he needs.'

'That's a shame. This job doesn't pay that well, and God knows I need the money.'

'I'll bear you in mind and will let you know if he needs any more hands.'

'OK, thanks, fair enough. As I said, the money would come in handy.'

The two men took another gulp of their drinks, before James turned back to carry on stacking glasses. Michael took his glass to an empty table, sat on the cushioned bench with his back to the wall and took out his smartphone. He selected WhatsApp and sent a one-line message to Paddy to check what time they were meeting.

As he waited for an answer, he considered the beauty of modern messaging. These new applications encrypted messages in a way that made them untraceable and impossible to decipher. That is, unless you were stupid enough to give your unlocked phone to the police. You could say anything to anyone, without fear of eavesdroppers. No more worrying about tapped phones or intercepted email, Paddy and the Brethren now used these applications all the time, other than when face-to-face communication was unavoidable.

Michael didn't have long to wait for Paddy's answer:

Meet me at the lock-up on Rivington St at 2.

Michael replied briefly:

Will do.

There was no need for pleasantries; after all, this was business. But before meeting Paddy, Michael needed some food. He had worked up quite an appetite this morning and he was ravenous.

'Hey, James, ask Carter to rustle up one of your big breakfasts will you, with double the fried bread?'

Michael leaned back and considered his earlier conquests. *I think I've earned it.*

6

Jacob rocked back and forth on his haunches to get his circulation going. Pins and needles had set in and his joints were beginning to ache, and he knew he would suffer later for crouching down low for so long. He had watched the hotel staff entrance for the past hour, but all he'd seen so far had been a procession of people coming out to smoke, chat, look at their phones or empty rubbish. The only mild bit of excitement was when a middle-aged woman pushed a cart of linen through the door and walked straight towards the bin behind which Jacob was hiding. He was convinced that she'd spot him and he squatted as low as he could, but she simply transferred the sheets and towels from her cart into the hopper and slammed it shut. The bin smacked against him and he stifled a curse, but the woman didn't notice. She returned to join two colleagues who were smoking by the back door.

He massaged his aching ankles and thought about leaving this fruitless reconnaissance. But then, everything changed. A loud bell sounded at the back of the second door, and a young man dressed as a bartender came out, walked across the tarmac and opened the double gates. Immediately, a deliveryman wheeled a trolley stacked high with boxes through the opening.

'Hi there, Nathan, we have five lots for you today, starting with the soft drinks.'

'Cheers Tony. Usual place, over by the back door.'

Tony pushed the trolley to the door and wiggled it to and fro to release the load, and whistled as he returned for the next batch. It took no time at all to deposit the crates and boxes by the door.

'There you go, that's the final load. The last pile is the hard stuff. There's some pretty expensive whisky in there, well, more than the likes of us can afford, anyway.'

'Speak for yourself,' Nathan said and he winked at Tony. 'There's always a way when you work behind the bar.'

Nathan signed the delivery sheet and handed it back to Tony. 'See you again in a day or two.'

'Thanks, see you soon mate.' Tony resumed his whistling and returned to his van, trailed by Nathan, who closed and bolted the gates behind him.

From behind the bins, Jacob watched with growing interest. This was just what he'd been waiting for. It struck him as odd that the boxes had been stacked outside, rather than being wheeled straight into a storeroom, but it might work in his favour. The question was, could he get over to the kitchen door, take something out of a sealed box, and then back to the cover of the bins, without being seen?

Nathan carried the boxes one or two at a time through the door, and Jacob counted how long each trip took. *Only about ten seconds, damn, that's never going to be enough time*. The stacks quickly reduced, and within three or four minutes Nathan had reached the last pile. Jacob had just about given up hope, when Nathan did something different. He looked all around the car park to make sure no one was watching, then opened one of the whisky boxes and took out a bottle, which he placed behind a crate of empties about two yards from the back door. He closed the box and took all of the remaining ones inside, and shut the back door.

All was quiet.

Jacob knew that theft from employers was relatively commonplace, not only in the hotel and pub trade but in all walks of life. Nathan was probably taking more than most, but Jacob didn't care about that; he just wanted to get his hands on the plundered whisky and make his escape. He drooled at the prospect. The trick now was to get his timing right, and make it to the bottle in between the employees' smoking breaks, and he decided to chance it immediately after their next one. Jacob put his aching joints out of his mind.

Minutes later, a group of three workers came out by the main staff exit. They all lit cigarettes and then took phones out of their pockets, which they stared at and prodded for the next ten minutes without exchanging so much as a word. Jacob looked on in bemusement, wondering if they spoke different languages, or if they were messaging each other instead. He would never know, as they returned to the hotel in silence.

Right, here we go. After a brief look around the car park, he dashed to the crate that hid the whisky, keeping as low as he could, then he grabbed the bottle and turned back towards the bins. The weight of the bottle was reassuring in his palm and the anticipation of drinking it was so great that Jacob could almost taste the whisky.

He was barely strides away from his hideout when he heard an angry bellow behind him. 'Oi, come back here with that, you thieving beggar!'

Jacob looked over his shoulder to see Nathan bearing down on him, and realised there was no way he could get out of the car park before he was caught. A strong hand yanked his collar and pulled him back. Jacob threw his elbow as hard as he could at his pursuer's arm and Nathan let go with a yelp, but he soon grabbed Jacob again and pushed him to the ground. The bottle fell from his grip and shattered on the tarmac, and the immediate, powerful smell of whisky hit them both hard.

'You'll be sorry for that, you low-life scum.' Nathan's face was florid and spittle sprayed when he yelled. Jacob knew that the barman was losing control and he covered his head with his arms to protect himself from the inevitable assault. Nathan punched him, then kicked him twice in the side, giving Jacob no chance of rising. Jacob knew he'd have to flee or fight back soon, otherwise Nathan would keep going unchecked.

Suddenly, another loud voice interrupted the flurry of blows. 'Hey Nathan, what the hell's going on?'

Nathan aimed a further spiteful kick into Jacob's ribcage and turned away. 'What do you think's going on? I'm teaching this sonofabitch a lesson for stealing my whisky.'

'What do you mean *your* whisky? How the hell did he get hold of it? You're not drinking on duty, are you?'

'No, of course not, you know I don't do that, Merv. I meant *our* whisky, the hotel's, not mine. It was a slip of the tongue.' Nathan looked down at Jacob and glowered. 'He must have got in during the delivery and got hold of it somehow.'

'Well, in that case, we need to review our security, don't we? But first, unless you want to call the police for *theft*,' Merv said, pausing to make sure Nathan understood the implication, 'I suggest we get him out of here and let him go with a warning. What do you reckon?'

Nathan looked livid and ready to explode. He wanted to pulverise Jacob, but he knew that he couldn't push it and he had no choice but to agree.

Merv didn't wait for an answer. He stooped down and pulled Jacob up roughly by the collar. 'Right, time to go, and count yourself lucky this time. Don't ever try this again or I might let Nathan give you a good kicking.'

He unbolted the gate and pushed Jacob through, but before letting him go, he leaned towards Jacob and whispered so that only he could hear, 'You were lucky I came along. He has a vile temper and would probably have put you in hospital. But at least I now know where that whisky has been going.'

Then in a louder voice he said, 'Don't even dream of coming back, you hear me?'

With that, Merv winked at Jacob and slammed the gate shut.

***

Brandon was struggling. He had spent most of the morning thinking about the next steps for *Proximity*. His initial flush of excitement on returning to the loft after his success at Stratford had gone, replaced by a dawning realisation of his system's limitations. He had grappled with a few possible solutions, to no avail, but he was determined not to be beaten.

The main problem was volume. How could he infect enough devices in a short time to generate the amount of internet traffic he needed? He knew of numerous ways to hijack computers and tablets using traditional hacking and infection techniques, but the major internet security firms were getting pretty good at identifying and neutralising those viruses. Brandon didn't want them to have time to do that; he wanted this to be a flash event that was over before anyone had even heard of it.

Volume was a problem for *Proximity* because he needed to be near the devices being infected, and it also relied on people reacting to the pop-up message. People were attentive to their screens when idle, like during their commute, but in other situations they wouldn't be looking at their phone when the message arrived. A large, dense crowd would be ideal, maybe at a concert or football game, but he would look conspicuous working on his laptop at such events, and he couldn't risk attracting unwanted attention. In any case, the number of infections might still be too low. Despite the increasing number of people who were glued to their screens all the time, many others still wanted to watch a concert rather than record the action or post comments about it on social media. They were no good to Brandon. For once, he wanted to see, and abuse, the users' addiction to their phones.

It was no good, he needed some air. He thought he was missing something simple, a solution that would transform his project and make it a reality, and sometimes inspiration came to him during his walks. A random event or sight might illuminate a light bulb; he certainly hoped so. Brandon locked his computers, grabbed his hoodie and left the loft. He pulled his hood over his head and turned in the direction of Mark Square, with no particular destination in mind, and let himself drift northwards.

At Great Eastern Street, Brandon headed towards Silicon Roundabout, colloquially named to reflect the technology entrepreneurship of the district, with its unsubtle comparison to Silicon Valley in California. Brandon was amused at the idea of this fringe of the City being compared with the sun-soaked home of Apple, eBay and Tesla, but what really tickled him was the absence of entrepreneurial inspiration in naming it so clumsily after somewhere else.

Brandon was less amused at his own lack of inspiration. Every so often he would stop, sigh and shake his head at another half-formed thought, a fragment of an idea tantalisingly out of reach. His footsteps became heavier and his energy waned, so he turned into Whitecross Street, where he knew that the stalls would be up and running, providing what people now called 'street food'. Perhaps he just needed to feed his imagination. When he arrived, there were well over a dozen stands and vans on both sides, serving numerous choices of food, from every corner of the globe. He queued at a burrito van surrounded mainly by City bankers, and bought a spicy chicken version of the famed Mexican dish.

It was a bright day and Brandon headed for the terraces of the Barbican. He trudged up the ramp at the end of Whitecross Street, but he didn't gravitate towards the open areas frequented by most visitors, where groups of workers would congregate during their lunch hours. Instead, he crossed to a quiet section near Ben Jonson House, which he knew was usually empty, where he could eat and think in solitude.

Brandon picked a bench shrouded by shrubs looking away from the Barbican towers, and opened his lunch, expertly rolled in foil. He took his first bite and looked across the street towards a local school, his attention drawn to the joyful laughter and shouting of the children at play during their lunch break. Four girls were skipping and chanting a song which sounded vaguely familiar to Brandon, but he couldn't quite remember the words from childhood. Another group of girls watched nearby, although a couple of them were giggling and pointing at some boys who were playing a game of tag the other side of the small playground. Even from where he was sitting, Brandon heard one of the boys shout, 'Got you!' as he slapped a classmate on the back, and then they both chased the other boys. They must be playing the version where everyone would eventually be caught by the ever-growing number of chasers.

Brandon thought back to his own time at school. He recalled the same sense that he had right now, of watching other people play. Even at primary school, he had never fit in; he was always on the fringes pretending to join in, or sometimes he just stood there, alone, and watched the girls skip and the boys chase around. From what he could see of this school, there weren't any obvious misfits like himself. Maybe they were better at concealing it now, or perhaps the other children were more accepting of their classmates' differences. Whatever the reason, Brandon wanted to believe that times had changed and that no child had to go through what he had at school.

Brandon watched the children play while he finished his burrito. He was conscious that if anyone saw him staring in the direction of the school, they may question his intentions, but he couldn't help it, he was drawn to them and the way they interacted. There was something in the children's behaviour that he felt was important, but he couldn't work out what it was.

Deep in thought, Brandon jumped when the school bell suddenly sounded. Lunchtime was over, and all of the children stopped what they were doing, gathered up their skipping ropes, jumpers and other belongings, and made their way off the playground. A couple of stragglers dragged themselves back to their classes, glum looks on their faces.

Brandon stared after them, stock still and unblinking, transfixed by what it was he had just witnessed. The peal of the bell had reverberated around this small corner of the City, amplified by the echo from the buildings so that all of the children had heard it. The sudden crescendo reminded Brandon of the final scene of a movie, The Lawnmower Man, when every telephone started to ring at once, signifying that the film's main character, Jobe, had infiltrated all computer networks on Earth. The film's plot was ridiculous, but that wasn't the point. It was the way the sound had built that had caught Brandon's attention, and he realised that he had been looking at *Proximity* all wrong. It needed to act like a real virus, self-replicating and spreading, contaminating other gadgets. *Amplifying, growing, living.* Like the boys' game of tag, in no time, everyone was caught, but not all by the same boy.

Brandon didn't know why it hadn't occurred to him before. Everyone's mobile phone, tablet or laptop was able to receive *and transmit* the virus, which would spread exponentially if it could self-replicate.

Brandon dropped the rest of his burrito into the bin and hurried down the ramp on his way back to the loft.

Refuelled and reenergised, he now knew how to make his plan a reality.

He had work to do.

7

Michael strolled along Rivington Street towards the railway bridge. He felt the buildings watching him, leaning over the narrow street to follow his progress, spying. Despite recent renovations, many of the buildings had that typical East End feel to them, scruffy and old-fashioned, and even this close to the busy High Street it was quiet and unhurried, as though an invisible curtain had been drawn across the end of the street at the entrance to a different world. The centuries old buildings brooded, silent at this time of day, but that would change as night fell, when the local bars and clubs opened their doors.

A train passed over the arches, the discoloured brickwork still standing after all those years of vibration and pollution. Michael saw that various businesses occupied the valuable space beneath the tracks, although a few of the arches were used solely as storerooms or as overflow for the neighbouring properties. Just like the one he had been summoned to.

He approached a pair of doors set in a wooden facade about ten feet high, selected a key from his key ring, and unlocked the heavy-duty padlock. He released the securing steel bar and the door opened with a faint creak. After the cloying street, the lock-up was dank, and he felt a faint breeze of cool, stale air escape as he stepped inside.

He reached for the light switch and the fluorescent tubes flickered into life.

Inside, the lock-up was Tardis-like and the light barely touched the gloom at the rear. Michael remembered that the railway tracks diverged as they approached the double bridge at Old Street, and therefore the lock-up didn't occupy only a single archway, but filled the void below and between the tracks and then carried on through the other side, into an area formerly used by a vehicle repair firm. It created an odd shape, impractical for many purposes, but ideal for storage and a perfect hiding place for all manner of craven activities.

Michael lit a cigarette and threw the match onto the floor, where it joined countless butts and charred scraps. Between puffs, he wondered why this dingy space had been retained by the Brethren. It clearly wasn't used very much. Hundreds of undisturbed cobwebs clung to the walls, the shelves were covered in dust, and discarded bottles and cans littered the place. He assumed that Paddy didn't want the lock-up for its cleanliness, but for its location in a quiet part of Shoreditch, off the beaten track yet close to the centre of London. But what else did it have going for it?

He heard a noise above and looked up. A second floor had been installed in the void between the arches, with a small loading hatch in the middle of the wooden floor providing access to additional storage space on the upper level. He was about to investigate when the sound came again, and he realised that it was only the scuttling of tiny feet. He peered into the loft space and thought he saw two small pin-pricks of light staring back at him. Rats. He'd leave that well alone for now, and perhaps Paddy would sort it out later if needed.

Louder footsteps outside the lock-up alerted him to someone's approach, and Michael forgot all about the rodents. Moments later, Paddy came round the door.

'Hey, Michael, great to see you. How are you doing?'

Michael opened his arms and stepped forward to embrace his old comrade. 'All the better for seeing you again my friend, it's been too long.'

Michael gripped Paddy's right hand in his and clapped him on the back with his left. He noticed that Paddy seemed thinner and, when he stepped back, he saw more lines in Paddy's face than he remembered and his eyes were bloodshot and sunken. The change in Paddy was more than just advancing years.

Paddy saw Michael's expression and pre-empted his question. 'Yes, I know, I've lost a little weight. But forget that, we've more important things to discuss. Like what you've been up to.'

Michael looked at Paddy and shrugged. 'Not much, this and that. All the usual stuff.'

'By that I assume you're still living the high life.' Paddy nodded towards Michael's cigarette. 'I can see you haven't quit the fags yet, and I can smell that you still like a Guinness or two, am I right? But what of your other weaknesses? How many women do you have in tow at the moment, eh?'

Paddy laughed at his own humour and the leer that had appeared on Michael's face, before adding, 'I never could keep up with you on that score.'

'Ha, you're right, you never could,' Michael said, 'and you never will. You're always too busy losing money on the horses, fool that you are!'

'Too true, but I'd rather lose money on my nags than on yours, any day.'

The two men laughed and it felt like old times. Except that it wasn't; something had changed in Paddy, and Michael wanted to know what.

'But seriously, Paddy, you do look a bit tired. Are you OK?'

'Well, I could say that I'm fine, just getting a bit old for these jaunts nowadays, and I must admit, it seemed a hell of a long journey getting here.' He paused before continuing. 'But I won't lie to you, Michael, we've known each other too long for that. I fear this may be my last job.'

'Why Paddy?' Michael asked, although he thought he knew the answer already.

'Well, I always said that the horses would be the end of me, or the bullet if I got careless. But it seems I was wrong. The fags got me first, my friend, the big C.' Paddy took a deep, wheezing breath. 'I've known for about a month. Funny, eh, you do all these crazy things in life, and then it's the little pleasure that kills you.'

Michael placed his hand on Paddy's shoulder, but said nothing.

'My doc says I have about six months, so it's not over yet, but I've got to finish this one last job. We'll make it one to remember and then I'll be happy that I've done my bit. Let's make this the big one, eh Michael, together, you and me, one last time, the best team the Brethren ever had. Agreed?'

'Yeah, of course Paddy, anything you say. But are you sure your doctor is right? Is there anything they can do, you know, like operate, chemo?'

'Doc said I could take the drugs and see what happens, although he didn't think it would make much difference. Might add a few months, might not. I really thought about it, I can tell you, but in the end I decided not to do it. What's the point of living a couple of extra months, if those months are spent even more unwell because of the chemo? No, that's not for me. I'd rather accept my time's up and do something with the short time I have left. So here I am.'

'God, Paddy, I don't know how you can talk like that.'

'That's because it's not happening to you, and I hope it never does. But you could help yourself by giving up those things,' he said, and nodded at Michael's cigarette.

'But now, no more depressing talk. I've told you my news and there's no more to be said about it. From now on, all we're going to talk about is the task at hand. And maybe women and beer!'

'OK, it's your call, whatever you want Paddy.' Michael was relieved to drop the subject, as he didn't know what else to say. 'So, what exactly is the plan?'

***

It wasn't the buildings that spied on Michael, as he walked down Rivington Street to his rendezvous with Paddy. Unknown to them both, dark eyes watched their every move through the grimy panes of a first-floor window, where a thin hand parted the jaded net curtain on their arrival at the lock-up.

Despite knowing that Paddy and Michael were up to the job and had delivered whenever asked before, this was too big an operation for the leader of the Brethren to stay at home. It was the start of the most significant week in the Brethren's history. Nothing could be left to chance.

Donovan saw the two terrorists arrive without a trace of emotion. This was just one small step and they had a long way to go before they could claim victory on the streets of London. There would be plenty of time for laughter and celebration afterwards. Until then, even smiling could wait.

***

At Great Eastern Street, traffic was bumper-to-bumper and the pavements were seething. A typical lunchtime, it was much busier than when Jacob had crossed it earlier in the day.

For most people, everyday bustle offers a sense of security, safety in numbers and the reassurance of daylight hours. But not for Jacob; all he saw were potential dangers. A line of people queued out of a sandwich shop and into the street, and Jacob imagined enemies concealed in their number, camouflaged by the distractions and hubbub of the throng. A woman leaned out of an upstairs window, and he saw a sniper in the shadows, shielded behind her innocent look. Even the schoolchildren who joked together on the corner weren't beyond suspicion, with their bulging backpacks and excitable high spirits.

No, Jacob didn't like daytime crowds. He preferred empty streets and the cold isolation of wandering alone at night. He told himself that he wasn't just adopting a habit common to many homeless people, who hid away during the day. It was different for him. Years of combat had taught him that an enemy was just as likely to be lurking in a group of people, in plain sight, as hidden away in dark corners. He could never relax in a crowd.

Low on energy after his scuffles with Bill and Nathan, Jacob traipsed along the pavement. Shoppers and workers on their lunchtime breaks gave him a wide berth, like shoals of wary fish parting for a shark. Their noses wrinkled and their eyes either rolled or widened, their disgust and fear mixed in equal parts. Jacob was used to this reaction and, although it pained him to experience the derision of so many people who thought him worthless and contemptible, he continued his journey as if oblivious to their mutterings.

At the corner of Paul Street, he stopped and paused for breath, then took a sip of water from the memorial fountain on the corner. He looked down the street at the jagged tip of the Shard in the distance, just visible above the much older buildings of this neighbourhood. Different worlds, different times.

'Hey, it's Jacob isn't it? Haven't I seen you at the Refuge?'

He started at the chime of the words, then found himself looking down into the engaging, smiling face of a slim, dark-haired woman in her early twenties. There was a flicker of recognition, little more, but the memory was just out of reach and he couldn't place her. Nowadays he often struggled to distinguish his dreams from the reality of his distant memories, although she did seem more familiar than the wraiths of his nightmares.

'Sorry, you probably don't remember me.' Her voice was quiet, but friendly, almost musical, as she continued her introduction. 'I'm Maria, and I live at the Refuge. For the moment anyway. I am right, your name is Jacob isn't it?'

Jacob nodded. 'Yes, that's me. Sorry, I was miles away and didn't recognise you. As it happens, I am on my way to the Refuge now. You know, for a little food.'

He looked away. He couldn't explain why, but he felt bitter and embarrassed at admitting he needed the Refuge's help. Surely if anyone understood, it would be one of the shelter's residents.

Maria saw the momentary look that crossed Jacob's face and she followed his gaze down Paul Street. 'Don't worry, I can go with you if you like. Or maybe I can buy you something to keep you going?'

This time it was Jacob who detected uncertainty in Maria's voice. He turned his head back to her, but she looked down at her shoes, like a child caught out. He knew she couldn't afford to buy him anything, not if she wanted to eat herself. She looked up again and, although she smiled, her deep brown eyes betrayed the sorrow she felt at their situation.

'No, thanks Maria, it's OK, I can manage. It's very kind of you to offer. Most people don't, but then I guess you know that.' He nodded in the direction of the other passers-by, as if indicating the world in general. 'Too many better things to spend their money on.'

A middle-aged woman was walking towards them, studying her phone, and only just looked up in time to avoid colliding with Maria.

'Like mobile phones,' Jacob said, louder than needed. The woman scowled, but said nothing and turned away to continue her walk. Maria laughed, relieved at the change in atmosphere, and looked up at Jacob's grinning face.

Jacob studied Maria and decided that he liked her. She had a light, easy manner, with an expression conveying an almost child-like innocence, and when she smiled her eyes lit up with warmth and kindness. She had olive skin, a slight frame and dark, almost black hair that reminded him of his wife, and a little of his daughter.

Maria saw him watching her and blushed. 'What, do you recognise me now?'

'No, sorry, I didn't mean to stare. You just remind me of someone I used to know.'

'Someone close?' she asked, perceptively.

'My wife. She died a few years ago.'

'Oh, sorry. Me and my big mouth.' Maria averted her gaze, not knowing what else to say.

'Don't worry. You couldn't have known and it was a while ago now.' Jacob saw the relief in Maria's eyes when she turned back and he smiled at her. 'So, where were you off to then, just now, before we met?'

'I'm looking for work. I've asked in shops and offices along here, although there doesn't seem to be much going. I'll head up to the High Street next, but if that doesn't work, I think I'll call it a day.'

'OK, I'll let you get on then. Good luck, I hope you find something.'

'Thanks, me too. See you around, Jacob.'

Maria turned away, then looked back over her shoulder and lifted her hand in a shy wave. Jacob smiled and watched her for a few seconds, before continuing his journey.

When he reached the Refuge, Jacob entered through the glass doors on the townhouse side of the shelter, the customary entrance to the soup kitchen. The owners had named it Refuge-Eat, but there was no denying its function and all of the regular guests called it what it was, and he wasn't sure why others were reluctant to use the term. Previous generations hadn't had any issue with it.

Jacob knew that the townhouse wasn't the site of the original Refuge, although no one who came to the shelter now, nor anyone who worked here, remembered the church hall where it had all started. But leaflets in the lobby gave visitors a brief history, and black-and-white photos that lined the wall allowed people a glimpse back in time, to when the Refuge started, and Jacob often stopped to look. It almost seemed ungrateful not to.

The first picture was a portrait of the local vicar who had started it all, immediately following the Second World War. It hung next to a sepia photo taken inside the church hall, where suited and pinafored parishioners ladled soup into bowls and handed out hunks of bread to scruffy, bearded men. The narrative below the frame described the beneficiaries as former military men living rough who needed a little help to survive. *Sounds familiar.*

Jacob looked at the next display, a collage of newspaper clippings that showed the strength of feeling and resistance at the time to the vicar's efforts. A few locals had complained that it was bringing vagrancy and undesirables into the neighbourhood, with accusations of increased crime and disorder. But other cuttings and copies of letters demonstrated that, through perseverance, willpower and a refusal to be bullied into closing the facility, the volunteers had stuck to their work, and ever since had provided charity safely to some of the poorest and most deserving in society.

The final few pictures were more familiar to Jacob, who recognised the buildings and some of the people. The Refuge outgrew the church hall and relocated to a converted townhouse, where Jacob now stood, and then expanded into the adjoining property. About ten years ago, a disused building behind the Refuge was bequeathed to the charity, and it now formed an annex containing offices and accommodation. As a result, the Refuge was now a rather odd, rambling collection of buildings that offered shelter, food, support and education to the area's homeless population.

He turned away from the photos. Despite feeling that coming here meant accepting both charity and defeat, Jacob always experienced a sense of relief when he passed through these doors. No one here judged him, he was made to feel welcome and, most of all, there was no pressure to accept any help and support he didn't want.

'Hi Jacob, how are you today?' came the customary greeting from Vicky on the front desk. She had worked at the Refuge for years and knew every regular visitor by name.

'If you don't mind me saying so, you're looking a little worse for wear today,' she said, looking him up and down. 'Even more than usual.'

'Thanks, I'm sure, and you look a pretty picture yourself,' Jacob replied, although his grin gave away his improving good humour at the thought of hot food. 'What's on the menu?'

'Oh, I see, no small talk and straight to business.'

Vicky paused, raised her eyebrows, and then added, 'Reminds me of my ex,' and exploded with laughter. Jacob joined in.

'Go on through, it's fairly quiet today, so you won't need to talk to anyone if you don't want to.' Vicky winked at Jacob.

The dining area was a spacious, airy room with high ceilings and a large bay window at the far end, opposite the door. It contained half a dozen wooden tables surrounded by chairs, and in the window stood two serving tables covered by white cloths. On top of the first were two large urns, a basket of bread and a tray of sandwiches, and on the second were tureens of mashed potato, rice and stews. From experience Jacob knew that one urn would contain vegetable soup and the other was most likely chicken or fish broth, which seemed to satisfy most religious and vegetarian tastes, and likewise with the casseroles. Jacob always chose one of the carnivorous options.

There were only five other guests in the room when he entered, as well as a young man Jacob didn't recall seeing before, who sat behind a serving table. He put down the book he was reading as Jacob approached and stood to serve him.

'Non-veggie soup please,' Jacob said and he grabbed a piece of bread and a spoon.

'Of course. It's chicken, if that's OK?'

Jacob nodded.

'There you go. Are you here frequently?'

'Yes, unfortunately,' Jacob said with a wry smile, 'but thanks anyway.'

Jacob took his bowl and shambled over to the table nearest the door. He recognised the man eating his soup there as Joel, a man in his twenties he had spoken to on a couple of occasions. They nodded at each other and Jacob took his seat, but said nothing. They both knew the unwritten rule: eat first, talk second.

He devoured his soup in seconds and then mopped up the dregs with his crust of bread. It tasted good and he returned to the serving table for a second helping. This one he ate more slowly and he savoured its warmth as his hunger abated. It always surprised Jacob that he could feel satisfied by so little soup, when he had previously had such a voracious appetite, especially during his time in the Army.

Joel was studying him across the table. 'Man, you look rougher than I feel. You been having those dreams again?'

'What is it with everyone today, saying I look so bad? I feel the same as usual, I just needed some food,' he replied.

'Hmm, OK, not convinced.'

When Jacob didn't respond, he changed tack. 'I haven't seen you here for a few days, so where have you been, your usual hiding places around the Barbican?'

'Here and there, you know, staying out of trouble. You?'

'Same, nowhere new. I was thinking of moving on, but you kind of get used to the same old places, don't you? Better the devil you know I suppose. Anyway, I'd miss this place. At least the food is reliable.'

Jacob's brief chats with other people on the streets were often the same. Most of them were on the look-out for new places to sleep or eat, but rarely gave anything away. If someone found a new, warm cubbyhole at night or a source of food, out of self-preservation they didn't want everyone else to find out about it. Camaraderie had its limits, so life was lonely for good reason.

'OK, I'll be off now,' Joel said after a few moments of silence. He rose from his seat and winced. 'See you again.'

'Yeah, see you.'

Jacob watched him go and noticed that he had gained a slight limp. Maybe he had aggravated a strain from sleeping rough, or else he had got into a scrape recently. He hadn't mentioned it, but then why would he? Whatever had happened, it was unlikely to get any better while Joel remained on the streets.

Jacob stayed where he was for a couple of minutes and looked around the room. He thought about going over to the man seated at the neighbouring table. He seemed about sixty, with grey hair and an almost white beard, creased face and bloodshot eyes, although Jacob knew that he might be younger if he'd lived on the streets for a few years. His clothes appeared loose and were torn and frayed in places, and no doubt the Refuge staff would offer him some replacements before he left. He might refuse them in any event, unless he wanted to trade in some fresh boots or a coat on the streets, maybe for alcohol or drugs. But that wasn't any of Jacob's business, and he'd let him be.

Jacob wondered if he appeared that way himself, given everyone's comments to him today, but he decided he couldn't look that bad or he'd have noticed more concern. However, he had no intention of checking his appearance in a mirror on his way out. Today had been tough enough already.

Incubation

In the beginning it is only a dream, a few unconnected ideas, a fantasy. But ideas take root, and left untamed and unrestrained, hidden from view in forgotten corners, they grow. Their tendrils touch and combine, drawing strength from each other, and fantasy becomes reality, an uncontrolled monster that rises up to devour everything in its path. Too late, the innocents see the teeth and smell the breath of the beast.

Orla woke with a start. She hadn't realised how tired she was, and during her lunch break she had fallen into a broken doze. Dazed and light-headed, she couldn't recall the details of her daydream, she just knew that it had filled her with dread. What was playing on her mind, why was she so jumpy? Was it something to do with Michael, the Refuge or something else entirely?

Orla looked at her watch. She had no time to think about it now; the children beckoned.

Forget it. It was only a dream.

8

Michael could hardly believe what he was hearing. Surely the plan wasn't as simple as Paddy had just suggested, there must be more to it than that.

'So, let me get this right. All we have to do is wheel the cart into the market, wait for lunchtime, then set it off?' Michael was exhilarated by its audacity and simplicity, and he imagined hordes of office workers descending on their explosive-laden trap, tempted by the promise of a free snack, then *Boom!*

'Yep, that's about the size of it,' Paddy said.

Michael pictured the scene of carnage at the City market and he laughed at how easy it sounded, but he soon stopped when he saw Paddy's serious expression.

'It's not meant to be funny, Michael. This is real, and it's going to be the biggest hit we've ever made, by far.' He looked around the lock-up and drew a long, rattling breath. 'Which brings me to next bit. Why we're here.'

'Yeah, I was wondering what it had to do with this place,' Michael said.

'OK. The thing is, it's important that we can bring in the crowds. We're relying on their greed, their weakness for a free giveaway, even if it's only a cheap one, and that's where the snacks come in. The Brethren have decided to use pots of yoghurt, which have to be kept in clean, cool conditions.'

Michael looked around the lock-up. It was cool, that was fine, but it certainly wasn't clean, and he closed his eyes and shook his head as he realised what this meant. Even though they wouldn't use all of the space, they would need to clean it up to ensure that years of accumulated dust and grime couldn't reach the yoghurt while it was stored at the lock-up. His earlier good humour at visions of slaughter had disappeared and he didn't feel like laughing anymore. Once again, he wondered why the Brethren had chosen this place, if not for its cleanliness.

'Why does it have to be yoghurt, Paddy? Why can't we give away cereal bars or something like that? People love those things.'

'Think about it, Michael. If we gave out cereal bars, we wouldn't have any reason to bring in any electrical stuff, you know, like the canisters and the barrow. We can disguise all of that as cooling equipment, like those ice cream carts you see on the seafront.' He looked at Michael and appealed to his bloodlust. 'Just imagine how much explosive we'll fit into something that size. And who on earth is going to question the intentions of someone wheeling one of those things into the market?'

'OK, I see your point, and yeah, it's a good idea.' He nodded despite himself. 'But I still don't get it. Why can't we bring a fridge into the lock-up to keep the snacks clean and cool until we need them, or just keep them wrapped up until we leave?'

'I thought that too at first,' Paddy said. 'But as part of the plan we've been told to put new labels on the yoghurts. That means removing the pots from their original packaging to make the changes, and we can't work in a fridge.'

'Yeah, sure, we need to have a little space to do that, but why are we changing the labels? I'd have thought we'd get more people to come to the cart if they see a brand they recognise, like Müller or Cadburys.'

'I agree, but it's something the Brethren want us to do.' He hesitated. 'They told me that changing the labels has another purpose too, some sort of message from us to the people of London. They didn't say what it was, but the order came from Donovan, so straight from the top. I didn't push them about it. These aren't people who take kindly to doubters. If you know what I mean.'

Michael wasn't convinced, but nodded his understanding and cast another dispirited look around the lock-up.

'OK, as you say, it's their call. I'd have been happier to keep it simple, but I suppose it isn't a big deal. I'm assuming we only need to replace a few hundred labels, which I guess will take no more than a couple of hours. We have the time to kill ... ha, if you know what I mean.' Both men laughed.

'But first we need to clean this place up, my friend,' Paddy said. He didn't look too pleased at the prospect.

* * *

Maria wasn't feeling very pleased either. She had trudged the streets for hours and had nothing to show for her time, not even a sniff of a job. She had known it would be hard, but hadn't expected the endless rejection of so many shopkeepers and office receptionists, even those who had vacancies advertised in their windows. A few had shown initial interest, as Maria was cheerful and personable, but their attitude would change when they discovered that she was living in a shelter and had no references to give other than from the Refuge. How did they expect her to have work references, if she couldn't get any work?

Maria had twice been offered a trial period without pay, and she shuddered at the memory of the second occasion.

'I'll give you a try, for a couple of weeks,' the balding, middle-aged man with the pot belly had said.

'Oh, OK. And how much will you pay me if I get the job, after the trial?' Maria had asked. She wasn't sure she really wanted to work in the hardware store, where the goods looked like they had sat decaying on the dusty shelves for several years, but she might as well ask.

'Oh, don't worry about that. I'm sure we'll come to some arrangement.' He looked Maria up and down, and there was no doubt in Maria's mind what he was expecting her to do for a chance of a job, or what he would be paying her for. She turned and ran out of the lecher's filthy shop to the sound of his laughter, as he revelled in her humiliation.

Maria felt like returning to the Refuge, but she was determined to reach the end of the street. She was not a quitter, she told herself between a couple of deep breaths, and she would not be deterred by a grubby little man with nothing better to do than taunt women. She had walked up the east side of the High Street as far as St. Leonard's Church and was now making her way back down the opposite side. She had fewer than twenty shops to go, so the end was in sight, and at least she was now heading back towards the Refuge.

She entered a linen and textiles store that was full to bursting with racks of ready-made curtains, bedding and fabric samples. Behind the counter at the back of the store stood an elderly woman, who looked up from the magazine she was reading and smiled.

'Hello, my dear, can I help you?'

Maria beamed back at the shopkeeper and tried to sound positive. 'I was wondering if you have any vacancies at the moment please? I work hard and I'm good with customers.'

The woman's smile faded. 'Oh no, I'm sorry, I don't need anyone else. I don't get that much business and can only just afford to pay myself as it is.'

Maria looked around the shop and imagined that on many days nothing would be sold. It wasn't the first time today she'd had that impression.

'Can I leave my name in case anything changes?' she asked.

'I don't think so. We both know nothing is going to change.'

'OK, thanks anyway. You don't happen to know of anyone else looking for staff do you?' Maria had asked this everywhere and expected the same answer.

The woman looked at Maria and shook her head. 'No, not any of the shops along here, but I've a feeling you've asked most of them already.'

'Yes, I have, but no joy so far.'

Maria turned to leave, but the shopkeeper hadn't finished. 'Is it just shop work you want, or are you willing to do other things, like cleaning?'

Maria turned back. A ray of hope? 'Yes, I'm happy to do anything, and cleaning is fine with me. Do you need a cleaner?'

'No, not me, and I don't know if there is a job going, but I saw that two men had opened up one of the arches round the back today. It used to be a car workshop and they were clearing it out this afternoon. It hasn't been used for years, but you may be lucky with your timing if they're starting up there again. It's just a thought.'

'Oh, thank you, that's great, I'll take a look now. Where did you say this workshop was?'

'Turn right after the takeaway next door, into Rivington Street. Go under the railway bridge, then you'll see the arches on the other side. Theirs is the second one along, and when I popped out a little earlier they had the door open. You can't miss it.'

Maria thanked the woman again and her mood brightened. She skipped past the kebab shop, headed down Rivington Street, then passed under the bridge and looked down the row of arches. As the woman had said, the door of the second one was open, with a pile of rubbish next to it, although she couldn't see or hear anyone as she stepped towards the entrance.

***

Michael and Paddy had made a start on clearing out the lock-up. They had removed some of the old boxes and garbage from the store area and piled it all outside, and then set to work sweeping the worst of the cobwebs and debris away. It was dirty work, and very soon Paddy started to cough and wheeze and after half an hour he was drenched with sweat.

'Hey Paddy, take it easy, I can do this bit,' Michael said. 'Take a break outside until I've cleared the worst of the dust.'

Michael was worried about Paddy's health, especially the effects of the dust and workload on his lungs, although his main concern was the mission itself. If Paddy exerted himself too much he might need medical treatment, and that was the last thing they needed. It would draw attention to what they were doing and could even jeopardise the bombing if Paddy became too unwell. He was on borrowed time and may not get another chance, and now that they were into the operation, Michael was keen to get on with it. He also didn't want to be associated with an aborted mission due to someone else's failure; he had his reputation to uphold.

'Yeah, thanks, I think you're right. Once the dust has cleared a bit, I'm sure I'll be better and I can help with the mopping. I'll go and fetch us some tea from the café around the corner. At least I can manage that. Fancy one?'

'Sounds grand. Take your time, I've got this covered.'

While Paddy was gone, Michael swept the rest of the ground floor. He then glanced up at the loft section and decided he should take a look. It might also need sweeping out to remove any dust, to avoid it settling through the hatch once the yoghurt was delivered.

He flicked the switch for the light, climbed up the ladder to the platform and surveyed the space. Several boxes lay scattered around, coated in a thick layer of muck and covered in cobwebs. He also recognised the tell-tale signs of rodents: tiny droppings and tracks in the dirt and nibbled holes in the boxes. He didn't think the rats and mice would disturb the dust, but they might be attracted to the food they'd be bringing in, so they'd need to take precautions against that.

A train rumbled overhead, as they had every few minutes since he'd arrived. However, unlike downstairs, up on the platform he felt a tiny vibration from the passing train, and there was also a very faint breeze up here that he hadn't noticed downstairs. On closer inspection, he found a couple of holes in the wall, which may have housed piping or vents in the past but were now just gaps. He guessed they would lead to the arches either side of this one, and ultimately into the open air somewhere, and maybe this was where the rats and mice got in. But he didn't think it would be worth trying to block them up, as there were probably other smaller holes they used too.

'Hey, Michael, where have you got to? Tea's here,' Paddy said from downstairs.

'Up here, I'll be down in a minute. I'm just going to push these boxes away from the hatch and up against the wall.'

Two minutes later, Michael took his tea from Paddy, who looked better than earlier but still not up to helping with the mopping.

'How are you? OK to go on?'

'Oh, I'll be fine, don't you worry yourself, Michael.'

Paddy then coughed as he breathed in the steam rising from his cup, and brought his hand to his chest with a wince. He looked at Michael. 'Honest, I'll be OK, once I've finished my tea. We have work to do.'

Michael was about to argue when he heard footsteps outside. He looked over Paddy's shoulder, immediately on guard.

'Hello, is anyone there?' a female voice said, accompanied by a tentative knock on the wooden door, and Maria stepped into view.

'What do you want?' Paddy demanded.

His terse tone left Maria in no doubt that she was unwelcome, but undaunted she answered, 'I saw the door was open and was wondering if you needed any help.'

She looked around the space and saw Michael. She addressed him and hoped for a more sympathetic response. 'It looks like you're cleaning this out, so are you starting up here? I'm looking for work and am happy to do most things. I'll work hard.'

'No,' Paddy said, 'there's no work for you here.'

Michael recognised the desperation in Maria's eyes, but she hadn't flinched or looked away at Paddy's curt response and she stood waiting for Michael to respond. He liked her. He put his hand on Paddy's shoulder and said, 'Maybe there is something she can do.'

Paddy shot him a look, but Michael whispered back to him, 'It's OK, I've got an idea.'

Michael stepped forward and smiled at Maria.

'Don't mind my friend, he's a bit of a grouch as he's a little unwell at the moment. As it happens, we may need some help, but it would only be for a day or two to start with. Is that any good for you?'

Maria was delighted that at last someone was talking to her. 'Oh yes, that's fine, but could it be for longer if I work well? What's it doing?'

'First things first, what's your name? Mine's Martin,' he said, 'and my friend here is Peter.'

He held out his hand in greeting. Paddy had seen this performance before from Michael, turning on the charm when he wanted something, particularly from women. But he still didn't know why he was encouraging this girl. They needed to keep their activities quiet.

'I'm Maria,' she answered, blushing as she took Michael's offered hand. 'Pleased to meet you.'

'Pleased to meet you too, Maria, and you may have arrived at a good time. Peter and I were just talking about the work we have to do in the store room here. We are in the food business and we really need this area cleaned before our first stock arrives tomorrow. I'm afraid we may have misjudged it, especially as Peter is feeling a bit under the weather.'

'I can help, but how are you going to do this by tomorrow, as it's already late in the day? And what happens after that, is it just one day's work?'

'Well yes, I'm afraid it would mean working late tonight, so we'll pay extra. But if you have family to get home to, does that work for you?'

Maria thought about it for a second. She had been out all day, but she didn't need to get back to the Refuge early and no one would miss her. She decided to keep quiet about the shelter. She mustn't lose this chance.

'No, that's OK, I live alone. I can do it. But I will need to get some food soon, as I haven't eaten much today.'

'Excellent, that makes two of us. I'm starving too,' Michael said, and then continued with his charade. 'You also asked what happens after tomorrow. Well, after the delivery has come in, we need to distribute it, which we'll probably do the following day. You can help with that too, and who knows, it may be the start of something big. You see, this is a brand-new product, all hush-hush at the moment, and if it catches on we could all do well out of this.'

Maria's eyes widened and she grinned at Michael. 'Where do I start?' she asked, not needing any further encouragement.

Within minutes Michael had her wiping down work surfaces and mopping the floor, but once she was occupied, Paddy signalled to Michael to follow him outside.

'What the hell are you doing? I know I was struggling with the work, but what makes you think we can trust this girl? She might go home and tell all her friends about it, and what if they all turn up looking for work? Our cover will be blown.'

'Trust me Paddy, she won't tell anyone. You heard what she said, she lives alone, and after tonight she'll be too tired to do anything but sleep when she gets in. And I bet she won't share this with anyone until she knows she actually has the job herself. It's human nature.'

'But after the event, she will lead the police to this place. Then they may be able to track us down,' Paddy said, still concerned at Michael's plan.

The veneer of charm he had adopted to recruit Maria fell away, and an evil glint appeared in Michael's eyes. 'Ha, that's the best bit, don't you see? There is no *after the event* for her. If we get her to hand out the yoghurts, she will go up in the blast. No, believe me, this is perfect. Not only is she helping us, she will also be the first one the police investigate afterwards. From the look of her, I'd say she's from Eastern Europe or the Med and there is nothing to link you or me with her, so they'll be looking in the wrong direction.'

'You better pray you're right, Michael. If they ever link us to that girl, we're dead men.'

Michael peered through the crack in the door at Maria, a young woman he had met barely minutes earlier, now sentenced to death. 'You worry too much. She has been sent to help us. God works in mysterious ways.'

Maria hummed to herself as she scrubbed shelves, unaware of the plot against her. What unbelievable luck to find this job. She would work as hard as she could to justify Martin's faith in her, and she prayed that the new product would be a smash hit.

9

There was a fresh edge to the late afternoon air as Jacob made his way past the former St Michael's Church and he pushed his hands deep into his coat pockets. It was going to be a long, cold night.

When he reached City Road, he noticed more people than usual walking the streets. Then he remembered overhearing that the tube strike started this afternoon, which meant that more City workers would be walking or cycling than on a normal day. The pavements would be busier and more hazardous and it would be best to stay away from the main roads, so Jacob decided instead to head for the relative tranquillity of Bunhill Fields. The home of the dead.

Jacob often passed through the historic burial grounds, but he didn't like spending nights there. Bunhill Fields closed every day just before dark, although it wasn't unusual for homeless people to evade the attendant so that they could spend the night undisturbed amongst the tombs and headstones. But this wasn't for Jacob. The park offered little in the way of shelter or warmth, and he preferred to find a doorway or recess at night, or a disused building away from the elements. Even in the summer it didn't feel right, the thought of all those bodies lending a chill to the sultry London air.

However, the grounds would be open for a couple of hours yet, so Jacob entered them by the City Road gate and clambered over the green railings to avoid the attendant's office. Even though he had no intention of staying for long, it was still likely that he'd be moved on if he was seen, so he wouldn't take that chance.

All was quiet in the grounds. It wasn't a tourist hotspot at the busiest of times, but maybe the transport strike was keeping away the few that might have visited today, and Jacob smiled at the welcome desolation around him. He extracted some newspapers from beneath his coat and laid them on the ground, behind a tomb of the Cromwells, then sat back against the wall. He took the photo from his pocket and stared at the image of his wife and daughter, before eventually closing his eyes. The buildings of the Honourable Artillery Company were behind him, exactly where he wanted them, and to the sound of the rustling leaves he soon drifted into a light doze.

The mood during the drive into the derelict village was sombre, heavy with dread at what they might find. The radioed message had told them to prepare themselves for the worst, to suspend all of their belief and trust in humanity and to steel themselves against the most unimaginable barbarity. This they did, and yet they were still unprepared for the horror that awaited them.

From the outside, the building appeared like any other; battered and bruised from shelling and gunfire, but still standing and capable of providing basic shelter. The first indication of what was to come was the image of hardened, grown men gagging at the open doors as they approached, and a sense of foreboding fell over the unit.

The first assault on Jacob's senses was the smell, a stench of decaying, rotting flesh peculiar to human remains. Flies swarmed around the doors and the air was thick with death. Hundreds of cartridges and shell cases littered the floor, and streaks of dark red, almost black stained the concrete where bodies had been dragged across the warehouse and piled to one side. The entire floor at that side of the building was covered in corpses, in places three or four deep. From the position and angle of some of them, it appeared that many of the victims had survived the initial shooting and had crawled across their prone friends, family or neighbours, only to be executed before reaching safety. Three of them still lay on the sills of the side windows where they had almost escaped, slain just as they believed they could reach freedom on the other side.

As if that wasn't diabolical enough, scores of dismembered bodies lay slumped against the right-hand wall, splashed with blood and bearing the marks of ritual slaughter. What possessed men to kill others like this, not only rounded up and executed in cold blood, but allowing them to suffer for hours from their wounds and then shooting them when they could no longer summon the energy to cry out in pain?

Jacob noted that all of the victims wore civilian clothes and all were male, several of them little more than boys.

What had they done to the women and girls, and the youngest boys? He found out, when he was led round the side of the building to a deep trench at the back. They hadn't spared the village's women and children; they had raped and butchered them and made the men of the village watch, before killing them too. And as he reeled in shock at the mass burial ground of the innocents, all Jacob could see was a sea of faces, all in the image of Selma and Leila. The field of the dead.

'Hey you, wake up, you can't stay in here. Come on, I'm locking up.'

Jacob jolted, suddenly wide awake. Dazed and confused, he struck out instinctively, his eyes wild and bulging, and caught the attendant with a glancing blow to his cheek as he leaned forward to pull Jacob to his feet.

'What the hell? There's no need for all that. I'm just doing my job and don't want any trouble.'

It was almost dark and Jacob was disorientated. But as his breathing slowed, he remembered where he was: in Bunhill Fields surrounded by the dead of long ago, not a mass graveyard of a foreign land. He took a long, deep breath and exhaled slowly. The attendant had retreated a couple of yards and studied Jacob with narrowed eyes, aware that he might lash out again.

'It's OK, I'm going. Just a little creaky in the bones nowadays. Give me a minute.'

The attendant watched Jacob in silence. He didn't offer any help, and was relieved when Jacob stood, put his hand to the small of his back and arched it as if relieving stiffness, then started moving back towards the path. Neither man said a word as Jacob left the grounds by the Bunhill Row exit or when the gate clanged behind Jacob. He heard the key turn in the lock.

Jacob looked up and down Bunhill Row, but already knew he would choose neither direction. Instead, he crossed the road and headed past The Artillery Arms on the opposite corner, one of his regular haunts when he was at the bank. He missed those days, when he had still believed he could leave his Army memories behind. He should have known better.

It had been a responsible, well-paid job in one of the largest banks in the City, where he was treated with respect by his colleagues and commuted daily from the suburbs. But nightmares and sleep deprivation blighted his life, and when his violent mood swings, heavy drinking and sudden eruptions of pent-up emotion spiralled out of control following the loss of his wife and daughter, the result was inevitable. But, even though his life in the City had been short, he still recalled plenty of good times, and people, from those days.

Jacob rested for a few minutes on a bench in Fortune Street park, but soon realised that a group of three youths watched him from the deep shadows around the children's play area, otherwise deserted at dusk. Whether they were dealing or taking drugs, or both, they would see Jacob as a threat or a target, but either way it wouldn't turn out well for him.

He pretended that he hadn't seen them, rose to his feet and ambled towards the park's exit on Golden Lane. Although he feigned disinterest, he listened hard in case the three young men followed, but he heard nothing. At the gate, Jacob glanced back and saw that the youths were still under the trees, ignoring his slow retreat, and he began to relax as the familiar, grey, concrete walls of the Barbican loomed ahead.

Despite their unsightly appearance, Jacob always thought of these buildings as his original sanctuary in the City, a refuge where he could find shelter, a warm doorway and sometimes food. He had wandered around the complex so often that he felt he must know it better than anyone else, and he varied his route into and around the estate to avoid the security patrols. They might have the advantage of technology, with their ubiquitous security cameras, but Jacob knew every entrance to the complex and was able to slip in and out largely unnoticed.

However, it wasn't the security patrols he needed to worry about this night, but a far more menacing and dangerous predator, closing in on him fast.

At the bottom of the long ramp that ran up from street level to the raised walkway alongside the apartment blocks of Ben Jonson Place, Jacob was suddenly aware of footsteps behind him. He turned around, half expecting to see the youths from the park, but instead a flare of alarm blazed through him when he recognised the barman from the City Road Inn that morning. For a moment Jacob was confused, bewildered by his appearance, but there was no mistaking his pursuer's intentions the instant Jacob heard his roar.

'Stay there, you thieving tramp! I knew it was you the moment I saw you. You're going to pay for smashing my whisky.'

His fists were clenched into tight balls and every sinew in his neck stood taut, and from the murderous expression on his face, Jacob was in no doubt that Nathan was hell-bent on revenge. It was time to go. Jacob wasn't going to confront him in his dark mood, not after the warning that Merv had whispered about Nathan's temper and violent ways, so he span round, back towards his Barbican refuge and sprinted up the ramp. After it doubled back on itself halfway up, Jacob saw Nathan snarling after him and grimacing from the exertion of the chase, although he wasn't wasting any further energy on cries or insults. But, despite being younger, Nathan hadn't gained any ground on his quarry, and Jacob knew he would reach the top of the ramp first.

He prayed that he would run into a patrolling security guard or resident, who could help him or deter Nathan from making an attack, but he looked around and saw no one. Jacob's best hope therefore lay in out-running Nathan and finding cover, and his mind swirled with the possibilities of which route he should take and the best way of evading him. He knew every inch of the way ahead, but any miscalculation could be fatal.

Jacob surged out of the top of the ramp, then immediately lurched to his right towards the exhibition hall entrances. Momentarily out of sight, he darted behind the wide concrete pillars and then round some shrubs where he would be hidden from view for a few seconds. His lungs burned from the effort of his run, but he could still hear the echo of Nathan's footsteps behind, albeit fainter than before, and he knew he hadn't lost him yet. No time to look back, Jacob forced himself to sprint along the walkway between the concrete pillars, and emerged into the open space adjacent to Cromwell Tower.

Jacob trusted his intuition. Nathan would be expecting him to cower behind a pillar or crouch down behind some shrubs, and would never imagine that Jacob would hide in the open area. It was a gamble, but one that Jacob thought would work. The terrace was surrounded by plants and wooden benches, often used by residents and visitors alike during the day but deserted in the growing gloom and worsening weather. In the middle of the terrace stood several low, brick-built structures, which Jacob had occasionally seen used as benches or tables. But tonight they'd have to serve another purpose. Underneath each one was a gap just high enough for a person to squeeze into, and Jacob dropped to the ground and wriggled into one of the openings. He pulled himself as far into the cramped space as possible, just as he heard Nathan's footsteps reach the edge of the terraced area.

Nathan stopped, and Jacob suddenly doubted his hiding place. Had he seen Jacob or guessed where he was? Had he made a huge mistake?

Nathan walked towards the low benches, his tread silent on the terrace, and Jacob forced himself to hold his breath. His lungs were bursting, but he mustn't make a sound, he couldn't give away his position. Jacob saw Nathan's boots as he made his way ever closer, the scuffed toe-caps rising and falling. But then he heard a welcome sound. Panting. Nathan leaned forward, put his hands on his knees and dragged air into his lungs. Each rasping breath exposed his discomfort and he spat hard, his venomous spittle landing just inches from Jacob, whose own battle with breathlessness was a silent agony.

'Damn, where the hell is he? He must be around here somewhere.'

Nathan stood back upright, hissed through his teeth, and turned away from Jacob, hands on his hips. He wandered over to the wooden benches and then up to the shrubbery to see if Jacob was hiding there.

Jacob could only see Nathan's legs from his vantage point, but he could imagine his livid face, crimson from the rage of losing Jacob and soaked in sweat from the physical strain of the chase. Jacob smiled at the thought, despite his vulnerable position and the possibility of being discovered at any moment, with no means of escape from his cramped space.

Nathan stalked all the way around the open area and looked behind its bins, plants and benches. After what seemed to Jacob like an eternity, Nathan eventually gave up and disappeared behind the concrete pillars, cursing loudly.

Jacob sighed. He hoped his adversary had gone for good, although he wasn't going to take any chances and he decided he would stay in his claustrophobic lair until he was sure that Nathan wasn't coming back. In any case, it was too early in the evening to commandeer a doorway, so this was as good a place as any to conceal himself for the next couple of hours. It might get cold, but he would survive until it was safer to move to a warmer spot by one of the apartment blocks later. It was cramped, but at least he was sheltered, protected from the weather and from the prying eyes of residents who might look out from their balconies or windows above. From the strands of fine mist that swirled in the air, Jacob concluded that the weather was a greater risk this evening than the residents. But at least it would keep Nathan away.

***

Orla was surprised to find the apartment empty when she arrived home from the crèche. Surprised, but also relieved that Michael wasn't there. She wanted some time to herself after her busy day and the last thing she needed was a tense atmosphere between them after his behaviour this morning. She hoped he had gone to work and hadn't spent the day at the pub, as she suspected he had a few times recently, judging from the smell of alcohol on his breath and in the flat when she got home. If he'd been there since lunchtime, there was no telling what mood he would be in.

Orla settled down to watch TV with a simple bowl of pasta in one hand. But it was all so dreary. Most of it was reality TV; cheap programmes that were as far from real life as you could imagine. Well, Orla's life anyway. She didn't spend her time frolicking almost naked around a Spanish villa trying to get the attention of iron-pumping boys, nor did she eat pig testicles in an Australian jungle so that people would pick up the phone to vote for her to eat more of the same tomorrow. She looked down at her pasta and was glad she had chosen a simple vegetarian meal.

But the real-life programmes were just as bad. One news station was showing the tragic scenes of an Italian earthquake and another was broadcasting an interview with a union leader, trying without success to justify today's rail strike. After five minutes of channel-surfing, Orla gave up. Maybe she was in the wrong frame of mind for TV. She left her empty bowl in the sink and decided to run a relaxing bath. She set her phone to one of her playlists, lit a couple of candles, and lay back in the bubbles.

'Ah, yes, this is more like it,' she whispered to herself, 'and not a testicle in sight!'

Orla burst out laughing at the thought and then slid down the bath to dunk her head under the water, enjoying her moment of pleasure. For the first time that day, she felt her troubles wash away, and she dozed, a contented smile on her face.

Orla awoke with a start, lying in a bath of tepid water.

She grabbed her phone. *My God, is that the time?* Then she saw the text from Michael saying he was working late. She reached for her towel, wrapped it around herself and walked through the living area into the bedroom. Sure enough, there was no sign of Michael. At least he was working and not at the pub, which was a good thing. Or perhaps he wasn't. Maybe he was avoiding her after this morning.

Who cares? It's fine with me, either way.

Alone, Orla pulled back the duvet. She was asleep by the time her head hit the pillow.

***

Michael was hard at work, but Orla wouldn't have slept so soundly if she had known what he was doing. His plot was taking shape and he was pleased with himself, despite the arduous activity. Maria and Michael had swept, scrubbed and wiped all evening, and although Paddy had contributed little to the manual work, he helped where he could and fetched cups of tea and a fish and chips dinner to keep them all going.

Shortly after ten o'clock, Michael remembered that he hadn't told Orla he would be late. He thought about giving her a call, but she'd probably ask too many questions about what he was doing and, in any case, she had seemed tetchy this morning. He decided to text instead.

'Hey, Maria, is there anyone you need to call to let them know where you are?' he asked, holding out the phone.

'Oh, no, that's fine thanks. As I said, I live alone.' She immediately looked away and carried on with her work.

'OK, if you're sure. I thought you might have a boyfriend? Or maybe someone like a neighbour, who might notice if you're not there?'

'No, no boyfriend. Just me.' She blushed and, not for the first time, wondered if he was trying it on.

'Fine, in that case, if there's no one for you to go home with, I will walk you home when we're done here. You know what these streets can be like at night.'

'No, don't worry, I'm used to this area, it's a short walk and I know my way around.'

'I insist, Maria, it's what anyone would do. Any gentleman anyway. And as you say, it's only a short walk, so it's no bother.'

'OK, thanks,' she conceded.

Maria knew that he wouldn't change his mind, which gave her a problem. If she went back to the Refuge, she would have to admit that she lived there and she might then lose this job. Maria couldn't think of anywhere else she could go that wouldn't give away her secret, and she looked up for inspiration as another train rumbled overhead. *Oh, why did I lie?*

Michael stepped outside for a cigarette. Something in Maria's manner told him that she wasn't being honest, but what was she hiding? Paddy may have been right that she was a danger to the operation. She had worked hard to clean the lock-up, so she had at least served one purpose, even if they did have to eliminate her before the attack rather than as part of it. He resolved to go home with her to find out for himself, and then he would decide what to do. The best time would be in the early hours, which reduced any chance of trouble if he needed to take action. It also meant they would get more work out of her in the meantime.

Michael extinguished his cigarette underfoot and glanced down the path towards the street. He noticed a couple of people outside the comedy club and wondered if the place would be closed by the time he left with Maria. The fewer people that were around, the better.

He wandered up to the bouncer on the door, who stared after a drunken City-type staggering down the road towards Shoreditch High Street. As Michael approached, the bouncer eyed him with unconcealed suspicion.

Michael ignored the look and nodded at the swaying man. 'Looks a little worse for wear, but I guess you get a few of them in here.'

He held out his hand to the bouncer. 'I'm Martin.'

The bouncer didn't take his hand or exchange any pleasantries. 'No entry after ten-thirty, no exceptions.'

'Oh no, I don't want to come in, I was simply checking what time you closed. I'm new around here and was thinking about coming along one night,' he lied.

'The final act will be finishing up in twenty minutes or so and we'll be shut by midnight. Monday is always a bit slow, but Thursday stays open a bit later, to about one o'clock.'

'Thanks. What other days are you open this week?'

'Just Thursday and Friday. Those are the nights the City boys and girls prefer.' He nodded up Rivington Street to where the drunken man was leaning against a building beyond the railway arches.

'Great, that's all I need to know. Maybe see you Thursday.'

Michael turned, happy in the knowledge that he'd be long gone by Thursday night. *Along with plenty of the City boys and girls.*

He returned to the lock-up and surveyed the space. He was pleased with their progress. They could easily stop now as it was clean enough for the deliveries, but he needed to keep Maria going for another hour or two.

'We seem to have this place pretty clean now, and you could almost eat your dinner off these shelves. Great work, Maria.'

Maria smiled at Michael, her eyes half-closed with weariness.

'We still need to do some tidying in the back room and a little sweeping up in the loft,' he said. 'It doesn't need to be as clean as the rest, just enough to stop dust floating around and into this area. An hour or two, and then I'll take you home.'

***

The Brethren's leader was mystified. Why did Paddy and Michael have a young woman helping them out in the lock-up? Donovan couldn't ask Paddy the question without giving away the fact that they were being watched, so this unwelcome development would need to be monitored closely.

All that could be done for the time being was wait. Sooner or later, this new recruit would have to go home, and then Donovan would decide what to do about her.

10

The cloying air intensified the silence and emptiness of his bunker and the mist lay thick and oppressive over Jacob in the dark shadows. He ached with fatigue and his body cried out for sleep, but his mind would not rest. The minutes dragged. Try as he might to focus his attention on his surroundings, and in particular any tell-tale signs that he had been discovered, Jacob's thoughts kept returning to his life before the streets, and after a while he gave in to his memories.

Not a day went by when he didn't think about Selma and Leila. Both loved, both lost. He had spent his life in service safeguarding people of all nations, races and religions, yet when it came to those closest and dearest to him, he had been an impotent bystander and had failed in his first duty as a husband and a father, to protect them. It wasn't as though he had been unaware of their troubles, he couldn't claim that defence. He simply hadn't been able to help them when they needed him most.

Following his time in Northern Ireland, Jacob had been posted to Bosnia during the conflict that tore apart the former Yugoslavia, where he guarded humanitarian aid convoys and helped protect safe areas in the region. It was here that he met Selma. Their deepening relationship raised a few eyebrows in his unit, but no one said anything to Jacob, he suspected because most of his colleagues thought it would end as soon as his tour did.

But his family and friends at home were more forthright. They disapproved of the match and told Jacob that Selma wasn't good enough for him, even though they hadn't met her and knew little of her background. When Selma fell pregnant and returned home with Jacob, they accused her of using Jacob as a way out of a war zone. However, she soon enchanted them with her natural patience, tolerance and charm, and from the evident mutual devotion of the couple it became clear that this was more than a fling or an escape route. Selma's detractors soon became her biggest supporters and, when Leila was born, they were viewed as the perfect family. And they were, for a while.

When Jacob had seen Maria earlier, he had glimpsed Selma in her face. There was a clear resemblance in their delicate features, but what had struck Jacob hardest had been her demeanour and expressions, those perfect reflections of his wife. The same kindness, compassion and gentle determination shone in her eyes and smile, alongside a tinge of vulnerability that Jacob worried would be exploited by others. He had harboured the same fears for Selma.

Jacob shook his head. Who was he kidding? In the end, the actions of others hadn't killed Selma; she had died because he hadn't been able to hold the family together. No, even that wasn't right, it was worse than that. Jacob had ripped the family apart.

He had allowed his horrors and demons to escape, and they'd overwhelmed them all, haunting and hounding Selma to her death. He had been so immersed in his own troubles and terrors that he hadn't understood what Selma was going through. Jacob didn't know whether she had intended to take her own life, or if it had been a cry for help or a tragic accident as everyone had told him. But to Jacob, whatever her reasons, the result was the same. Selma was dead because his own torment had inflicted pain and misery on her, and he had failed to stop her suffering. It was dereliction of duty, through and through; there was no other way to describe his crime.

Jacob screwed his hands into balls as tightly as he could and his nails dug into his palms. He had to stop punishing himself with his past; it wouldn't change anything.

He forced himself to concentrate on his Barbican surroundings. The concrete buildings, canopies of plants and thickening fog cocooned him in eerie silence, punctuated only by the occasional drip from leaves that soaked in the enveloping fog. It was time to move. Unless he found a sheltered and less cramped spot, he would soon seize up in the dank atmosphere, and then he would be unable to shake the cold. He was already feeling stiff and damp, having brooded too long in his hiding place.

Jacob poked his head out from beneath the brick structure, looked around the courtyard to ensure that no one was about, then slid out commando-style. Once on his feet, he massaged his agonising knees, then tottered forward, each small step bringing more life to his tingling, aching limbs. In the gloom, he could see no more than ten metres ahead and he listened intently for signs of danger, but the solitary sound was his own breathing. Jacob reached the dry path beneath Ben Jonson House, and in the improved visibility he could tell that he was the only soul around. He relaxed for the first time in hours.

Jacob skirted the shadowy pillars and recesses of the building, all the time keeping away from the security cameras, and headed towards one of the maintenance entrances facing Beech Gardens, sheltered from the worst of the cold and next to one of the block's air vents. Although still outside, it would be several degrees warmer than most other doorways and was a favoured spot for those living on the streets. Unfortunately, it was also popular with the security patrols, who would remove any homeless people and then use it themselves for a smoke or coffee. The trick to maximising warm time was to wait for the security guards to move on, and then take the space as soon as they left.

Jacob saw that the entrance was occupied by another man he didn't recognise. Lying next to him was a Jack Russell Terrier, whose eyes locked on Jacob as he approached.

'Howdy friend,' Jacob said, his usual greeting to someone he didn't know on the streets. 'How long have you been here?'

'About ten years, I'd say,' the man replied, his toothless grin giving away his attempt at humour. 'No, only kidding. Best part of an hour, I guess. Nice spot.'

He looked at Jacob without blinking, but he put a hand on the dog's back, not sure if Jacob intended to take his place or join him.

'Ah, OK, I'll leave you be then, you'll be nicely settled,' Jacob said. 'I'll head up to the next one.'

'No need for that, there's space here for two, and Mitzy here doesn't mind shuffling up a bit.'

'Thanks, I appreciate it, but I'd think about moving if I were you. The patrols are pretty frequent around here and they'll probably move you on soon if you've been here an hour already.'

Jacob suspected that the man already knew this, if he really had been living on the streets for ten years. But it felt only right to warn his comrade that he was running the risk of being turfed out into the damp chill of the night, even though Jacob would be the chief beneficiary if he was. There was nothing he'd like more than the warmth of this space.

'Obliged for the warning, but I think we'll stay put. It's hard to give up a spot like this, as I'm sure you know.'

Jacob knew that feeling only too well, the need to stay a few minutes more in the warmth, even if it meant possible discovery. But as he had learned in the Army, you had to be disciplined about how long you stayed in one place, and the more comfortable you felt the less alert you became, and that's when things went wrong. Eventually they always did.

Jacob nodded to the man and walked back the way he had come. He'd only passed two sets of resident staircases when he heard voices ahead, and he dashed out from under the building towards a screen of bushes close by. The two approaching men patrolled in the light of the walkway underneath the building, keeping them out of what had now become a light drizzle, and Jacob was confident they wouldn't see him hiding in the dark garden. He waited for them to pass before he returned to the dry walkway behind them, but he didn't retreat any further. He wanted to see what would happen to Mitzy and her owner.

Jacob didn't have long to wait. A few seconds later he heard voices, and despite being too far away to hear the exact words, he knew what the two guards were saying: this is private property, he had to leave immediately and he wasn't to return. The words were always the same, although the tone and aggression varied from guard to guard. Jacob was relieved to hear no obvious anger in their voices tonight and no shouting as there sometimes was. Maybe they felt guilty at sending the man out into the worsening weather, or perhaps they were animal lovers. Jacob had noticed that homeless people with dogs were sometimes treated with more sympathy, although occasionally some of the more vicious guards, or members of the public on the streets for that matter, felt that they could vent their anger on an animal, so it worked both ways.

One of the two guards led the man and Mitzy to the same ramp that Jacob himself had used to flee from Nathan, but he didn't accompany him very far; it was too damp for that. He stepped back under the cover of the walkway and turned away once the man reached the bend and disappeared from sight. Jacob watched the scene from the shadows and reflected on his own wretched luck over the past few hours, and for the second time that miserable day a homeless man left the Barbican to Jacob's same muttered words.

'Time to go.'

***

Maria dragged herself forward. She ached all over and every so often she jerked as her eyes sprang open after she'd started to drift off. It was almost as if she was sleepwalking home through treacle. She wanted to get back to the Refuge before the mist got any thicker, but despite the allure of a nice warm bed she was dreading getting there, and her footsteps became shorter and shorter.

What was she going to say when they arrived at the shelter? Perhaps she should stay quiet, as Martin might not register the name of the building and could just assume it was a normal apartment block. Yes, that might just work. It was a dark street and it would be easy to mistake the sign above the door for the building name, and in the absence of any other ideas it was her only hope.

One thing was for sure, though: it didn't look like Martin was trying anything on with her. She had wondered earlier if his questions about a boyfriend meant he was interested in her, but now he appeared preoccupied during the walk. There was little conversation and he kept looking around rather than at her, almost as if he thought someone might be following them. He didn't make any attempt to take her hand or brush against her while they walked, but kept his hands firmly in his pockets. It seemed that his offer to escort her home was courtesy after all, nothing romantic. Maria was disappointed, as she liked him, but maybe he was just a little old-fashioned and took things slowly.

Maria was right about one thing: Michael was preoccupied. He visualised what he'd do if Maria turned out to be living with her family or a boyfriend. He didn't want her talking to them about her job, and he was beginning to regret his decision to rope her in. But if he hadn't, who would have done the work, as Paddy had been too unwell? Maria had been a godsend and might still have her uses, especially as she was the perfect choice for a starring role on the big day.

Michael was torn, but he'd have to decide what to do by the time they arrived at Maria's home. He knew he could handle Maria if needed, after all he was a warrior and he'd dealt with far more dangerous foes in the past. He also had the element of surprise on his side, and in his jacket pocket he felt the reassuring presence of his silenced pistol.

Their route was quiet at this time of night, other than the point where they crossed Great Eastern Street, a road that never seemed to sleep. But even there no one noticed them, wrapped up in their own lives and hurrying to be out of the worsening weather.

They walked the short distance along Luke Street to a corner where, to Michael's surprise, Maria suddenly stopped and said, 'Here we are then.'

'Where, which is your place?'

He then looked in the same direction as Maria and froze. His hand tightened around the pistol and he gasped. Surely not, he must be mistaken.

'The Refuge... you're kidding me, right?'

Maria was shaken by his response. She'd hoped that Martin wouldn't have heard of the shelter, and certainly hadn't expected him to react to it like that. Something was wrong, she knew it from his tone, and she took a step back.

Michael stared at the building through the thickening mist and tried to think. *What does this mean? Orla works here and she's bound to know Maria.* Despite everything he'd said to Paddy earlier, his words of warning echoed around his head. There was now a way of linking Maria with Michael.

He needed to act, now. If he dealt with Maria tonight, no doubt the Refuge would raise the alarm by the morning and Orla might somehow make the connection. Unlikely, but possible. On the other hand, he was certain that Maria would talk to others about what she had been doing today. He felt the pistol in his hand. There was only one thing for it.

Michael took his hands out of his jacket and raised them towards Maria.

He spoke with no emotion, although he was still in turmoil inside, and forced a smile onto his lips. 'I had no idea. Why didn't you tell me you lived here? This isn't living alone.'

'I didn't want you to know I was homeless. No one ever gives a job to someone like me. Anyway, it is like living alone. I have my own room and I have no real family or friends here, or anywhere.'

In her tiredness and distress, tears welled up in Maria's eyes. She saw her chance of a job slipping away, but she was determined not to cry and she needed to defend herself. She might not get another opportunity.

'But as you saw today, I can work hard, as hard as anyone else, even if I don't have a home to go to!'

Maria's outburst had given Michael time to think and he now realised what he needed to do to make this work. First of all, he had to get Maria back on side, and he stepped forward.

'Hey, it's OK, I'm not mad at you. I was just a little taken aback, that's all. It's not what I was expecting. Look, you have been great today and, if you still want it, the job is yours.'

Michael watched the relief wash over Maria as she briefly closed her eyes and wiped them quickly with the back of her sleeve, but she said nothing. Keen to press his point, he turned to the oldest trick in the book.

'And to prove it, I'll give you the money now for today's work, plus a small bonus. You deserve it.'

Michael extracted three fifties from his wallet and held them out to Maria with a smile. Her eyes opened wide. This was more money than she'd ever received from anyone, and for just one day's work. What a wonderful day it was turning out to be after all, and how much more exciting might it be in the next few days?

'Oh, thank you, Martin, I was so worried you'd think I'd lied to you. I won't ever do that again.'

She held out her hand to take the money, but Michael pulled the cash back a few inches.

'There is one condition, though. As I said earlier, this product launch is top secret and no one, and I mean no one, can know about it. Not your family, friends or anyone working here.' He pointed at the Refuge. 'If anyone else gets wind of what you're doing, then there will be no more cash like this. That's a lot to give up, for two or three days' silence, isn't it? Do we have a deal?'

Maria nodded and held out her hand again. 'Of course, I promise, cross my heart and hope to die.'

'You bet!' Michael said, and he laughed at the childlike yet prophetic response. 'Come to the store tomorrow, mid-afternoon, and I'll tell you when you'll be needed back. It will probably be Wednesday, but I'll know for sure by tomorrow.'

Maria turned, skipped across the road, and disappeared through the Refuge's front doors without a look back. The frowning terrorist watched her all the way, deep in thought.

As Michael walked to Orla's flat, he considered the next steps of his heinous plan. It wasn't how he had imagined his time in London would end, but maybe Maria walking into the lock-up had been divine intervention. It was more complicated now that both Maria and Orla were involved, but it would be a neater way to end his time here. His mood brightened. Yes, the more he thought about it, the more he liked it, and his steel eyes glinted in the light of the streetlamps.

At Orla's door, he smiled, and three minutes later he slipped naked into the bed beside her, possibly for the last time, his smile now a malignant grin in the darkness.

11

Donovan stepped through the door, soaked to the skin. Tailing Michael and the young woman through Shoreditch had been an unwelcome way to spend the early hours of a cold, wet Tuesday morning, but it had to be done.

Michael hadn't seen his commander-in-chief following behind, despite his training. The weather had helped Donovan to avoid detection, but Michael wouldn't have regarded the person pursuing him of being any danger anyway, even if he had been more observant. Donovan knew Michael's reputation well, and the last thing he would have suspected if he'd seen Donovan would have been a fearless, predatory and unforgiving leader of men, with a history of unimaginable savagery. After all, he wouldn't have believed a woman capable of such things, would he?

Donovan was keen to encourage such thoughts amongst the Brethren's members. She had kept her identity a secret for years, with only a few close disciples aware of the truth, and she was determined to maintain the pretence as long as she could. Not only did the name of the organisation imply it was a group of brothers, of males, giving her the ideal disguise and minimal suspicion, it also helped to confuse her trail amongst the security services and allowed her to come and go almost unchallenged. The mystery created its own folklore of rumours, speculation and conspiracy theories, most of them wide of the mark and invariably concerning ruthless acts of barbarity. Few men pictured a woman in this role, which was just the way she wanted it, as men who underestimated women were blind. Men like Michael.

But there were more important matters to think about right now. Donovan couldn't dispel the concerns she now had about this operation after tracking Michael back to the homeless shelter. What on earth had they been thinking and how could the mission be kept a secret? She might need to deal with their new recruit herself, if Michael or Paddy didn't dispose of her first. Donovan knew she could do little tonight, now that their helper was back at the Refuge, so it would have to wait a few hours.

She would discuss it with Paddy in the morning and maybe by then a solution will have presented itself. If not, it would be the end of the line for their homeless new recruit.

***

'Bitcoin.' Just saying the word was enough to conjure a multitude of images in Brandon's mind. Wild speculation, greed and volatility in financial markets; computer hijacking and coin mining that depleted the world's energy reserves; dark corners of the web where terrorists organised financing for their atrocities; but most vividly of all, a gleaming opportunity to create limitless wealth, brighter than sparkling diamonds or glistening gold.

Brandon was excited by the prospect of using Bitcoin to commit such an ambitious crime. It wasn't that he wanted to take advantage of the so-called cryptocurrency's anonymity to hide his ill-gotten gains. His main motivation was the prospect of creating real money from what he viewed as a system built on thin air. He admired the technology and principles behind Bitcoin, the concept of a 'blockchain' to verify, authenticate and provide an audit trail of transactions. That part he liked, it made sense to Brandon. It was just unfortunate that the hype and hysteria surrounding cryptocurrencies had overshadowed the technology itself. Unfortunate, but hardly surprising.

The world's media had jumped on Bitcoin and exaggerated and demonised something they didn't truly understand, and in doing so had fuelled the bandwagon. History was littered with examples of the public's clamour for apparent one-way financial bets that often ended in heartbreak and destitution for those who were late to the game. But to Brandon, Bitcoin was nothing more than a scheme designed to line the pockets of its secretive founders, with no substance to the claim that it was a currency. Instead, he viewed it as a speculative financial instrument akin to an investment plan with no underlying assets, where the plan's shares were called coins to create the illusion of value, but with no rational way of valuing them.

He knew that people bought the digital coins because they assumed they would increase in value, not because they wanted to spend them. To Brandon, this was the sort of thing that happened in the playground, and he thought about the schoolchildren he had watched earlier that day. What if one of the pupils had convinced a friend to exchange a Monopoly note for a sweet? To record the trade, the children could write the details of it on the note, establishing the first block in the chain. The second child, as the new holder of the note, might later trade it for two sweets and then a third might use it to buy three. Just like the game of tag, eventually the whole class could be swept up by it, and by the time the note reached the last child it might pay for a whole bag of sweets and thirty transactions could have been scrawled on it. The blockchain would have done its bit, faithfully recording each transaction. But did that make the Monopoly note real money, and was it worth a bag of sweets?

Brandon was haunted by a similar experience at school, where a special marble had become more and more sought after in the playground, so that every time it changed hands it was harder to buy or to beat in a game. He'd coveted it and eventually traded it for all of his other marbles, only to find that no one else wanted it afterwards. He ended up losing it to another ordinary marble, and he still recalled the nausea he'd felt afterwards and his embarrassment at having been tricked into believing what the marble was worth, based on an irrational concept. Perhaps that's why Brandon didn't trust Bitcoin.

However, for the purposes of his cyber-financial crime, a cryptocurrency's illusory value was a perfect way to create real money, and it helped his cause that so many people had been pulled into it through the clever use of familiar expressions borrowed from the real world. His work would be camouflaged by the countless other people doing the same thing, and so he spent much of his evening putting together a complex web of new wallets, accounts and aliases, and one-by-one he loaded the details into his programs for the big day. He may not have liked Bitcoin, but that didn't stop him using it for his own illicit ends.

As he worked into the night, Brandon smiled at the thought of putting his childhood scars behind him. *This time I won't be left with an overpriced marble when the music stops, and I will decide how much someone else pays me for it.*

***

After witnessing the ejection of his comrade from the Barbican, Jacob waited for the security patrol to move on.

He had considered leaving himself and following Mitzy and her owner towards Golden Lane, the nearest other place where he'd be able to find a sheltered doorway. When it was wet, the housing estate became a magnet for those living on the streets, with its sprawling blocks and alleyways, numerous parking areas and covered pavements. Many of society's forgotten souls would be taking shelter there this evening; people of all ages, races and gender, some with obvious disabilities, others with pets like Mitzy. A real mix of humanity, but all with one thing in common: they had nowhere safe to stay. A pitiful sight, although to those like Jacob it was just another cold, damp night on the streets of London.

But Jacob decided to remain where he was. He felt more secure in the Barbican's grounds and he was enticed by the prospect of a warm vent in one of the quieter corners. After about five minutes of listening for any sounds or conversation, but hearing none, he crept towards the maintenance entrance. He was about to round the pillar past the last resident stairway, when he saw a plume of smoke billow from the final corner, and he darted back behind the column.

Thank God for vaping! He would never have seen the smoke from a real cigarette, whereas the thick cloud of vapour from an e-cigarette couldn't be missed, even on this gloomy night. Seconds later he heard the crackle of a radio. From where he was standing, the words and static were indistinguishable, and Jacob couldn't help smiling to himself that some things were still done the old-fashioned way.

Again, he waited. Given how close he was to the guards, he decided to stay put rather than risk being heard returning to the garden to take cover behind the plants or turning back the way he'd come, and he pressed himself hard against the dark side of the pillar. His ears strained for any sound. After five minutes of hearing nothing but the dripping of water from the leaves and gutters, Jacob decided that the patrol must have moved on, so it was time to take his chance. They couldn't just be standing there in silence, could they?

With his back pressed against the pillar, he inched round it. The space was empty, and with a sigh of relief he settled himself into the shadowy recess. Maybe he'd be lucky tonight after all.

Huddled, his knees brought up for warmth, he tried to sleep. In truth he never slept on the streets, not properly. The best he ever managed was a doze, as he was constantly alert to sudden sounds and he expected to be moved on or harassed by people far more fortunate than himself, who wouldn't understand what it felt like to find a few degrees of warmth next to a heating vent. Thankfully, on damp nights like this, fewer people ventured out and the security patrols became lazier, so Jacob was hopeful that he'd be left undisturbed until the morning.

After an hour of nodding off, interrupted by the occasional siren in the distance, he napped. His restless mind returned to memories of his wife and daughter, blessed relief that for once he wasn't plagued by atrocities of war. Therefore, he didn't jolt awake to horrific scenes of mass death and destruction, as he usually did. Instead he woke to a different nightmare, something present here and now, and in its own way, just as brutal.

Jacob sensed a sudden change in the light and he opened his eyes to see two men silhouetted in front of him, one of whom leaned in close.

'Well, well, well, who do we have here then? If it's not the thieving tramp. Ha, ha, what did I tell you? I knew we'd find him around here.'

The voice cried with glee, mixed with a chilling malevolence, and when the man turned towards his companion, Jacob recognised Nathan's menacing profile.

'Right, this is payback time!'

The vile stench of alcohol on Nathan's noxious breath engulfed Jacob. There was no telling how much drink-fuelled suffering he intended to inflict, but it was not a good sign that he'd come back to the Barbican with a friend to look for him. There could only be one reason. The familiar sensation of adrenaline flooded Jacob's veins at the prospect of imminent conflict, and he knew he'd be lucky to escape serious injury from these two young thugs.

Nathan grabbed both sides of Jacob's collar, yanked him forward as if to pull him up, but then slammed him backwards. Jacob's back smacked against the wall and he heard a sickening thud inside his own head as it bounced off the alcove. His vision exploded momentarily with spiralling light and he felt oddly detached from his body, but he was lucid enough to cover his head with his arms to shield himself from the inevitable onslaught. Deep down, he knew he couldn't just take a beating, he would have to resist, even though the odds were stacked against him, but he would have to choose the right moment to strike.

'Ha, not going to fight back, eh?' Nathan taunted. 'Good, makes it easier for me.'

Nathan stepped back and kicked Jacob in the ribcage. A sharp, agonising pain surged through his body and he cried out. Nathan looked down at Jacob with satisfaction, then lunged forward and stamped on his leg, and his eyes lit up as the intoxication of his violence overpowered his alcoholic inebriation.

'Come on beggar, fight, you old coward.' He aimed another kick at Jacob, this time his boot glancing off Jacob's arms, still clasped around his head.

'Hey, Nate, take it easy mate, you'll kill him,' said the second man. Jacob had forgotten all about him, but it was clear from his slow, slurring voice that he had been Nathan's drinking partner this dismal evening.

'That's exactly what I mean to do. This is the guy I was telling you about, the one who smashed my whisky this morning. Now Merv is onto me, so this vermin deserves everything he gets. You can either help me as promised or get out of here, like a wimp.'

Nathan looked down at Jacob, curled on the ground as he had been that morning, and in his mind the damp patch next to him was whisky on the hotel tarmac. He was going to pay for that. He leaned forward and grasped the thick lapels of Jacob's coat, then yelled at him in a fit of uncontrollable anger as he pulled him up.

'Are you going to fight or not?'

Jacob staggered to his feet. An excruciating pain shot through his chest and he suspected he had cracked a rib, but he was relieved to be upright and out of the corner. He would have struggled to stand unaided, and he felt a glimmer of hope that Nathan had made a mistake by helping him up. That small corner could have been his grave, but on his feet he had a chance.

But then Nathan's fist pounded into Jacob's jaw, and he staggered backwards and collapsed against the wall. Jacob's fingers grasped the brickwork, and through force of will he pushed down hard on his thighs and remained on his feet. He knew the next blow might send him to the floor, and having pulled him up once he doubted Nathan would do so again. Jacob steadied himself, raised his hands and faced his enemy.

'That's more like it, stand up and fight, like a man.' Nathan smirked at his foe. 'Not that it's going to help you much, you're pathetic, but it'll be more fun for me.'

Nathan stepped in and released a frenzied attack of punches to Jacob's body and head. A few of them caught him in the mouth or around the eyes, or on the left side of his chest, where the dizzying agony of successive punches to his ribs brought loud moans from Jacob. However, despite the burning pain, Jacob managed to parry several of Nathan's blows and landed a few in reply. Slowly, the pace and power of the younger man's barrage waned, and Jacob stepped forward to inflict some of his own. He felt he had a chance, just a small one, of getting out of this.

'Are you going to just stand there, Ray?' Nathan realised that he hadn't finished Jacob and that it would take two of them to do it. He turned and snarled at his partner-in-crime. 'Come on, do something. Grab him.'

Ray looked unsure of himself. After a moment's hesitation, he stepped in, pulled Jacob's left arm and attempted to clasp it behind his back. Jacob caught him with a couple of blows but Ray held on, and the two men pirouetted, locked together. However, the younger man finally managed to wrap his arms around Jacob and, standing behind him, squeezed his arms against his side. Jacob cried at the crushing pain in his chest, and he knew that he was now exposed, unable to defend himself against a further attack from Nathan.

Nathan had caught his breath and saw his chance to finish the contest. He stepped forward to punch Jacob whilst his arms were trapped by Ray's embrace. But even through the pain, Jacob saw him coming. He gritted his teeth and used all of his remaining strength to lift both of his legs up, kicked out at the approaching Nathan and caught him in his stomach. Nathan shuddered against the blow and gasped for air. Jacob's sudden shift in weight caught Ray off guard, he lost his balance and fell back against the wall. Jacob heard a loud grunt and felt Ray's clutch loosen.

Jacob sensed his chance. He shrugged off Ray and staggered forward into the drizzle towards Nathan, like a tired boxer in the ring close to the knockout blow. Nathan's energy was sapping, and breathless from his exertions he took a couple of paces in retreat. The two combatants glared at each other.

Ray had seen enough. From the start he had been wary of injuring himself for Nathan's vendetta against this homeless man. Despite their age advantage and superiority of numbers, he wasn't convinced they'd win the battle, and he had no appetite for defeat.

'OK, Nate, that's enough now. He's cut up pretty bad and you don't want any trouble with the police. Leave it now.'

Nathan wiped the back of his hand across his brow, and a glistening streak of Jacob's blood appeared on his rain-soaked face. He surveyed his adversary. Jacob was still on his feet, but only because he had now stumbled backwards and was supported by one of the pillars. He had an open gash above one eye that had already begun to puff up, numerous cuts on his face and a swelling lower lip. Blood dribbled from his nose and mouth. Nathan was satisfied with what he saw.

'Yeah, I guess you're right, I reckon he's learned his lesson.' Nathan looked at Ray and nodded towards the exit ramp. 'Let's get out of here.'

Ray relaxed, turned his back on Jacob and took a step away. Without warning, Nathan swivelled and launched one final, crunching blow to Jacob's head. He slumped to the floor.

'That's one for the road, arsehole. And don't you ever steal from me again.' Nathan held his right fist in his left as if he had damaged it from the last punch. He grimaced, but his expression turned to a malicious smirk when he looked down at Jacob.

'Nate, come on, I think someone's coming. Let's go,' Ray said urgently.

Nathan turned, glowered at his companion and stalked off. Ray looked down at Jacob, shook his head and then backed away into the fog.

Jacob groaned from the pain in his chest and head, and although he kept his swelling eyes open for as long as he could, fearing that his assailants might return, he drifted in and out of consciousness. Between a feverish, trance-like state and blackness, faces of people he had known appeared and then faded; Selma and Leila smiling at him, Orla greeting him at the Refuge, Nathan and Bill snarling and spitting. They fell silent, but before he gave in to oblivion's welcome embrace, Jacob heard one final voice.

'Oh, my good sweet Jesus, no Jacob, who did this to you?'

12

Orla arrived at the Refuge as usual at about six o'clock, but when Ginger stepped forward to greet her as soon as she came through the front door, she knew that something was wrong.

Ginger was one of the shelter's administrators, whose duties included managing the staff roster and approving access to the Refuge's facilities. Despite his nickname, he had a thick mane of white hair, and it was assumed by everyone at the Refuge that he must have been a redhead when younger. Either that or it was a silly joke that stuck.

He addressed Orla with his customary politeness, although she could tell from his frown and low voice that he wasn't in his normal good humour.

'Orla, can I have a quick word please? It's probably best if we do it in private,' and he beckoned her towards his office behind the reception desk.

After closing the door, Ginger told Orla about Jacob, that he had been brought to the Refuge earlier that morning after suffering a severe beating on the streets. A parking attendant at the Barbican, who knew Jacob somehow, had discovered him while on her way to work.

'She wanted to call an ambulance,' Ginger said, 'but she said that Jacob grabbed her arm and demanded to come here instead. He refused to go to hospital. By all accounts he was feverish and babbling, and if I'd been her I would have called an ambulance anyway. But he was brought here, old Jenks let them in and then rang the emergency doctor.'

'Oh Ginger, that sounds awful. Is he going to be OK?'

'I understand he was pretty bloody when he arrived, but he has cleaned up fine and I'm sure he'll be alright. The doctor says he'll have a headache for a while and he appears to have a cracked rib, but she's happy for him to stay in the sick bay here today rather than send him to hospital. He probably wouldn't get a bed anyway. The thing is, Orla, the reason I wanted to speak to you about it is that he said your name whilst muttering in his sleep, so I think he wants to see you.'

'Really? And is it OK to see him? Do we have enough people in for breakfast?'

'Oh yes, of course you can.' Ginger smiled at Orla. 'I can hardly say "no" can I, especially to a regular volunteer like you? In any case, we're OK at the moment, we'll manage for an hour or so without you.'

Ginger looked down at a sheet of paper on his desk and shook his head. 'It's later this morning I'm worried about, as I'm not sure how it will pan out with the tube strikes today. We always have at least a couple of staff not turn up on these strike days. As usual, it's the people at the bottom of the ladder who suffer most from these things.'

Orla thanked Ginger and headed for the medical bay, situated in the refurbished block at the rear of the Refuge. When she reached the room, Doctor Fernandez was just closing the door and she updated Orla on Jacob's condition.

'Most of his injuries are superficial, other than the rib, but even that isn't too bad and it isn't affecting his breathing at all, so I don't think he needs an X-ray. He'd probably refuse anyway from what I've heard. The rest will heal quickly, a few cuts and bruises and a bit of swelling, that sort of thing. It looks worse than it is and it could have been far more serious. He could easily have damaged his eyesight or suffered internal injuries, but I think he's escaped the worst. He's either a strong man, or a lucky one.'

'Oh, that's such a relief,' Orla said, and she let out a long sigh.

'Well, he's not quite out of the woods yet. We'll observe him here for the next twenty-four hours in case any complications arise. Just to be sure.' The doctor saw Orla's furrowed brow, her concern clear in her face. 'I'm sure he'll be fine, don't worry. He's still a little delirious, but you can sit with him now if you like.'

Muffled voices, bright lights, then silence and the dark.

Jacob floated in and out of consciousness. He sensed people around him, felt their touch and heard them, but he didn't recognise their voices. He knew that he was in a bed from the rub of the sheets on his body, but not where he was.

Dull aches, stabbing pains and agonising loneliness.

His head throbbed, and whenever he forced open his one good eye, he experienced blinding light and dizziness. He tried to say a few words, but his lips were cracked and dry, and only a hoarse whisper emerged.

Searing heat and sweats followed by cold, clammy damp.

He trembled, delirium taking hold, and he stared into the bottomless abyss of his nightmares. But then at the precipice came a voice he knew, accompanied by a tender touch, holding his hand. Was he hallucinating?

'Jacob, can you hear me? It's Orla. You're at the Refuge and you're safe now. If you can hear me and understand what I'm saying, please squeeze my hand, if you can.'

Jacob gripped Orla's hand and a single tear ran down her cheek. 'That's good. Now all you need to do is rest. Don't worry about anything and we'll look after you. I'll be back again later, at the end of my shift.'

A door closes, then blackness returns, all-enveloping, cloaking like Death.

***

At the sound of the front door closing, Michael opened his eyes. He usually stirred as Orla got ready for the Refuge, but tired from his late-night exertions at the lock-up he had slept through that today. Tempting as it was to turn over and go back to sleep, he forced himself to get up. He knew he wouldn't sleep again, not with so many devious thoughts swirling around his head, and he still needed to finalise his plan for dealing with Maria and Orla. There would be plenty of time to sleep when it was all over.

Halfway to the bathroom, he paused. He heard the door across the hallway close, soft footsteps on the floor outside the apartment, and then a knock on his front door. *Jenny.* He smiled. What better way to take his mind off such things? He didn't need to be back at the lock-up early this morning, and Paddy could let himself in if he got there first.

Michael opened the door and Jenny stood there, barefoot and dressed only in his Killers T-shirt that she'd borrowed last week.

'Ha, ha, way to go, you're keen this morning,' she said, and laughed as she looked Michael up and down and stepped forward.

'What are you on about?' Then he realised, and burst out laughing too. He had answered the door still naked.

'Well, let me join you then,' Jenny said, her tone playful. She lifted the T-shirt above her head and dropped it to the floor, then stepped backwards to close the door with her bare body. Michael reached for her.

Even though their relationship had never been based on anything but sex, they surprised each other with the intensity of their lust. Returning to the bed breathless from the living area, Jenny was first to speak.

'My God, Michael,' she whispered, 'I don't know what you put in your tea this morning, but it's unleashed a beast. Not that I'm complaining, of course.'

Michael pulled up his pillow and sat back. He lit a cigarette, took a long drag, and exhaled with his eyes closed. 'I could say the same for you.'

'It's almost like it's the end of the world and you're getting as much sex as you can,' Jenny said, then tilted her head to one side. 'You're not leaving, are you?'

Eyes still closed to avoid her enquiring look, Michael wondered how she could be so perceptive. He'd have to be careful with this one, keep it simple.

'No, of course not. Perhaps we're just getting to know what we both want.'

'In that case, why don't you move in with me? Leave Orla, it's not like you've been with her for long.' She paused, irked by Michael's lack of reaction to the idea. 'I'm serious. How about it?'

Michael realised he was on risky ground, but decided it was best to play along. After all, it wouldn't matter in a few days' time.

'You know, maybe you're right. Do you really want that?'

Jenny nodded and beamed at Michael. 'Absolutely!'

She took the cigarette from his fingers and placed it in the ashtray, then straddled Michael and put her arms around his neck. 'I hate being across the landing at night thinking of you two together in this bed, and I'm tired of all this scurrying about behind Orla's back. I'm not sure how she's going to take it though.'

'Give me a couple of days to find the right moment to tell her.' He pulled Jenny in closer and his eyes flashed. 'She'll be history in no time, I promise you that.'

***

Orla was relieved to be approaching the end of her shift. Just a few more tables and then she would be finished. She was still distressed by the images of Jacob that kept returning to her, and the thought of what had happened to him. He had clearly been viciously assaulted, judging from his swollen eye and lips and the bruising around his face and chest, and she had been distracted all through breakfast thinking about it. She wondered how he was doing.

She glanced up and saw Maria approaching. She looked tired. Maybe her search for work yesterday hadn't gone well, and Orla hoped that she wasn't too down on herself.

'Hi Maria, how are you this morning?'

'Hi Orla. Great, thanks, although I'm so tired that I almost didn't get up for breakfast. I found a job yesterday!'

'Oh, that's great, where is it?'

'It's just off Shoreditch High Street. At the moment we're clearing out the place, but I think I'll also get the job selling the food afterwards.'

'Oh, is it a food store? That's good, that would be regular work for you.'

Maria nodded. She remembered that she had promised not to tell anyone about it, but she was excited by the job. Surely there was no harm in telling Orla a little more, as long as she didn't mention the product.

'There are two men running it. One of them, Peter, doesn't look very well, which is why they needed my help, but the other one, Martin, he's really nice. And guess what, he's already paid me for the first day, so you needn't have worried about that yesterday. Isn't that great?'

'That's good, I'm happy you've found something.'

Maria detected something in Orla's downbeat tone that suggested she wasn't paying much attention. She was usually far more enthusiastic, especially when it was good news. 'Orla, are you OK? You don't seem yourself this morning.'

'Oh, I'm sorry Maria. I'm OK, and it is great about your job. It's just that one of our men was brought in last night after being attacked, and I'm a bit worried about him. You may have seen him here, one of our armed forces guys, Jacob.'

'Jacob? Oh no, I only saw him yesterday. He was on his way here when I was looking for work. Is he OK? Do you know what happened?'

'I saw him when I arrived this morning and he was barely conscious. He has been cleaned up by the doctor, who thinks he'll be OK, but it's still worrying. But I can't see why someone would attack a defenceless and penniless

156

man like that. People can be so cruel.' Orla finished wiping the table. 'Anyway, I'm going to call in on him again when I'm done here, before I head off.'

'Do you mind if I come with you?' Maria asked. 'I can sit with him for a while if he wants. I don't have to be at work this morning as we finished late last night.'

'That's a good idea, I'm sure he'd like that. If you can hold on a few minutes, I'll quickly clear these things away.'

With Maria's help, within five minutes the two women were at the medical bay. But Orla frowned when she saw a policeman outside Jacob's room. He turned at the sound of their footsteps, smiled at Orla and held out his hand in greeting. He was about the same age as her, tall and wide-shouldered, with an engaging smile and deep brown eyes.

Orla offered her hand in return. 'Hello, I'm Orla. Are you here to see Jacob?'

'Hello Orla, I'm Detective Constable Harry Saunders. Yes, I need to speak to him about the attack. I was hoping he'd have come round by now, but he's been drifting in and out, so I was thinking of going back to the station and returning later.' He paused and his smile widened. 'I've been expecting you, as I'd heard he mentioned your name, and I'm glad I waited a little longer.'

Harry shook hands with Maria, but immediately turned back to Orla. Maria smiled to herself.

'How is he, do you know? I only saw him briefly, a few hours ago,' Orla asked.

'According to Doctor Fernandez he should be OK. She checked his breathing, sight and hearing, things like that, and she was happy enough to leave him in the care of Corinne. You're lucky to have a qualified nurse here, you know, otherwise I think she'd have wanted Jacob moved to hospital for observation.'

'Oh, that's great news,' Orla said, relieved that Jacob's condition hadn't deteriorated. 'But why do you want to speak to him? I wouldn't have thought an assault on a homeless man would be high on your list of priorities, and certainly not an immediate call out.'

'We've had a spate of these attacks recently and we're keen to find the culprits. It may be the same attackers each time, maybe not, but either way we want to look into it. And if we don't ask right away, we find that the victims of the assaults, like Jacob, just disappear, and we often can't find them again. Not that he'll say much I suppose. Most of them haven't so far.'

'Can I see him first please?'

'Actually, I thought we could go in together, as he's more likely to speak to you. You don't mind asking him a few questions about the attack, do you?'

'Not at all. If he's awake we can try now, as I don't have long. I need to get to the crèche.'

'Crèche? Do you have children?' Harry asked.

'Oh no, they're not my children. I work at a crèche during the day; it's what pays the bills. I'm only a volunteer here.'

Harry smiled.

Corinne wouldn't let all three of them crowd by Jacob's bedside at the same time. She agreed that Orla could see him with Harry, as long as he wasn't disturbed by any questioning, and Maria said she'd wait outside until they had finished.

When Orla entered, Jacob looked up and smiled, but his smile faltered when he saw Harry following behind.

'Why have you brought the police with you?'

'And good morning to you too, Jacob,' Orla said. She bent over the bedside to touch his hand. 'How are you feeling now? We've all been worried about you.'

'Splitting headache, otherwise I'm alright,' he said, but he stared over Orla's shoulder at Harry, still suspicious of his presence.

'Oh, come on Jacob, be nice. I don't have much time before I have to go to work.'

Jacob looked back to Orla and his look softened.

'Don't worry about Detective Constable Harry Saunders here.' Orla turned to Harry, who had taken his place on the spare chair next to the door. 'He has orders from Corinne not to quiz you, and I won't let him anyway. He will want to ask you a few questions about the attack, but only when you're well enough.

'But I'd like to know what happened, Jacob. All I've heard is that you were brought in last night after being attacked by thugs. Apparently, a parking attendant at the Barbican brought you in. Do you remember?'

Jacob closed his eyes. 'So, I didn't dream about Whoopi, it was her.'

He looked at Orla, who remained silent while he collected his thoughts. Just when she thought he wasn't going to continue, Jacob recounted the events of the night before, whispering at first so that only Orla could hear what he was saying.

'There were two of them, but only one was really violent. He was nasty, vicious, you know the sort. They were both drunk, seemed they might have been drinking hard all night. I was simply in the wrong place at the wrong time. It's not exactly unusual is it, for someone like me?'

'Did you recognise them Jacob, or can you tell me what they looked like?'

'No, I've never seen them before,' he replied. It was obvious to Jacob that Orla had asked this for Harry's benefit, and he had no intention of revealing how he had first met Nathan at the City Road Inn. 'Two guys, both white, in their twenties. The one that did all the punching and kicking, he was clean-shaven, the other had a beard. I can't remember much else, I was trying to defend myself and it was pretty dark. The Barbican lights aren't that bright, and it was misty too, so it was hard to make anything out. The last thing I remember is Whoopi's voice, but that was after the guys had gone and I was well out of it by then. That's all, sorry.'

'That's OK,' Orla said. 'If anything comes back to you, you can tell us later. But there's nothing else you can remember now?'

'No, nothing.' Jacob paused, and then added, as if to himself, 'He did remind me of Bill, though.'

'Did you say "Bill"? Who's he?' Harry asked from behind Orla.

'I thought you weren't asking any questions,' Jacob said, but on seeing the reproachful look from Orla, he sighed and continued. 'I mean Bill Conran. He wasn't involved last night, but he's the same type, you know, sneering face and violent ways. Angry with everyone and everything. He also makes sure he has a mate with him for back-up.'

'But who is this Bill, Jacob?' Orla asked.

Jacob told Orla about his altercation with Bill at Broadgate the previous morning. When he had finished, Orla shook her head and looked into his eyes. 'Jacob, I know there are people around like Bill and these other guys last night, looking to pick on others less fortunate than themselves. But most of us aren't like that, we care and will help fight bullies like them.'

'Really? Well no one helped me yesterday against Bill,' Jacob said. 'They all stared and watched as he kicked me. Just another tramp, getting what he deserves, isn't that what they're all thinking?'

The memories of his continual conflict the previous day came flooding back, and he couldn't stop himself from letting it all out. 'And who was there helping me last night? Everyone behind their doors, minding their own business. Someone must have heard me being attacked, but no one cared enough to look, did they? I was lucky that Whoopi came along when she did, and at least she did what I wanted.'

The mood had changed and Orla tried to ease Jacob's rising anger.

'Please don't be angry with me. You came to the right place, the Refuge, which is full of people who will help you. And there's also someone waiting outside who wants to see you, who will be a friendly face for you this morning. You know Maria, don't you? I think you saw her yesterday on your way here?'

Jacob nodded. 'Yes, I've met her, although I wouldn't really say I know her.'

'Well, Maria will come in to give you a little company, as I have to go now. Just do one thing for me, will you? Please stay away from Liverpool Street and that Bill man. He sounds like trouble to me.' She looked at her watch. 'But I really must fly or else I'll be late for work. I'll try to stop by later if I can.'

'I probably won't be here,' Jacob said, before realising how ungracious he sounded. 'But if I am, thank you, that would be nice.'

Orla squeezed his hand and smiled as she stood to leave. Jacob smiled back, and the sorrowful expression deep in his eyes told her that he regretted his ungrateful outburst.

Harry nodded at Jacob, who responded in kind, and followed Orla out. He held the door open for Maria, who entered the room and closed the door behind her.

'Well, he's a lucky man to have you and Maria, but he doesn't seem to appreciate it much,' Harry said. 'But then I suppose he has had it pretty tough. Sounds like he's been in a few scrapes in the past couple of days.'

'Yes, most of our long-term homeless are frequently attacked and abused. With the men it often ends up like that, or even worse, so Jacob can probably count himself lucky he doesn't have any major broken bones, although the rib is bad enough. With the women the abuse is usually more sexual, and the scars aren't only what you can see on their bodies.'

She sighed. 'But at least we manage to get more girls off the streets, whereas the men, especially the ex-servicemen like Jacob, have to fend for themselves.'

The couple reached the locker room, where Orla turned to Harry and held out her hand.

'Well, it was nice to meet you, Detective Constable Saunders. I guess you have what you need from Jacob, so you won't be visiting us again.' She lifted her gaze to meet his.

'Oh, I wouldn't be so sure. I may have to follow up my enquiries here sometime, so you never know, we may meet again. I hope so. But please call me "Harry", not "Detective Constable Saunders" ... unless, of course, you're being interrogated.'

Orla laughed and Harry grinned back.

'If I see you again, Harry, then I'll try to remember.' She turned to the locker room and pushed the door open, before looking back over her shoulder to where Harry was watching her.

Even after she had disappeared from view, Harry stared after Orla for a moment longer, disappointed at the brevity of their meeting. He was determined to find a reason to return to the Refuge, even if he would have some explaining to do at the station.

13

Brandon's alarm went off at the same time every morning, but today he was already wide awake, his head swarming with bugs, codes and other images of his latest version of *Proximity*. He was certain he had solved it and had tested the program on a few of his own devices last night, but he needed targets for a live test. That was his task for the morning, the excitement and anticipation of which had kept him awake through the small hours. But, despite his sleep deprivation, Brandon leapt out of bed as The Ride of the Valkyries blasted from his alarm, and the loft resonated to its battle-cry and the prospect of another victorious day.

Brandon wandered into the den to review the overnight market news, but within minutes he gave up. He was too distracted by his visions of malware, computer viruses and secondary infections to concentrate on the news and, after a cursory look at the headlines, decided he could catch up later.

With his laptop in his satchel, on his way out of the building he waved to the ever-present Elwyn on the reception desk and headed to the testing ground. Brandon had thought long and hard about where to try out his newest version of *Proximity*. He needed a regular stream of people, enough to see how their devices interacted with each other, but not so many that he couldn't observe individual secondary infections. A handful of stationary devices would be ideal, as that gave the virus time to install and start replicating. And then it had clicked. Of course, a coffee shop would be perfect, as customers would queue at the counter for their drinks, or sit eating breakfast, while *Proximity* attacked their gadgets. He knew just the place.

Gianluca was handing a customer his change when Brandon entered Il Miglior Caffè.

'Buongiorno, Brandon,' he said in his usual enthusiastic manner, although a quizzical look crossed his face. 'But this is a little early for you isn't it, my friend?'

'Hi Gianluca, yes, I guess so, but I couldn't sleep last night. Too much on my mind.'

'Ah, sorry to hear that. Hopefully you can catch up on your sleep later. Your usual black coffee and cookie to take away?'

'Well actually, no. I think I'll have it here today and try to catch up on a few things. I have come prepared.' Brandon held up his satchel. 'I will take that small table at the back. Same coffee and cookie, though, as I haven't won the lottery yet.'

'Well take a seat and I'll bring them over.'

Brandon sat at the table with his back to the wall, from where he had a clear view of the door and the counter. He set his laptop on the table and placed the satchel behind it to discourage anyone else from sitting opposite him, although the shop wasn't full and Brandon suspected that most of the trade would be take-away.

Brandon opened up his *Proximity* program and set the power to its lowest setting, more than enough range to reach the café door. He highlighted his new pride and joy: the *Replicant* file he had tested successfully on his own devices. It was more invasive than the benign *Sleeper* bug he had released at Stratford. This time he needed to check self-replication and transmission, so he had no choice but to let something more dangerous into the wild, but it was still only a slimmed down version of the final virus he had developed for the ultimate cyber-attack. That one would have far more serious and sinister consequences, and Brandon couldn't risk letting that into the open until the day itself.

Finally, he selected the pre-prepared lonely-hearts message that would appear on the target devices. He was all set.

Two of the other tables were occupied. In front of him, a young couple held hands and chatted, with their phones on the table in front of them. To his right, seated side-by-side against the wall, two men studied a tablet screen, which the younger one prodded every few seconds. He appeared to be demonstrating something to the older man, who looked every inch the fintech entrepreneur.

At the counter, a uniformed security guard poked at his smartphone as he waited for his coffee, and a middle-aged woman looked at the chalkboard behind Gianluca, deciding what to order.

Looking good. With a deep breath, Brandon pressed the button to transmit *Replicant*. He concentrated on his screen, but out of the corner of his eye he kept tabs on his targets and listened for tell-tale signs that *Proximity* was working. He didn't have long to wait.

'What the heck? Bloody cheek!'

Everyone in the café looked at the security guard. Brandon saw that the man's screen had turned bright purple, but he jabbed it to close the message box and the colour disappeared. He muttered something under his breath and then returned to the game he had been playing.

As far as the guard was concerned, that was the end of it, but Brandon looked at his own screen and saw that one new live version of *Replicant* had been activated and was preparing to replicate itself. Within a second, it had accessed the connectivity and transmission functions on the security guard's smartphone and had started to broadcast an identical message to the one it had just received. This was invisible to the guard, who was oblivious to the fact that his smartphone was now a miniature version of *Proximity*.

A faint chime sounded from behind the shop counter and Gianluca reached for his phone. One of the two phones on the table occupied by the young couple vibrated and the screen lit up. Only Brandon appeared to notice the coincidence of their timing and, like the security guard before them, the phones' owners dismissed the message and went back to what they were doing.

Brandon looked down; the *Replicant* count had risen to three.

Another ping sounded. 'Did you just get that message too, the one about feeling lonely?' the young woman asked her partner, and she tilted the man's screen towards her. 'Yes, same one, very odd. But, in our case, I reckon the answer is "no", eh?'

Four. Brandon smiled.

He glanced at the two men by the wall. Why hadn't their tablet been contaminated? Then he saw that the younger man was putting it away in his bag, which would explain it, but didn't they also have phones with them?

Brandon was delighted with the results of his first test, which proved that *Proximity* could infect other people's devices with *Replicant*. He'd never doubted it, but the key to his project was that these devices would then go on to transmit the same bug to others. A secondary infection, and then a third, a fourth and so on, and theoretically the infected population would grow exponentially.

So far, all of the infections had come from his laptop, but now came the moment of truth. Would the virus live up to its name? It was easy to test. All he had to do was stop his own version of *Proximity* from broadcasting.

He turned off his transmission, and waited.

A smart young woman entered the café and approached the counter. 'Buongiorno, Louisa, my princess, how are you?' Gianluca said, throwing his arms in the air with typical gusto.

'Oh, not so bad, thank you, other than this dreary weather. A strong latte please.' She fished around in her bag for a few seconds, but then looked up at Gianluca with a furrowed brow. 'Sorry, I don't have my purse. Can I pay on my phone?'

'Of course, that's fine, go ahead, almost everyone does it now.'

Louisa held her phone towards the reader but, before it reached, it chimed. She glanced at the purple screen, shook her head and pressed the display, and then held her phone back to the reader.

Brandon held his breath and looked at his laptop. Five.

He sat there staring at the screen for a few seconds. *It works!* The woman's phone could only have been infected by one of the other *Replicant* viruses, not his own. He trembled at the implications. Now the rate of infection would accelerate, and every device that left the café would be capable of transmitting the virus further afield.

For another ten minutes, Brandon watched the count rise, by which time he had recorded a total of twenty-five new infections of *Replicant*. But there wouldn't be many more after that. Brandon had built a time limit into the program to avoid the replication process running out of control. He knew how vital it was to keep a low profile, and the last thing he needed was to have a runaway pop-up reveal his program before the big day. He felt a bit like the scientists involved in the first test of the atomic bomb during the Manhattan Project, where legend has it that no one knew for sure that the chain reaction wouldn't keep going and ignite the Earth's entire atmosphere, engulfing mankind in the ultimate nuclear holocaust. Brandon had some doubts about this popular myth, but he wouldn't take such a chance with *Proximity*.

Satisfied with his morning's work, he rose from his table. The two men by the wall were leaving at the same time and Brandon thanked the younger one who held the door for him. It reminded Brandon about his only unanswered question. Why had neither of them received the virus? Deep in thought at the question, Brandon almost walked into the back of the older man, who suddenly stopped a few yards along Worship Street.

'Oh, sorry, excuse me,' Brandon said and he stepped round him.

The man reached into his pocket and addressed his companion. 'Sorry, Jake, I need to get my phone. It's been buzzing incessantly and I've been trying to ignore it, but it's beginning to bug me. Sorry.'

Brandon glanced at the smartphone's purple screen and smiled. *Twenty-six.*

***

The key turned in the lock. Michael sprang up, dashed into the kitchen and tipped his cigarette ends into the bin. Just in time.

He had only just finished clearing away the evidence of Jenny's earlier visit. He was prepared to be caught in the act of smoking, but Jenny was another matter entirely. She had left less than quarter an hour earlier and he'd almost had to push her out of the door, but not before she had demanded that he say it again. *Of course, I will tell Orla about us soon.* He scowled. She had left it so late that he would have said anything.

Fortunately, Orla was home a little later than usual, otherwise it would have been a close-run thing. It was almost as if Jenny wanted Orla to arrive home to discover them together. He just hoped that he could stall her for another couple of days, then it would all be over.

'Hi Orla, how was the Refuge?' Michael asked. 'You're home a bit later than usual.'

Orla placed her keys on the table and dropped her bag onto the sofa, then looked at Michael for a few moments. It was unlike him to ask after her work at the Refuge. But she took his question as an encouraging sign of his interest in what she was doing. Or maybe it was his attempt at an olive branch after yesterday.

'Sorry I'm a bit late. One of our homeless men was brought in last night after being beaten up. I've known him for a while and have mentioned him to you before. His name's Jacob, the one who wanders around the Barbican. He's been caught a couple of times taking trips to the top of the towers, remember him?'

Michael nodded, although he wasn't interested in Jacob. He had only asked about the Refuge in case there was any news about Maria.

'So, I popped in to see how he was before coming home. He was a bit of a mess, but I think he'll be fine. But it means I'm in a bit of a rush for work now, sorry.'

Orla expected Michael to object and ask her to come to bed, but to her relief he appeared to be listening to her story.

'That's too bad, and I hope the guy will be OK. I guess the homeless often get into scrapes.'

'Yes, unfortunately they do.' She pulled off her top and trousers. 'In fact, Jacob was attacked twice in one day. The first time was in broad daylight at Liverpool Street yesterday morning, and of all people it was one of the Broadgate security men there who assaulted him. You'd expect more of people who are supposed to be there for our safety. I've a good mind to report him when I get to work. I'm sure our bosses wouldn't be happy with someone like him providing security for our firm.'

Orla took off her bra and turned to the bathroom. 'Actually, that's not a bad idea. I know his name, after all,' she said, more to herself than to Michael.

Michael watched Orla's back all the way to the bathroom and then heard her turn on the shower. He sauntered to the door and spied on her through the crack for a few moments, the water running down her back and over the curve of her buttocks. He was tempted. He knew he wouldn't get many more chances, but he also suspected he'd be pushing his luck and he didn't want to get on Orla's wrong side right now. What a shame. But at least he'd had a good time with Jenny this morning, so he returned to the bedroom, where he reclined against his pillow and grabbed the TV remote. He flicked through the channels, but found little of interest. He yawned and glanced to the side.

His Killers T-shirt lay crumpled on the floor by the front door.

How on earth had he missed that and, more to the point, how had Orla not seen it? With no time to worry about that, Michael snatched up the T-shirt, buried it in a drawer and dashed back to bed, just in time to hear Orla turn off the shower.

The TV had stopped at a news channel, where the newsreader was talking about the London Underground strike. Michael was about to turn it off, when the newsreader's next comment caught his attention.

'And this was the scene at Liverpool Street station earlier, as thousands of commuters queued for buses and taxis.'

The screen switched to long queues of people filling the upper walkways of Liverpool Street, three or four deep, as they waited for buses from Broadgate or Bishopsgate.

'Others waited in vain on the main concourse for the Underground station to open, but many of them have since given up and have now started the long walk to work.'

The picture switched to a seething mass of people crowded around the shutters to the Underground station, but as the camera angle panned out to reveal the whole chaotic scene, Michael wasn't looking at the queues, and he certainly wasn't feeling sorry for the commuters. He got up from the bed and peered at the centre of the screen, where two temporary stalls were inundated with people, swarming around them and reaching over each other to grab free snacks, even in the melee of the tube strike.

'Oh my God,' Michael whispered. 'This is it, this is what we have to hit. Forget the market, this is far bigger.'

He marvelled at how many hundreds of people stood there, packed so close together, and at the centre, someone was giving away food. *That could be us. There's hardly anywhere to escape and it would be carnage; an absolute bloodbath. Why didn't we think of this earlier?* 'I need to call Paddy, he'll love this.'

'Are you OK Michael?' Wrapped in a towel, Orla was surprised to see Michael talking to himself by the TV. 'You seem a little agitated.'

'Oh, yes, I'm fine, I was just watching the TV. All those people trying to get to work. Lucky you can walk, eh?'

Michael had recovered his poise, but as his devious mind whirred with the logistics of it all, an inspired thought struck him.

'Actually, Orla, I was thinking about what you said before, you know, about the man who was assaulted.'

'Jacob, you mean? What about him?'

'Yes, that's the one, Jacob. These pictures of Liverpool Street reminded me. What did you say was the name of the security guard who attacked Jacob yesterday? If you want, I can go down there later and warn him off, you know, make it clear someone knows he's stepping out of line. I think that would be better than you reporting him.

He could cause you trouble, but he doesn't know me, does he?'

Orla studied Michael. For the second time since she'd arrived home, she couldn't work out if he was up to something. He'd never offered anything like this before and he generally had little sympathy for anyone at the Refuge.

'I don't think I said his name. And what if you get into trouble? Jacob said this guy is always surrounded by his thuggish colleagues. You might get hurt.'

'Oh, don't worry about that, I'll turn on the Irish charm,' he said and gave her a silly grin. 'If that doesn't work, I will still have made my point and he'll know he's being watched. You can always report him through your work tomorrow if he turns nasty. How about it, deal?'

Orla couldn't think of a reasonable objection and it was clear that Michael was determined to do it. She wasn't sure why it was suddenly so important to him, but she had little choice but to concede.

'OK, but be careful. I don't want you getting beaten up like Jacob. The security guard's name is Bill. I can't remember what surname Jacob gave, something starting with a "C" I think, but I can't imagine there are too many guards called Bill working down there.'

'Great, I'll have a quiet word with this Bill creep. I'll do it when you're at work, no fuss, just a man-to-man chat.'

'Talking of work, Michael, what were you doing yesterday? You finished up pretty late. I didn't even hear you come home.'

'Oh, it was an urgent call-out for one of our clients. They had a bit of an emergency at their IT centre. It may be the same today, but I'll let you know later.'

'But why are all your clothes dirty? The ones you took off last night look like they've been through an army assault course.'

'Oh, those...' He was irritated with himself for such a simple error. 'Yes, there was quite a bit of crawling around on the floor, and this company's idea of a clean environment for their computers leaves a bit to be desired. I'm sure they'll wash up alright.'

Orla frowned and Michael wondered if his tale had been too flimsy. But it wasn't his clothes that perplexed her, but hers.

'Michael, have you seen my jumper, the long turquoise one? You know, the one you always say is green. I thought I'd left it out last night to wear to work today, but I can't find it now. That's really odd. You haven't moved it have you?'

Michael knew instantly where it was, but he shook his head. 'No, I don't remember seeing it.' He closed his eyes and saw Jenny, wearing nothing but Orla's jumper.

'Well I don't have time to search for it now as I'm going to be late. This one will have to do.' Orla took a cardigan from the shelf and pulled it on.

'Must fly, see you later.' She kissed Michael goodbye, before turning and rushing out, grabbing her keys from the table as she left.

Michael sat back down on the bed and exhaled loudly. The last few minutes had been a whirlwind of conflicting thoughts and emotions, and he needed time to think. What had just happened?

His weakness for the fairer sex was catching up with him and he wondered whether he now had to deal with all three women. Maria's elimination had already been decided. She knew too much about the lock-up and would see the merchandise, so she had to go. Orla's association with Maria and her knowledge of Michael counted against her, and she was also asking too many questions. Orla therefore had to go as well. But what about Jenny? She wasn't directly involved, but she was starting to become a danger, possibly even a bit crazy with the risks she was taking trying to let Orla know about his infidelity. Why would she steal Orla's jumper and leave his T-shirt where it could be seen? *Damn, she may have to go too.* It was getting complicated.

But now, just as these three women had threatened to blow the mission off course, the clouds had parted with the news report from Liverpool Street. Michael was confident they could pull off his alternative plan, and surely Paddy and the Brethren would buy it. This was going to be bigger and far deadlier than they had ever imagined. Better still, there was a clear way to ensure that all three women were included in the slaughter. With that, no one would come looking for him. He'd be just another missing person statistic, one of the many presumed lost, along with Orla, Maria and Jenny.

He laughed at the thought. *Happy days.*

***

Michael wasn't the only person enjoying the news that morning. Brandon plugged his laptop into its cradle after his successful test at Gianluca's coffee shop, then flopped into the chair in front of his screens. Although he was tired from lack of sleep and the nervous energy expended during the test, he couldn't stop smiling, and every few seconds he chuckled to himself as he imagined his victims prodding their purple screens. What a morning.

He needed to take his mind off *Proximity* and *Replicant* for a while, and what better way than to catch up on the markets? It wouldn't be most people's chosen way to unwind, but Brandon loved to relax at work in his den. Where others would read a book or play a puzzle, Brandon would review financial charts or work on a complex algorithm. He liked music but rarely remembered the lyrics, yet he never missed a word when listening to the market news. He enjoyed the drama and tension of a good action movie, especially science fiction or anything with futuristic technology, but he preferred the cut and thrust of finance and the thrill of beating the professionals with his computer-generated models. There were no two ways about it; the markets won every time.

Brandon watched his screens. Every so often he would lean forward, flick to a different display or inspect a chart. In the background, his computer programs monitored market trends and prices and executed automatic trades. When the rolling news became repetitive, he changed channels. He was in his element.

It was in this laid-back pose that Brandon had his epiphany.

Like Michael, he became mesmerised by the reports of the transport strike, the sea of people at the rail terminus, who filled the walkways whilst they waited for buses or crammed themselves against the drawn shutters to the Underground station. But where Michael saw people crowded around pop-up stalls and visualised death and destruction, Brandon saw thousands of phones and gadgets clutched in commuters' hands, and imagined the virulent cyber havoc he could wreak.

This is what *Replicant* had been designed for. It was the perfect target.

Convergence

The union leader spoke confidently into the microphone, his back-drop the bright, expansive Liverpool Street concourse, his audience a group of reporters clamouring for his attention.

'Our members' actions will change the face of travel in this country. No longer will our workers suffer so-called technological advances that replace drivers and signalman with computers. The proposals of the railway companies are nothing more than penny-pinching; insidious measures that will cost many of our members their jobs and will put our passengers' lives at risk. We understand our customers' frustration at having to make alternative travel arrangements at this time, but their pain will be short-term. Mark my words, our industrial action will protect the jobs of our members and will make our passengers safer. In short, it will change lives forever.'

Michael and Brandon couldn't help smiling at the pompous official's grandstanding.

Two men, two very different weapons of terror.
One place, one time: Liverpool Street on strike day.

14

Switch on your TV news, pictures of Liverpool Street. We need to talk. I have a new plan.

Michael's message to Paddy was deliberately vague. Whilst he was confident that WhatsApp communications couldn't be intercepted, he was worried about Paddy's health and the risk that his phone might fall into the wrong hands if he took a turn for the worse. There was no telling who could get hold of it, and Michael wasn't taking any chances.

The response from Paddy took only a few minutes:

OK, watched TV. See you @ lock-up asap. Our delivery is this pm.

Adrenaline surged through Michael without warning as the magnitude of what they were about to do struck him. He hadn't felt this excited for a long time, so psyched up for battle. This time tomorrow, London would be soaked in blood, cowering from the ferocity of their attack, and he would be a hero of the Brethren. Revenge would be sweet.

***

When he arrived at the lock-up, Paddy was already there. He looked pale and drawn.

'So, Michael,' Paddy said with no preliminaries, 'I'm guessing that you now want to hit Liverpool Street, rather than Spitalfields. Is that it? It's a little late to change our plans.'

'Yes, too right I do. It's a much larger target and imagine how many more people we can kill.'

'But larger targets have more security.' Paddy wasn't yet convinced that the last-minute change was a good idea. 'And think about it. Liverpool Street is harder to get into, whereas you can drive right up to the entrance of Spitalfields and wheel the bomb straight in. It's all been planned.'

'Ah well, that's where you're wrong. You can easily wheel it into the station too. Didn't you see the two stalls in the TV shots today? Apparently, it happens almost every day with demonstration stands and giveaways. You know the kind of thing. Right in the middle of the station, no problem.'

'OK, well what about reconnaissance? We haven't even looked at where things would go or escape routes.'

Michael felt that Paddy was ticking off a list of objections he had already rehearsed and he was happy to play along. This was an easy one to quash.

'Oh, that's fine, we can do it today. No one will take any notice if we wander round and take a few pictures, they're so busy down there. As an added bonus, I have the name of one of the security guards, and I'll go see him this morning. I reckon I can convince him to let us in with the carts.' He rubbed his thumb against his middle finger to indicate he'd bribe him. He paused. 'But actually, there's one more thing I want to change.'

'Tell me you're joking. Isn't changing the target hard enough for you?'

'I want two carts, two bombs.'

'What? Are you crazy?' Paddy threw his hands up in exasperation and stared at Michael. 'I haven't even told the Brethren we've changed the plan yet, although I think they will go along with that. But there's no chance they'll get two carts organised in time.'

He took a deep breath. 'Look Michael, I admire your ambition, but I don't think this is going to work. And haven't you forgotten something? We'd need two people to man two carts, and we only have one, your new friend Maria.'

'Actually, it's worse than that, but hear me out on this.'

Paddy rolled his eyes, but then nodded to Michael. 'Go on, let's hear it.'

'In the TV pictures, I counted four helpers handing out bits, probably to avoid mayhem as people grab their free stuff.'

Paddy opened his mouth to object but Michael cut him short. 'I can get four people, and in fact I think it helps us in other ways. I'll get to that in a minute. But the reason I think we go for two carts is that it's a big target, it can take two bombs. I was originally going to rig it up to detonate remotely, and I can still easily do that with two. And imagine, one goes off, carnage. People panic and they end up running straight into the second one, which I detonate a few seconds later.'

Michael's eyes blazed as he pictured the horror of mass murder.

'What about the four people? Where do you get them from?' Paddy asked.

'You know one of them, Maria, and she's keen, as you saw yesterday. But I've also been thinking about how I cover my tracks once we've finished here. Orla knows too much about me, and I found out last night she also knows Maria—'

'What? Oh, that's just great, a link back to Maria!' Paddy's face turned crimson and he looked ready to explode. 'I told you it was a mistake to use her.'

'Calm down, yes, you did, but don't you see? It's divine intervention again.' Michael put his hand on Paddy's shoulder. 'Orla was going to be a problem, so we'd have to get rid of her anyway. Shooting her and dumping her somewhere isn't without its risks, whereas if she goes up in the explosion, no one will ask any questions. And Maria and Orla will make one team.'

'Hmm, I suppose so. And the others?'

'Well, one of them is a guy I know, a barman at my local. He needs the money and I'm sure he'll do it. It's also one less person who knows me who may wonder afterwards where I've gone. Good riddance. The other is Orla's neighbour, who lives across the hall. She and I, well... we're friends.'

'Which means you're screwing her too. Christ Michael, what's the matter with you?' Paddy shook his head in frustration and disbelief. 'And what makes you think she'll do it?'

'I think she'll do whatever I say at the moment,' he replied, and he grinned at the memory of their recent early mornings. 'I've a feeling Orla will be hardest to convince. But she'll get there. Don't panic, it's all under control.'

Paddy closed his eyes and considered the options. He liked the boldness, the daring of Michael's plan, but what if he couldn't recruit the four sacrificial lambs? It wouldn't matter anyway if the Brethren couldn't give them two carts, but he may as well try. What did he have to lose? After all, he wouldn't be around much longer, and he certainly wasn't going to die from the embarrassment of having only one cart at Liverpool Street if Michael couldn't deliver.

'OK, OK, I'll give them a call. Be it on your head, though, if they don't like it.' Paddy reached for his phone. 'Your turn to get the teas.'

When Michael returned with two steaming cups and two bacon rolls on a cardboard tray, Paddy was leaning back against a table, smoking. He took his tea and nodded.

'Yes!' Michael cheered, almost spilling his tea as he clenched his fist. 'Two carts, two bombs?'

'Yeah, that's right, you lucky bugger. It seems they have a spare cart, a back-up in case the first one gets damaged. Standard procedure, apparently. The extra explosives, well, they were never in doubt, as they're always available.'

Michael whistled and clapped Paddy on the shoulder, the ecstasy clear in his face.

'A word of warning, though, before you get carried away. They like the new plan, but they've warned us both, Michael, any screw-ups and it'll be on our heads. We can't leave the second cart unused to be found afterwards. No trail back to them, or us. I get the feeling this operation is being closely watched from the very top. I just spoke to Donovan, who even seemed to know about Maria, God knows how. This is a big one for the Brethren, and they won't be very forgiving. You know what I'm saying, don't you?'

'Relax man, relax. Have faith. I'll get onto it now. When's the delivery?'

'Nine o'clock tonight. The load isn't coming very far, but they didn't say where it is now. We'll have all night to rig it up and make the changes to the snacks, which should be enough time between the two of us. At least one of us will have to be here all the time once it arrives, as we can't let it out of our sight.' He looked around the look-up. 'But at least it will all be over soon, and we won't have to spend much more time in here.'

Paddy took a wheezy breath, straightened his back and spoke with greater determination and urgency. 'Right, let's do it. We've got a lot of work to do, especially you. It's time we got to Liverpool Street and took a good look at our new target.'

***

Donovan stared at her phone with a frown. She had been surprised to receive Paddy's call, and taken aback at his request for two weapons for a new, larger target. Now that Paddy had explained it to her, she was annoyed that her advisers hadn't suggested Liverpool Street in the first place, as it would cause much more damage and give the Brethren far more exposure and publicity. She made a note to check that out, once she returned home after the event.

Paddy had credited Michael with the idea, maybe to avoid potential recriminations for himself if anything went wrong, or possibly as a sign that he wanted to pass the mantle of leadership to Michael after this operation. He was unwell, so that was natural, but Donovan wasn't sure Michael was ready yet. She hadn't been impressed with him so far on this mission, recruiting a helper off the streets on a whim, then not detecting Donovan when she had tailed him last night. But he was ambitious and committed to the cause, and she needed that in her men.

She watched the two men leave the lock-up. Paddy, a jaded figure, pale alongside Michael, who strutted along Rivington Street as if he owned it.

A new leader? Maybe. Just don't get ahead of yourself Michael, with the prize so close.

***

Maria watched Jacob doze, and yawned. What was it about seeing people sleep that made you feel drowsy yourself? But maybe it wasn't that. After getting back to the Refuge late last night, her mind had been buzzing with the excitement of her newfound job and it had taken her a while to get to sleep. How annoying, now that she wanted to stay awake, she couldn't help nodding off every few minutes.

She watched the clock and concentrated on the second hand, ticking round the dial, and counted in her head. But she soon found herself drifting off again. In her boredom, she studied her hands, still pink and blistered from all that scrubbing yesterday, but she smiled at the thought that the cleaning was over. She had proved herself to Martin and the next part should be much easier. After all, how hard could delivery be?

She couldn't wait to return to the lock-up, not only to be involved in the new product launch, but also because she was keen to see Martin again. *A good-looking man, and kind too*. He'd offered her a job when everyone else had ignored her. He had walked her home and had been very chivalrous, and he'd even paid her more money than they had agreed. He had an air about him, something she couldn't explain, an edge, and she remembered his reaction when he'd found out she lived at the Refuge. For an instant he had felt dangerous; Maria shivered at the memory. She recalled being a little scared at the time, but in the light of the new morning, it felt exciting. Maria didn't think life would be dull with Martin.

She looked at Jacob. Although he was now covered in cuts and bruises, she remembered thinking when she spotted him yesterday that he was striking for someone who had lived on the streets for a few years. He was tall, yet didn't stoop the way people often do after sleeping rough for a while. His slow deliberate walk was graceful, not lethargic, and he gave the impression of possessing great physical strength. Yet when he spoke he was hesitant, almost humble, as if his unkempt appearance and reduced status in life were sources of embarrassment to him. But her most vivid recollection was the way he had looked at her before saying she reminded him of his dead wife. In his eyes she had seen utter desolation, as if he was haunted by his past. A deep sorrow that he couldn't dispel.

Jacob opened his eyes. He looked around the room until his eyes settled on Maria, and he smiled.

'How do you feel,' Maria asked. 'Any better?'

'Not much, although the headache's not quite so bad. Can you help me up please?'

Maria held Jacob's arm and then propped the pillows up behind him. He shifted up in the bed and grimaced from the obvious pain in his chest, but once he was comfortable, she gave him a glass of water.

'Thanks, I needed that,' Jacob said and he sat back for a few seconds with his eyes closed. When he opened them again, he looked at Maria and she saw the same sadness from yesterday. She waited for him to speak, feeling herself blush under his gaze.

'You don't have to sit with me, you know, I'll be OK. I'm sure you have better things to do.' Jacob spoke gently, without any bitterness or hostility, and Maria took no offence at his words.

'I know, but I want to be here, as long as that's OK with you.'

'Thanks, yes, it's fine with me.' He paused. 'So, I guess you didn't have any joy with the job-hunting yesterday then?'

'Oh, you remembered. It couldn't have been that bad a knock to the head then,' she said, grinning at him. 'Actually, I did find a job. But the hours aren't regular yet, so I can sit with you for a while. I will need to go in about an hour or so, though, sorry.'

'That's OK. I expect they'll kick me out soon enough,' he replied. He looked around the room. 'I don't think I can take much more of this anyway. This room is so stuffy and these sheets are really itchy. I'm not used to beds and I won't get any rest here, especially with that nurse fussing about, poking and prodding me.'

'They said you should stay here in case you have any problems with your head.'

'You mean I might have concussion? No, I feel fine now, just a slight headache, and my chest will be OK. The rest is cuts and bruises, nothing serious. Believe me, I've had much worse. There's nothing they can do about my rib, so I may as well get out from under their feet in case someone else needs this bed. It's no use to me, I won't be able to sleep in it anymore.'

'Oh, come on, it's not that bad, and surely it's better than going back to the streets. You asked to come here, remember?' Maria reminded him.

Jacob grunted but said nothing.

'I can grab you some lunch if you want,' Maria said, changing the subject. 'Maybe you'll feel a bit better after that. You must be hungry.'

'Thanks, yes, I am. As long as it's not the veggie option.' He chuckled, then winced and held his hand to his chest. He looked up at Maria. 'Then I will leave.'

Maria rose from her chair and turned for the door. 'You're a pig-headed idiot,' she said, and left the room.

But Jacob heard Maria laugh as she went to fetch his lunch and he slowly shook his head. *I was right, she really is just like Selma.*

***

Michael's plan relied on the cooperation of the Liverpool Street security guards to give them access to the station. Michael knew it would be easier to buy Bill's allegiance than to sell him a sob story about helping hungry commuters during the strikes, and he had come to the station prepared to pay whatever it took to turn this busy London rail terminal into a slaughterhouse.

Paddy went ahead to the station concourse, leaving Michael to find Bill. In Broadgate Circle, the bars and fast food outlets were bathed in bright sunlight, burning away the dampness from the previous evening. A group of three

193

security guards stood to one side, apparently with nothing to do but watch office workers at lunchtime, who sat in small groups eating their lunches. The trio appeared to be paying particular attention to a cluster of young women on the top step of the raised podium in the middle of the bowl-like amphitheatre, who reclined on their forearms, heads tilted back and their eyes closed, taking in the sun.

'Hello guys,' Michael said with a forced smile.

The three guards looked at him with a mixture of disdain and hostility, but Michael ignored their reaction. 'I was looking for a guy named Bill and wondered if you knew him?'

'What do you want him for?' the shortest of the three guards demanded.

'I have a business proposition for him,' Michael replied, without looking away from the man who had answered. From the way the other two guards were staring at their colleague, Michael guessed he had struck lucky first time. 'I think he'll find it very interesting.'

The guard glared at Michael, as if challenging him to continue, but when it was clear that Michael wasn't going to venture any further information, he stepped forward.

'I'm Bill,' he said, then turned to his colleagues. 'I'll be back in a minute. Keep an eye out.'

Bill walked a few paces and stopped by the wall of the office block. 'OK, what do you want?'

'I understand you are responsible for security at Broadgate,' Michael said, pandering to Bill's ego. 'I was therefore wondering if you could help me with a project my employer is planning?'

'What sort of project?'

'Well, we wanted to give something to the commuters during the strikes, by providing them with a snack for breakfast as they come off their trains. It looks like they're queuing for hours for buses and cabs.'

'Yeah, my heart bleeds for them,' Bill replied. 'But what has that got to do with me?'

'We'd be in Broadgate and Liverpool Street, so wouldn't we need your permission to set up a stall handing out the snacks?'

'I don't give the permission. That's handled by the estate office over in the corner. If you book a date with them, you'll be put on the list and I will then tick your name off before you come on site.'

'Ah, well, that's our problem, you see. The next strike is tomorrow, so we don't have enough time to go through all that paperwork to book a slot. I was therefore thinking that, if you knew we were coming, you could let us in without all that fuss.'

'It doesn't work like that. If you're not on the list and my boss finds out I let you in, my neck will be on the line. I'm not risking that for you, just because you feel sorry for people during the strikes.'

Michael had anticipated this objection and had rehearsed his response.

'Bill, I understand what you're saying, but perhaps I didn't explain myself properly. Ordinarily we would have gone through your usual process, and it's only because we have limited time that we decided to come straight to you, as we'd heard you were able to get things done.'

Michael was conscious he was laying it on thick, but Bill was still listening. He probably knew what was coming and Michael didn't intend to disappoint him, much as it pained him to suck up to this pathetic guard.

'We want to make a business offer to you, businessman to businessman, if you know what I mean. We will, of course, pay you for your services and, if you wish to share it with your colleagues, that's entirely up to you.' Michael nodded towards Bill's two stooges.

'I'm not sure about this, it's not how we do things around here.' It was clear to Michael that Bill had taken the bait and it would just come down to price. 'I'll have to think about it.'

'Bill, we don't have time for that. If we can't do it tomorrow morning, then I may as well book another date for the next strike day through your office. And then, of course, this opportunity for you will go away.'

'OK, let me think for a minute.' Bill fell silent and Michael stepped back, giving him time and space to think and also dropping an unsubtle hint that he was prepared to walk away.

'A monkey, that's what it will cost you,' Bill said, after a few seconds' deliberation.

'What? How much is that, a hundred pounds?'

'No, and I'm not doing it for that, no way. This is a big risk and I won't do it for less than a monkey. That's five hundred to you.'

'You're not serious,' Michael replied, although he knew that he was. 'I was thinking of nearer two hundred.'

He thought Bill was being greedy and he had been expecting a lower demand. However, if it ensured the mission succeeded, it was a small price to pay.

'Five hundred. Take it or leave it, and I'll want it all up front today.'

'OK, OK, five hundred it is. But I'll only pay half today, and you'll get the other half in the morning when you let us in. I'm taking a risk too, and that way I know you'll be here tomorrow when we arrive.'

Bill pretended to think about it before nodding. Michael turned away, reached into his jacket and counted out five fifties. The last thing he needed was for Bill to see how much money he was carrying, as he'd no doubt want to renegotiate. Bill stepped forward and Michael handed him the notes, out of sight of Bill's colleagues.

'We'll be at the entrance to Liverpool Street over there,' Michael said, pointing, 'by that tall, rusting girder thing, at about seven o'clock tomorrow morning. I will be with four or five other people, who will be helping to hand out the snacks. We will be taking them into the station, understood?'

Bill nodded his agreement and turned away.

It was only when Michael watched him go, that it occurred to him that Bill hadn't asked anything about the product. Just as well, he thought with relief. Whilst Bill's lack of curiosity struck him as odd, he realised that he wouldn't have been able to answer much about it. He didn't yet know exactly what they were giving away, what it would be called or even what the promotion would say. He'd only know all that once the delivery came tonight. Michael wasn't as prepared as he thought, and he prayed that his luck would last for another day.

Only one more day. The thought made him smile.

***

Liverpool Street station was barely recognisable from the morning's news broadcast. No long queues in the walkways, no jostling throng in front of the London Underground ticket hall and no pop-up stalls offering promotional snacks to anxious commuters.

Brandon stood at the railing on a walkway directly above the centre of the concourse, below the huge, double-sided departure board suspended from the station's Victorian roof. He looked towards the Broadgate exit, where hundreds of commuters had queued for buses earlier, but where only a dozen or so people now waited. Below him, a couple of teachers shepherded a party of schoolchildren towards the escalators, and in front of them a few people mingled in front of the cash machines. This would be the perfect spot to launch *Proximity*. From here, Brandon would be able to check that everything was working, and there were several escape routes in case anything went wrong.

But why should it? Brandon closed his eyes and he could almost feel the touch of the button that would activate his program, and his stomach fluttered at the vision of his plan coming to life.

Brandon knew the layout of the station well, but he walked around every part of it, checking that none of the exits were blocked or temporarily closed. He was sure that no one would be suspicious of him tomorrow, but it was best to be prepared. He paid particular attention to the position of the CCTV cameras and there were even more than he had expected. Perhaps he should adopt a disguise, just to be safe. In the event that Liverpool Street was identified by security services as the initial source of the cyber-attack, he wouldn't want his image to be scrutinised in their recordings, picked to bits and digitally enhanced, and then broadcast in news reports. It seemed unlikely that he would be traced, but although he was confident in his technical ability to hide his tracks and make himself invisible to the online community, his physical presence was another thing entirely. He had always hated being the centre of attention and it seemed that he'd spent his whole life shunning the limelight, and he hoped that his practice would be rewarded when he needed it most.

Brandon left the station by the Bishopsgate entrance and walked towards Spitalfields Market, where he would grab something from one of the fast food stalls. On his way out, he didn't notice the two men who stood on the raised walkway, deep in conversation as they leaned on the railing and looked down at the concourse.

Like Brandon, Paddy and Michael were considering emergency exits, although they looked for places where panic-stricken commuters would struggle to get away from the chaos, not escape routes for themselves. They had no intention of being anywhere near this cavernous terminal during the carnage.

'One of our carts should be placed there,' Michael said, and he pointed at an open space next to one of the staircases that ran from the concourse to the raised walkway. 'I reckon it will catch anyone running away from the first explosion. Yes, that's a perfect site for the second blast. What's more, it's also going to be surrounded by people coming off those platforms there, who will be grabbing their free snack.'

Paddy followed Michael's hand and visualised the commuters coming off their trains and walking straight into the blast zone. He was right, there really was nowhere else they could go from that side of the station.

'And the first cart, of course, should be this end,' Michael continued. He walked towards the Broadgate end of the concourse, where the main entrance to the Underground, the front entrance to the station, its steps and escalators up to street level and the bus station, all converged. It would be teeming with people, as it had been that morning.

'This is where the carts will come in, past those shops there, and it's where most of the displays and promotions are put, so it won't look out of place. No one will suspect a thing.' Michael stopped at the railing beneath the departure board. 'When this one goes off, it will catch people coming off the platforms this end and anyone queuing for buses or waiting by the Underground. What do you think?'

Paddy nodded. 'Yes, I reckon you're right. It will block the escalators and stairs, and probably the exit into Broadgate. Anyone who isn't caught in it will naturally run that way.' Paddy pointed back to where they had agreed the second cart would be situated.

'My God, Paddy, it couldn't be better, could it?' The excitement in Michael's voice was palpable, and Paddy saw a look in his eyes that made even a man of murder like himself shudder.

'Yeah, it's looking good. But let's stay calm and think everything through. We haven't been downstairs yet, and who knows what we'll find? We need to check the signal strength down there too, although I don't imagine that will be an issue.'

The two men wandered down to the station concourse. The chosen sites for their deadly carts seemed even better close-up and they could think of no reason to change their plans. They left by the station's side entrance towards Exchange Square, satisfied with their target's potential to generate maximum bloodshed. Michael glanced into the small shops lining the passage and wondered which of these shop assistants and customers would die in the morning. All of them, he hoped.

'Until tomorrow,' he said under his breath. 'Strike day.'

15

He had forgotten how good this felt. He bounced along the pavement in a way he hadn't done for years; energised, full of purpose and battle-ready. At last, after months of waiting for a mission, here it was, just like the old times again.

But this time it was even better, as he was driving the operation, the baton of leadership having clearly passed from the older man, Paddy, to himself. He didn't have direct contact with the Brethren executive yet, but surely it was only a matter of time. The heir-apparent, he had staked his claim. Michael looked at Paddy, who dragged his feet as if tormented by every step, each one bringing him closer to his grave. Paddy was a fighter, but it was clear that his illness was winning the battle and he was enduring his role, not enjoying it. He just had to survive the next twenty-four hours and then he will have fulfilled his final mission, and Michael assumed he would then quickly give in to life's only certainty. Leaving Michael with the spoils.

'Hey Paddy, you look worn out. Perhaps you should get some rest this afternoon. It's going to be a long night.'

Paddy's bloodshot eyes were barely visible in his sunken eye sockets. Since leaving Liverpool Street he had suddenly become overwhelmed with exhaustion, and he could hardly keep pace with Michael. Whether it was the thought of the job or the strain of yesterday's physical exertion catching up with him, he didn't know, but it was clear he'd need time to recharge before tomorrow.

He nodded at Michael. 'Yes, I think you're right. I could do with a kip.'

'Great. I'm going to the pub now to get James on side, so why don't you head back to the lock-up? I said to Maria to come over mid-afternoon, so you can tell her the plan and then crash out.'

'OK, I'll wait for her and tell her to be back in the morning. We agreed six o'clock, didn't we?'

'Yes, that's it. After the pub, I'll go back to the flat so I'm there when Jenny and Orla get home, and then I'll be back to Rivington Street for the delivery and night shift. I'll be too wired to sleep until this is all over, and anyway, there will be plenty of time for that afterwards.'

Michael stopped walking to let Paddy catch his breath. 'Now go and get some sleep. You need it. I'll see you later.'

They parted ways. At Luke Street, Michael glanced towards the Refuge and wondered what Maria was doing. He hoped she was making the most of her last day alive. He shrugged and put it out of his mind.

It was nearing the end of lunchtime service and James was collecting glasses at one of the tables when Michael walked in.

'Hello Michael, a bit late for you today isn't it?' He wiped the table and carried the glasses back to the bar. 'The usual?'

'Thanks, yes, I've time for a swift one. And have one for yourself.'

'Now I am worried about you, that's two days running.'

'Just being friendly,' Michael said, 'and in fact that's why I popped in here. It was you I wanted to see.'

'Really?' James looked at Michael and raised an eyebrow. 'You buy me drinks then say you've come to see me. Sorry, Michael, you're a nice enough fella, but you're not my type!'

Both men laughed. James set a Guinness on the bar and waited for Michael to take a swallow before asking him what he wanted to see him about.

'You may remember yesterday morning, I said I was meeting an old friend of mine who wanted help with a new business venture.'

'Yes, I remember.' James took a sip of his ale. 'What's he up to then?'

'Well, it's not what I thought,' Michael said. 'He's involved in the launch of a new breakfast product. I've not seen it yet, as it's all hush-hush at the moment. The main publicity and advertising will be next week, but he's got the job of promoting it this week, starting tomorrow.'

'OK, but I don't follow, what does this have to do with me?'

'I was coming to that. For tomorrow's promotion, we are handing out free samples at Liverpool Street in the morning, trying to catch the commuters on their way to work. But he's had someone drop out last minute. He's asked me if I know anyone who could get to Liverpool Street before seven o'clock and then help to hand them out for a couple of hours. Are you interested? You mentioned yesterday that you could do with the money.'

James puffed out his cheeks. 'Yeah, you could say that again.'

'What time do you start work here? Fancy two hours of easy work? As it's last minute, you'll get a good rate.'

'I usually get here at about half-nine to help clear up after breakfast before my main shift. Sounds like I could do your job before then. What did you say, a couple of hours starting at seven?'

'Yes, that's right. But if you could get there a few minutes earlier to help unload the gear, that would help thanks. It will be all over by nine, don't worry about that.'

James was keen to help out and the two men finalised the arrangements for the morning. Michael drained the rest of his pint, satisfied with his work, and before leaving the pub he typed a brief message to Paddy:

Two down, two to go

But Michael wasn't kidding himself. He knew he'd done the easier half. Enlisting Jenny and Orla to his band of killers might prove much trickier.

***

Paddy jerked awake when Michael's message pinged on his phone. He sat forward in his chair, rubbed the heels of his hands into his eyes and yawned. Since getting back from Liverpool Street he had been dozing inside the lock-up, with the door ajar, waiting for Maria. He hoped she'd turn up soon, so that he could get a good sleep undisturbed, ahead of the delivery that evening. It was going to be a long night.

He smiled at Michael's message and lit a cigarette. The smoke caught in his throat and scorched his worn-out lungs, but Paddy was beyond caring. He deleted the message and contemplated how this operation was now wholly within Michael's control. It was clear that he had usurped Paddy as team leader and he was revelling in his role. Not that Paddy minded, it was the right time for that. Michael was ambitious, he wanted the credit for this job and, having learned his murderous trade from Paddy and others in Ireland, he was now an increasingly zealous member of the Brethren. Donovan had also been impressed by Michael's thinking, when Paddy had called to agree the new plan, so he was definitely on the way up.

But Michael wasn't yet the finished article. Paddy harboured a few doubts about his professionalism and he was still impetuous, as evidenced by his constant womanising and hasty inclusion of Maria in this operation. Michael was also bloodthirsty, his appetite for slaughter greater than anyone else Paddy knew, and he had a deep-seated ruthlessness, an ice-cold detachment that enabled him to kill without regret. But would it be his undoing if he allowed his lust for death and destruction to compromise his judgement? Time would tell.

Paddy stubbed out his cigarette underfoot and settled back in his chair. Within seconds his head lolled back, open-mouthed, and his laboured wheezing was the only sound in the lock-up.

'Hello, Martin, Peter, are you there?'

Paddy's head lurched forward again and he gripped the arms of the seat. But the moment he saw Maria in the doorway, he let out a long, rasping breath and wiped the drool away from the side of his mouth with the back of his hand.

Maria peered round the door and stepped over the threshold. 'Oh, sorry, I didn't mean to surprise you. Is Martin here?'

'No, he's not, he's getting some things sorted before tomorrow. I assume you're still OK for the morning?'

'Yes, of course, I'm free to help, although I haven't been told what the plan is yet.'

'Oh, OK, I thought Martin had explained it to you. It's straightforward enough. We'll be handing out free samples of the snack at Liverpool Street tomorrow morning. If you meet us here at six, you can come with us. We'll drive over there in the van with the stuff, unload it at the station, and then you and the other helpers will hand them out. Once they're all gone, we'll pack up and pay you all. We'll be done by nine o'clock. Easy as that.'

'But where are the snacks?' Maria asked, looking around the lock-up and stepping further into the space towards the old vehicle bay, as if the goods might have been concealed behind the units. She glanced up at the hatch to the upper level for good measure.

'Oh, they arrive tonight. Don't worry, they're on their way. I will be here all night, guarding them with my life.'

'OK,' Maria said, accepting his explanation without question. 'Mind you don't fall asleep again then.'

'Oh, you saw me dozing? Well, if I get to sleep now, I should be alright tonight.'

Maria didn't think that Peter looked like he could stay awake all night. His pallor matched the ash at his feet, and with his sunken, half-closed eyes, he looked shattered. But she didn't press the point. He seemed a little cranky.

'OK, see you tomorrow at six then,' she said, and walked to the door. She turned back to wave goodbye and saw Peter slump back in his chair.

Before leaving, Maria glanced up again at the upper floor and an idea took shape in her mind. On her way down Rivington Street, one image kept returning to her: a tired, unwell man asleep in his chair, beneath a cosy loft. Maria hurried back to the Refuge.

***

Brandon paced from one end of the den to the other, biting his nails, deep in thought, not even glancing at his screens.

He'd heard of numerous masterminds who had experienced moments of uncertainty when so close to their moment of destiny, but he'd never expected it to happen to him. Usually any last-minute doubts would be on technical grounds, whether something could be achieved with the skills, capability and knowledge of the people executing the plan. There might be practical considerations, such as time, budget or logistics. But none of this worried Brandon, so why was he getting cold feet now, when he was confident that *Proximity* worked?

The moment he'd let *Sleeper* loose at Stratford station the previous morning, in his mind he had commenced an unstoppable process, where he would test the program, prove its ability to infect and control other people's devices, and then use his undeniable technical skills to deliver the plan. Until now, Brandon hadn't questioned the morality of his actions. Why would he, when he had already convinced himself that he was doing this for the greater good?

He knew that elements of his plan were personal crusades, such as his loathing of greedy institutions, his antipathy towards Bitcoin and his quest to show the world the frailty of their gadget-obsessed lives. He also knew that he was about to commit a crime, actually several serious crimes rolled into one, although he was sure that most people would support the eventual outcome regardless of how he would achieve it. But did that really make it the right thing to do?

Brandon gave up on the markets and left his den. He stood at his huge living room windows and stared into the distance, looking at nothing in particular. He couldn't shake the feeling that he had missed something, an unforeseen consequence of his actions that would only become apparent once the plan was underway. He thought back to his reconnaissance of Liverpool Street, the walkways, the cashpoint machines and the departure board. He played back the success of *Replicant* at Gianluca's café. Nothing. He couldn't work out what the problem was. Just a nagging feeling that something wasn't quite right.

It was time for a walk, and he knew his destination before he left the loft. As he had the day before, Brandon pulled his hood over his head and set off in the direction of Mark Square.

But, on this occasion, he went no further. He sat down on one of the benches in the former grounds of St. Michael's Church and rested his forehead in his hands, his elbows digging into the top of his thighs. His face hidden from view, to any bystander he would have appeared the very picture of despair or, to the more morbidly inclined, an anguished, hooded spectre in an ancient churchyard.

Brandon knew the history of this place intimately. He had spent over a year of his life at the Refuge, sheltering from the streets during his teenage years, and he was aware of its association with the church. He had always been inquisitive, and even as a vulnerable and abused teenager he had researched its past and taken the time to understand the people who had rescued him. He had learned about the sacrifices they had made and the kindness that had been shown over the years to the destitute and defenceless. Brandon had been one of those unfortunate souls welcomed into the shelter, and he would never be able to repay the debt.

But in many ways, Brandon considered himself lucky. He had discovered skills and talents which, with the crucial support of the Refuge, had enabled him to escape life on the streets. He now lived free of poverty and he wanted for nothing, at least in any material sense. He no longer worried where he would be sleeping or where his next meal would come from, which was more than could be said for many of the Refuge's residents, past and present. His time at the Refuge was the source of his confidence, of his strength and his courage.

But Brandon still felt alone and isolated. Like today, sitting in the churchyard, he had no one to talk to, no one he could confide in, and no warm, human contact. How he missed the camaraderie of the Refuge. He didn't hanker for that life again, he couldn't go back, but he longed to rekindle those feelings of unconditional acceptance and inclusion. But it wouldn't happen now, not with the paths he had taken since leaving the Refuge. It was too late for that.

Brandon looked up at the shelter's walls. He had never given even one hour of his time to help anyone within, despite knowing from personal experience how much it meant to those in need. He told himself that other people made better volunteers, because they knew how to handle the homeless, with their natural patience and tolerance. But deep down he knew that these were convenient excuses that simply protected him from his own insecurities; he was scared of failure, of being rejected again, just for being who he was.

But he took solace in the fact that he could still contribute to life at the Refuge, by helping in the only way he could. With money. It was not the same, he knew that, but the shelter relied on benefactors like Brandon to survive and he was determined to make a difference. Giving money to the Refuge was what motivated Brandon to beat the markets at their own game, it had driven him to develop some of the most advanced trading programs in the market, and it had inspired him to create *Proximity*.

Brandon sat in the churchyard in the shadow of the Refuge and stared at the blank walls, thought of his time there and those still inside, and felt his sense of purpose renew.

***

Orla took her bag from the locker and pulled its strap over her shoulder with a sigh. She had enjoyed her morning with the children, but for some reason she felt more tired than usual, although she didn't know why. Was she coming down with something, or was she just over-exerting herself by combining her voluntary work every day at the Refuge with her full-time job at the crèche? She was certainly shattered most nights by the time she got home.

Orla shook her head. She couldn't bring herself to reduce her hours at the Refuge, even if her voluntary work was contributing to her frazzled state, because she knew how important it was to the people there. People like Jacob. Even whilst semi-conscious last night after the attack, he had asked for Orla by name, showing how much he valued her. She wasn't conceited by nature, but Orla did feel proud that he had asked for her, even if it felt like a guilty pleasure.

Once out onto the street, Orla tilted her head back and closed her eyes, stopping for a few seconds to soak up the early afternoon sunlight. She had always preferred working the second shift at the crèche, as her break avoided the normal lunchtime rush, when thousands of City workers would descend on the local sandwich shops, salad bars and fast food outlets, and the streets and terraces would be overflowing with people. But a late lunch felt unhurried, and during dry weather she would often wander down to Broadgate Circle or take the slightly longer walk to Finsbury Square and sit on the grass to eat her lunch.

But Orla took a different route for her lunchtime walk today. She decided that it would be better to revisit Jacob sooner rather than later, as she didn't know if he would still be there if she left it until she'd finished work. She should just about have enough time if she hurried. It also meant that she could go straight home after work. Orla had found Michael's behaviour this morning disconcerting and she wanted to ask him a few questions. She had a disturbing feeling that he was up to something.

At the Refuge, Orla went straight to the medical bay and checked in with Corinne.

'Jacob's doing fine, and he's a bit brighter than this morning. Maria sat with him for a while, but she left after he finished his lunch,' the nurse said. 'He's had a painkiller for his head and ribs and he was dozing when I last looked in. You're welcome to sit with him.'

Orla thanked Corinne and entered the room. Jacob appeared to be asleep, propped up against his pillows, so she sat on the chair nearest the door. But within a few seconds of Orla sitting down, Jacob opened his eyes and smiled when he saw her. 'It's OK, I'm awake. I heard you come in.'

'How are you doing? You look a bit better than this morning, but then it would be hard not to.' Orla's voice was soft, conveying concern for his welfare but also an optimism that the worst was over.

'Not too bad, thanks, better for a little grub. Maria fetched lunch for me. She's a nice girl, that one, kind-hearted.'

'Yes, she is, very thoughtful. But do you know where she's got to now? I thought she might still be here with you.'

'She said she had to go and see her boss. Apparently, she's got a new job. I saw her looking yesterday and she didn't seem very hopeful at the time, so I'm glad she found something.'

'Oh, yes, she mentioned that to me this morning. Working in a food shop I think she said. Good for her.'

'Talking of which, shouldn't you be at work?' Jacob asked.

'Oh, it's OK, it's my lunch break, so I thought I'd come to see how you're doing. I don't have long, but I have other things to do tonight.' Orla shifted in her seat, suddenly feeling guilty at the suggestion. 'It's the only time I can spare. Sorry.'

'What are you apologising for?' Jacob looked at Orla. It dawned on him that she may have felt pressurised into visiting him because he had asked for her during his delirious ramblings the night before. 'You have done more than enough and I didn't expect you to come out during your lunchtime, or after work. Please don't feel you have to.'

'Honestly, I don't mind. I don't usually do much in my lunch hour anyway.'

They fell silent. Orla realised that, in his own way, Jacob was expressing his gratitude for the effort she had made. But he was also embarrassed that he'd been the cause of it, and he didn't want her to spend all of her free time with him.

After a few moments, she stood to go. 'It's good to see you looking better, and hopefully when I see you next, you'll be back to fighting fitness. Just remember what I said this morning. Stay out of trouble, and keep away from that Bill man at Liverpool Street.'

Jacob nodded and they exchanged smiles as she closed the door.

On her way back through the lobby, Orla saw Maria coming up the steps of the Refuge towards her. She was flushed and panting, as if she'd been running.

'Hi Maria,' she said and she held the door as Maria caught her breath. 'I popped in to see Jacob. He seems quite a bit better, and I'm sure he'd like to see you if you have time.'

'I was on my way there now,' Maria said between gulps of air.

'Great! But I've got to get back to work now, sorry, I can't wait. I'll probably see you at breakfast in the morning. Bye!'

Maria opened her mouth to answer that she wouldn't be at breakfast because of her job, but closed it again. Orla had gone. *Never mind, I'll tell her about it another time. It'll keep.* But what couldn't wait, she decided, was the idea that she wanted to discuss with Jacob, and she hurried off to see him.

Orla grabbed her phone to check her messages. Concentrating on her screen, she almost collided with someone coming the other way.

'Oh, I'm sorry,' she said instinctively, 'I should look where...'

Orla's apology tailed off as she recognised who it was, and her words stuck in her throat.

'Hi Orla,' Brandon said. 'Long time no see.'

'Oh my God, it really is you. Hello stranger!' Orla threw her arms wide and hugged Brandon. She squeezed him tight for a few seconds, before stepping back to look at him.

'I had no idea you were still in the area. Mind you, if you're always wearing this thing,' she said, pointing at his hood, 'then I'd probably walk right past without recognising you. How have you been?'

'Oh, not too bad, getting by. I only live around the corner, between here and Liverpool Street, and I often walk up this way, for old times' sake. You know how it is, I owe a lot to this place.'

Brandon looked up at the building and Orla could see in his eyes the genuine affection he still felt for the Refuge.

'Yes, it is a special place and I'm sure many of our old friends feel the same way.' She paused but then screwed up her eyes in apology. 'Oh, I'd really love to stand and chat and hear what you're up to, but I'm on my way to work now, so I don't have much time. If you live close by, we must get together another time. Do you have a mobile?'

Brandon told Orla his number and she entered it into her phone. Almost immediately, he felt his phone vibrate in his pocket.

'Right, now you have my number too, so no excuses, eh?'

'Thanks, I'll call you. Do you still work at the crèche? If so, I can walk with you, it's not out of my way.'

They headed towards Orla's workplace and small-talked about the weather and nothing in particular. Anything important could wait until they had more time together. However, as they approached Orla's office, there was one thing she couldn't leave unsaid.

'I hope you don't mind me asking,' Orla said, a slight tremor in her voice, 'but are you living with anyone at the moment?'

'Oh Orla, of course I don't mind you asking. You probably know more about me and who I really am than anybody else.' He thought about the best way to reply. 'No, I'm not living with anyone, and I haven't since I left the Refuge. I don't think it's the right time and it would be tough, not only for me, but also for whoever I was with. Maybe I will in future, I don't know.'

Orla stopped and looked at Brandon. She tentatively raised her hand to his face, half expecting him to flinch or step back. But he stood perfectly still and let her slide her hand under the hood and touch his unshaven skin.

'I'm sorry, I didn't mean to pry, but I couldn't help noticing. Is it why you wear a hood?'

'Partly, I guess. But mostly I like hoodies because they are baggy and comfortable, and it's not as though I need to look smart to go to work. I work from home, programming and stuff like that. You'll remember how good I was at it.'

'So, you're going ahead with it then? I always thought you would, although it must be hard for you.'

Brandon shrugged and started walking again. 'Compared to what happened to me on the streets, it's not so hard. But the Refuge, and you in particular, picked me up when I needed it, and here I am, looking forward and not back at the dark days.'

They had reached the entrance of Orla's employer. She hugged Brandon again and then stepped back, looking him up and down.

'Well, here's to the future then. The hoodie suits you, it's the right look. I always said you were too pretty anyway, for a boy.' She gave him a wistful smile, then span on her heels and marched away over the tiled floor.

Brandon watched Orla recede until she disappeared from view. Seeing her again had brought back so many memories, and now he knew that he had made the correct decision. He was doing the right thing.

16

She turned her key in the lock and pushed open the door. She bent down, picked up her mail from the mat, sifted through it, then, without thinking, put her hand to the door to close it behind her.

'Boo!'

Jenny screamed and jumped back from the door. Her letters cascaded to the floor.

'For Christ's sake Michael, what do you think you're doing? Jeez, you almost gave me a heart attack, bloody fool.'

Jenny held her hand to her chest and leaned back against the wall, breathing deeply in an effort to regain her composure. When she could speak again, she looked up into Michael's grinning face. 'It's not funny. You'll be the death of me,' she said between gritted teeth, before laughing herself as her adrenaline rush passed.

'Couldn't resist it Jenny, only a bit of fun.'

'I'll give you fun, idiot.' She gave him a playful punch on the chest and he howled in mock pain.

'Now we're even, eh?' Michael said and he winked at her.

'What are you doing here Michael? You don't usually welcome me home. If you can call that a welcome.' She took another deep breath and then her eyes widened. 'You haven't told Orla have you, about us?'

'No, not yet, I've not seen Orla much today. I'll see what mood she's in tonight. Don't worry, I will do it, I just have to pick my moment.'

'I can't help it, I just can't wait until you're all mine, that's all.' Jenny stepped forward and put her arms around his neck, and teased him with a seductive whisper as she looked up at him. 'Anyway, you still haven't answered my question. What are you doing here if you haven't told her?'

But his answer surprised her and she pulled her head back and looked at him questioningly when he said, 'I came to ask a favour.'

'What sort of favour?' she asked, with a hint of indignation in her voice.

Michael retold the story he had given James about his business colleague being let down last minute, and again emphasised that the money would be good. However, Jenny wasn't interested in the money or the motivation of helping out commuters with a free snack, and Michael couldn't resist a smile when he heard her self-serving objection.

'But that's *our* time. What you mean to say is, I won't be able to come over tomorrow morning because you'll be giving out snacks to complete strangers.'

'Come on, I can't help it. He's an old friend of mine and I can't let him down. It's only one morning. I'll make it up to you, I promise, and as soon as I've told Orla about us, we will have every morning together, and every night too. Will you do this for me?'

Jenny pouted. She was going to extract as much out of this as she could.

'Please Jenny.' Michael hoped he didn't sound too desperate. If only she knew what was riding on this.

Jenny strung it out for a few seconds longer, before finally surrendering. 'I'll do it, but it's going to cost you. Two things.'

'What?' asked Michael, suddenly suspicious.

'First, you're going to tell Orla about us by Friday, or I will do it myself.'

'Easy, I've already said I'll do that. And the second?'

Jenny reached for Michael's belt and pulled the leather tongue through the buckle.

'You're going to give me now what you won't be able to tomorrow morning. Let's call it payment in advance.'

Michael smirked as she unbuttoned him. He contemplated what lay ahead and submitted himself to Jenny's desires. She had no idea what price she was paying for this final pleasure, and he was determined to make it worth it. *Once more for old times' sake.*

***

Always the perfectionist, Brandon was leaving nothing to chance. Meeting Orla had invigorated him and, with renewed enthusiasm for his project, he returned to Liverpool Street to check everything one final time.

Satisfied that he hadn't missed anything, he bought the last few items that he needed to execute his plan, silently thanking Orla for giving him the courage he needed.

Brandon left the station by the long passageway that ran behind the offices on Bishopsgate and glanced into the lobbies of the banks along the tranquil walkway. But it wouldn't be calm for long. This time tomorrow, these same banks would be in a state of sheer panic, unable to stem the onslaught of Brandon's attack, and these now quiet lobbies would be teeming with despairing and frightened people.

He emerged into Exchange Square and drifted home, playing over and again in his head the sequence of events that would be set in motion when he let *Proximity* loose. All of the inputs had been separately tested, but only when he pushed the button tomorrow would he know for sure that they all worked together. He felt as though he was creating a living organism from scratch, where he had tested all of the parts in the laboratory and then stitched them together. Like Doctor Frankenstein, Brandon needed a catalyst to jolt his monster into action. Not a lightning bolt in Brandon's case, but *Proximity*. Brandon smiled at the thought. A surge of electricity brought both creatures to life, but he was confident that his creation would behave more predictably than his fabled predecessor's.

He let himself into the loft and dropped his shopping and hoodie onto one of his sofas. He then did something that he hadn't done for years, not since he'd had them installed as part of the renovation of the loft: he activated the blinds in his huge windows. The blinds were of the type often used in offices, where the narrow slats occupied the space between the glass panes, and they glided slowly down with the faintest whirr of their electric motors. Brandon had thought them a good idea at first, as they were easy to operate and matched the modern, minimalist design of his living space. But after the novelty had worn off, he found that he preferred to keep the windows clear, even at night, so the blinds hadn't been used for months. Until today.

He grabbed a couple of marker pens from his den and a cloth from his kitchen, and by the time he returned the blinds had completed their descent. The windows had been transformed into oversized whiteboards, illuminated by the light of his room. *Picture windows, why didn't I think of this before?*

Brandon took the black marker pen and stood back from the windows for a few seconds, deciding where to start. 'Right, let's take this logically, from the beginning,' he said aloud.

He often talked to himself whilst watching the markets and constructing charts in his den. He sometimes wondered if he talked to himself more than he did with anyone else, and wasn't sure if he did it to keep himself company or as a way of working things out, but either way it was part of his ritual. Tonight it was particularly important, as he needed to verify every step and every detail of his plan and check that nothing had been missed, and this was no time to change habits that had served him so well.

He stepped forward and drew his first box on the glass, which he labelled *Proximity*. To its right, he drew an arrow, above which he wrote *Replicant*. The arrow ended at a new box that he labelled *Gadget*. 'OK, that's the first level, the attack from my laptop. Now for the secondary wave.'

Brandon added three further arrows to the right of the last box, at angles as if they were radiating away from it, and the marker pen squeaked as it moved faster across the glass. He wrote the abbreviation *Rep* above them and ended with three new boxes, also each labelled *Gadget*.

'And then another level, mobile-to-mobile, tablet-to-tablet.' Faster than before, he added more arrows and boxes to the diagram, and his drawing became more feverish and his writing almost illegible. But Brandon didn't care. His excitement reflected his vision of the utter mayhem and chaos that would trail in *Replicant's* wake as the infection multiplied.

He stood back and surveyed his work. He had constructed a simple hierarchy, with the *Gadget* boxes multiplying at each level, like the diagrams he recalled from school of a nuclear chain reaction.

'I wonder how far *Replicant* will get. It may keep multiplying forever.' He stepped forward and printed *INFINITE?* on the window.

'Maybe it will stop when it reaches the coast. Even if it doesn't go that far, it should still reach millions of devices.' His eyes sparkled. 'And they will all be under my control for as long as it takes to complete the Bitcoin swap.'

Around the *Gadget* boxes, Brandon drew a large circle, beneath which he scribbled *Botnet*. He didn't like the word, but he hadn't thought of another one that described the illicit hijacking of numerous internet-connected devices to use in a concerted attack. Underneath, he drew a series of downward arrows, each ending at a box he labelled *Bank*. 'You'll have no idea what's hit you,' he whispered, remembering his earlier walk from Liverpool Street. Over the top of these arrows he wrote *DOS* in large letters, before adding a dramatic flourished exclamation mark after this acronym for Denial of Service. He laughed and stepped back from the window.

'OK, let's check everything. Once a gadget is infected, *Replicant* will first disable all manual commands, then activate any mobile banking apps and connect to those banks. If the phone doesn't have one, it will access the browser and connect to one of the default banks.'

He switched to the red marker pen, and wrote *Default Bank Apps* beneath the *Bank* boxes, to remind himself to check this part of the program again later. After deliberating for a few seconds, he also added *On/off disabled?* as a further reminder.

'The banks won't understand what's happening when their systems flood with this much internet traffic, especially as most of it will be from devices they have previously authenticated. If *Replicant* really does go as far as the coast, this would be the biggest DOS attack ever, literally millions of hits all at once.' He smiled. 'It will be carnage. Banking Armageddon.'

He traced another large circle around the *Bank* boxes, and stooped down to draw two further circles, side by side, beneath the first. Brandon drew a double-headed arrow between each circle, resulting in a triangle of arrows with a circle at each point.

'The final act, the Bank of England, the Old Lady herself, will be at my mercy.' He wrote *BOE* inside the first of the lower circles.

'All the banks will be floundering. While they sort out their mess, contingency plans invoked and their guard down, I'll be in the centre of the mayhem.' Brandon printed *ME* in capital letters in the middle of the triangle.

'And finally, the Old Lady's gold will be turned into Bitcoin.' His eyes were wide and he spoke in an excited whisper. He stepped forward once more and wrote a capital *B* in the final circle, and scored it with two vertical lines; the symbol for Bitcoin. Suddenly, he recalled a line from his childhood and he laughed aloud. 'It doesn't have quite the same ring to it. Dick Whittington, the streets of London are paved with Bitcoin!'

He stepped back a couple of paces and reviewed his work. After a few seconds of muttering under his breath, he nodded, then retrieved his laptop from the den.

Over the next couple of hours, Brandon tested and retested his systems and programs. At each stage he crossed out various boxes with his red marker, added further boxes and comments, or rubbed out others, chuntering to himself. He loved it, the thrill of solving problems, and his master plan bloomed before his eyes. He had set himself the greatest challenge imaginable, and his whiteboard was proof that it could be done.

***

When Maria told Jacob of her plan for him to rest in the lock-up, a dry space safe from thugs roaming the streets, he decided it was worth a try. He knew he would soon outstay his welcome at the Refuge, and he didn't want to be a burden anymore to people who had already helped him so much, to say nothing of his desire to get away from itchy sheets and a fussing nurse.

'You're not ready to go yet. Can't you stay another night?' Corinne said when Jacob told her he was leaving. 'You're still under observation.'

'Thanks Corinne, but I feel in the way, and I don't need to stay. I'm fine, honestly.'

She was reluctant for Jacob to leave, but she knew she couldn't force him to stay and he had made good progress. 'Take these painkillers with you. At least do that. I can't give you anything stronger without the doctor's say so, but they will ease the pain in your ribs a little. But if your headache gets any worse, make sure you come back, OK?'

Jacob nodded, although they both knew that he wouldn't return unless his head felt ready to explode, and maybe not even then. She placed his clothes on the bed and left the room. If he was well enough to go, he could dress himself.

During their walk to the lock-up, Maria reminded Jacob that he would need to be careful he wasn't discovered sheltering there. Martin and Peter had sworn Maria to secrecy and they didn't want anyone else to know about it.

'OK, that's fine, I'm sure I can stay hidden, although I've no idea why their new food is such a big secret. I won't drop you in it.'

'I'm sure you'll be OK, as long as we can get you in. That's probably going to be the tricky bit, especially if they're both there, but I think I know how to do it.' Maria paused, as if thinking through her plan. 'You'll be fine getting out in the morning, once we've all left for Liverpool Street, as long as you leave before we get back. Is that OK?'

When Jacob didn't answer, Maria realised that he was no longer by her side, but had stopped a few steps earlier. He was looking into the shop they had just passed.

'Jacob? Are you alright?'

She walked back and, when he didn't react to her presence, she followed his gaze. Jacob was staring into the convenience store, where at the back the shopkeeper stood at the counter, in front of the shop's alcohol and cigarettes.

'Come on, Jacob, we've got to get to the lock-up.'

'Do you have any money with you, Maria? For a bottle of something? I really need a drink.' He put his hand to his chest. 'For the pain.'

Jacob reached into his pocket and then looked down at his hand, now holding the box of painkillers he'd been given by Corinne. 'These won't be any good tonight.'

'I don't think that's a good idea. You're not supposed to mix them with alcohol.'

'I wasn't thinking of mixing them, but replacing them. Please Maria, just this once. I'll get the money to repay you.'

'It's not the money, you know that. It's just not right. Come on, we've got to go.'

Maria looked at Jacob, who was now imploring her with his big, brown, sorrowful eyes. If she wasn't mistaken, he'd even stuck his lower lip out in a questionable pout. She knew he was doing it on purpose, but in spite of herself she laughed at him. He grinned back.

'Jacob, you're impossible,' she said, but then walked into the shop. Two minutes later, she emerged clasping a small bottle of whisky and thrust it at Jacob. 'I hope you bloody well choke on it.'

Maria turned and strode away. Jacob looked at her ramrod straight back and bobbing hair and chuckled. 'Thanks Selma,' he said, then slipped the bottle into his coat pocket and followed in her wake.

When they arrived at Rivington Street, Maria told Jacob to wait round the back of the lock-up, by the disused entrance to the former vehicle workshop. She continued alone under the bridge and then sidled along the arches. One door of the lock-up was a few inches ajar, as it had been earlier that afternoon, and slivers of light spilt through the gaps to illuminate the path outside.

Maria poked her head cautiously round the opening and saw Peter in his chair, head tipped back and snoring. Everything was as she'd left it hours before, and it didn't look like the delivery had arrived yet. Maria took several deep breaths to calm herself, then eased the door open just enough to squeeze through the gap. Her heart fluttered at the faint creak of the hinges, but Peter slept on and Maria slipped through the opening. A few tiptoed steps later and she was past the slumbering Irishman, and she headed for the back entrance where Jacob would be waiting. The further she crept, the darker it became, and Maria took her time to navigate the final stretch. She was wary of tripping over ancient tools and machinery scattered over the workshop floor, although she was relieved they had swept away most of the rubbish the day before.

Maria reached the back doors, nothing more than thick metal panels with vertical lever-operated steel bars that slid into housings in the floor and upper door frame. A heavy-duty steel chain was coiled around the levers, secured with a padlock, but Maria wasn't concerned. She ran her fingers along the shelves to the left side of the door, remembering that she had seen a small bunch of keys there when sweeping the floor of the lock-up the day before. After a few seconds of probing, Maria started to doubt her memory, but then her fingers curled around the welcome, cold metal ring and she exhaled with relief.

The third key she tried operated the lock, and Maria grinned when it turned easily. She pulled the padlock out of the chain and set it on the shelf, then unwound the chain. At every small clink, she looked over her shoulder at Peter and slowed her breathing, and little by little she unshackled the mechanism. Everything was going smoothly. Finally, she pushed the levers to release the bars and leaned against the door.

Nothing. The obstinate door remained where it was. Maria examined the frame and could see no reason why it wouldn't open. She looked around again to check that Peter was still asleep, closed her eyes in silent prayer, and pushed hard against the door. She felt it move, just a fraction. Encouraged, Maria pressed the lever, put all of her weight against the door, gritted her teeth and forced down through her legs as if trying to bury her feet in the concrete. The door budged less than an inch, stopped, then burst open.

The rusted hinges shrieked in anguish. Maria tumbled through the doorway and her palms smacked against the concrete outside, leaving her feet and ankles still inside the workshop. Jacob sprang forward to help, but undeterred by the sudden burning in her palms and knees, Maria brought her finger to her lips in warning.

'Shush. Peter must have heard. He is in there now.' The rattling and screeching of another train passing overhead drowned out her words, but Jacob understood the message from her actions.

Maria peered into the lock-up. She was dumbfounded by what she saw. After all the commotion, Peter was still in his chair, not rushing towards her as she had expected. All he had done was change his position in his seat, perhaps disturbed by the noise of the hinges or the passing train, and was now motionless again and snoring even more loudly.

'Unbelievable,' she whispered to Jacob. 'He must be damned tired to have slept through that, thank God. But that's good news for us.'

They edged into the workshop and Maria pointed to the opening that led to the upper floor. 'There, that's where you'll be. They won't see you up there and it isn't too dusty. Martin made me sweep it out a bit, although I don't know why as I don't think they're planning to use it.'

Jacob nodded, then looked around the rest of the lock-up, checking for exits, hidden dangers and potential weapons, a habit that had saved his life more than once.

'I'll be fine, thanks Maria. I'll stay out of their way and they won't know I'm here.'

Maria pointed to the chain and padlock. 'You'll have to put those back around the bars when I've gone, otherwise they may realise something's up.'

'Thanks, will do.'

'Well, that's it, I guess. Time for me to go, before Sleeping Beauty over there wakes up.' Maria glanced at Peter and then stepped up to Jacob and hugged him. He winced from the pain in his ribs, but didn't push her back.

'Thanks Maria, I appreciate it. See you again soon.'

Maria turned and stepped out of the workshop. 'I'll push from this side as we close it, but I guess we should wait for the next train, just in case it's noisy again.'

As it turned out, the door closed with a mere squeak, and afterwards Jacob wrapped the chain around the bars and levers with as much care as Maria had uncoiled it. He clicked the padlock closed, then cursed silently to himself. He had forgotten to ask Maria where she'd found the key ring, so he decided to leave the key in the lock. It wasn't a bad idea anyway, as it would aid a quick getaway if needed.

He inched his way along the walls, keeping to the shadows and carefully placing each step softly on the freshly swept floor. He stopped at the foot of the ladder and studied the man slumped in the chair. He was old, or at least he was frail, and it was clear from his haggard features and creased face that he wasn't well. Why was he involved in setting up a new food business in his condition, and in this run-down lock-up beneath the arches of all places? It seemed an odd choice. It wasn't exactly clean or hygienic.

The next train rumbled overhead, and Jacob took his chance. He climbed the ladder, settled into a corner away from the hatch, and waited for his eyes to adjust to the inky darkness. It wasn't as comfortable as the Refuge's bed, although thankfully he found it no more painful to sit upright than to lie down. *This will be just fine.*

He sat in the black, bottle in hand, and felt a faint breeze with each passing train. After the fire in his throat had subsided, the whisky started to work its magic, and he felt almost human again.

***

Michael was in a quandary. After prising himself away from Jenny, he had spent the last half-hour rehearsing aloud his story for Orla. But the more he practised the words, the hollower they sounded, and he was convinced that she would see through his tale. She was smart and she wouldn't be fooled as easily as James and Jenny. Why had he lied to her about why he had been late the night before? She would now realise that his explanation for his dirty clothes was untrue and, with her suspicions raised, she might refuse his request. This could get ugly.

He paced back and forth, weighing up his options. Either he could find a way to coerce her, or he would have to come clean about his deceit and throw himself upon her mercy. He knew which route he preferred, but it was no good; he had hardly any leverage and almost no time to think of an alternative. With a shake of his head, he concluded that his best chance lay in a quality he barely possessed. Honesty. Well, up to a point.

When Orla arrived home, she kicked off her shoes and flopped onto the sofa.

'Phew, I'm whacked,' she said. 'Give me a few minutes and then I'll fix dinner. Can you pop the kettle on please?'

'Sure. How was your day?'

'Busy, but it's over now, thank goodness. How about you? Did you get to see that Bill chap?'

'Yeah, all sorted.' Michael thought back to his conversation with Bill and the cash he'd paid. 'I can be pretty persuasive, and I don't think we'll have any more trouble from him.'

'Really? Jacob said he was a pretty horrid character. Oh well, typical playground bully I suppose, only brave when someone can't fight back.'

Orla closed her eyes for a few seconds before looking up at Michael. 'So, what happened to that job you had? I'm a bit surprised you're home, as I thought you might have to go back to it tonight.'

Michael took a deep breath. 'Well, actually, I wanted to talk to you about that. The thing is, you see... I have a confession to make.'

Orla blanched at Michael's words and sat up. She had sensed that Michael was up to something and here it was, about to be revealed. Wild thoughts suddenly overwhelmed her. Was he seeing someone, having an affair? Was he leaving? Did he have a clandestine life she didn't know about?

'I lied to you about the job. I'm sorry, I know I shouldn't have, but I didn't know what else to say.' Michael recited the words he had practised. 'I was helping an old friend who's in a spot of bother, and I was embarrassed to tell you.'

Michael saw the colour return to Orla's face at the mention of helping a friend, and he was encouraged. Orla had always been a soft touch for a sob story and this was going to be easier than he'd thought. It would do no harm to stress the good cause he was supporting or to exaggerate his act of humility. Orla was bound to be more sympathetic to his final request if she thought he was genuinely sorry.

'My friend, he needed help organising a charitable event, and I couldn't turn him down. I spent most of yesterday and last night helping him clean up a store room, ahead of the event, and in fact I'm going back to help him again tonight with the final arrangements. I hope you don't mind.'

'Oh Michael, why would I mind? And why didn't you tell me the truth? Jesus, for a minute there, I thought you were going to tell me you were seeing someone else.'

Michael laughed, more in relief that Orla had swallowed his story than that she'd dismissed thoughts of his infidelity. What did that matter now anyway, as he'd had his last time with Jenny? Buoyed by the unexpected ease with which his tale had been accepted, he decided it was time to move in for the kill.

'The thing is, Orla, I need to ask you a favour, for my friend.'

For the third time that day, Michael related the lie about his friend being let down last minute and needing help at Liverpool Street. When he'd finished, he smiled expectantly at Orla.

Despite her initial relief at Michael's revelation, Orla was suspicious. He had initially described the event as charitable, but it now appeared to be more commercial in nature, promoting a new product. Something wasn't right. Why was it so last minute, and why had Michael hidden the nature of his involvement? Not that it mattered anyway, as she couldn't do it. She had other priorities.

'No, I can't help Michael. You know I'll be at the Refuge in the morning and, to be honest, I think my work there is a bit more *charitable* than your friend's business. I'm sorry, that has to come first. You know how important the shelter is to me.'

'And this is important to me.' Michael's voice rose, despite his effort to remain calm. 'It's one morning, only a couple of hours, and the Refuge will survive without you. Oh, come on, I'll make it up to you.'

'Really, and how can you do that? You're asking me to let the Refuge down last minute, and the other volunteers will have to cover for me. It's not fair on them, or the people I'm trying to help.'

'Fair? You already do a huge amount for them, for no money, and I'm asking for one favour. Is that fair?' Michael knew that he sounded churlish, but he couldn't help himself. 'You seem to think more about this Jacob guy than you do of me.'

He glared at Orla, all pretence of charity and charm gone, and they both fell silent. Michael wondered whether he should reveal that Maria had been drafted, possibly hinting that he could make life difficult for her should Orla not cooperate. But that was a dangerous tactic. Orla might tip off Maria if he told her she was involved, and they couldn't afford to lose Maria at this stage. But what else could he do?

A heavy silence settled over them, suffocating as it dragged on, but eventually Orla spoke. 'Look Michael, I'm not happy about this, but maybe I can do it. I could call in at the Refuge first, work for an hour or so and still get to Liverpool Street by seven o'clock. I'll tell Ginger that I've had a last-minute problem and he'll understand. But this is a one-off, OK?'

'Thanks Orla, that's great,' Michael said, triumphant that his plan was all coming together. For a moment he'd had his doubts, but as usual Orla had found a compromise to avoid conflict, only this time her sacrifice would cost her more than she imagined. 'I'll make it up to you, honest.'

'Yes, you will. And you'll start by making dinner, while I have a bath. And don't get any ideas, I'm locking the door.'

17

Paddy awoke with a start to a loud rap on the door, followed by the bellow of a powerful voice. His head jerked up at the sudden din, and his wide eyes darted all around the lock-up, disorientated, until he found himself staring at Michael's scornful face, just inches from his own.

'C'mon, wake up sleepyhead, we have a delivery!'

A tall, muscular man had followed Michael through the door. He was huge, and Paddy guessed he spent much of his time in the gym.

'You've been asleep for ages. When I got back earlier you were dead to the world, but now it's time to get to work. Our man here has come bearing gifts,' Michael said, indicating the colossus at the door. 'We'll bring them in and then he'll be on his way.'

Up above the three men, roused by the sound of voices below, Jacob set his bottle to one side. He inched forward to the opening, careful to stay in the shadows and away from the edge to avoid disturbing any dust or debris. After a tedious couple of hours, at least it was something different to look at from the blackness of his secret hideaway.

The first items off the van were two three-wheeled ice cream carts, each with a pair of bicycle-sized wheels at one end and a smaller supporting wheel at the other. A canopy above each cart was painted with vivid white and emerald stripes, clearly designed to stand out in a crowd, and the carts themselves were a gleaming white, with the words 'Blarney Yoghurts' written on the sides in large green letters. The top of each cart had two sliding lids that covered the food compartment. The carts were wheeled into the lock-up and positioned side-by-side against one wall, and half a dozen T-shirts in the same green colour were placed on top of them.

The courier carried two portable air conditioning units into the lock-up and Michael shook his head. 'Damn Paddy, I hoped you'd been joking about that. It's going to be a chilly night in here.'

Next into the lock-up was the main cargo; hundreds of snack-sized, miniature yoghurt pots arranged in trays and wrapped in polythene. The courier set the trolley to rest and started transferring the trays to the recently-cleaned worktops, obscured from Jacob's view by a shelving unit. But then he stopped. He looked puzzled and turned to Paddy. 'That's odd. These don't have any labels on them, only the flavour on the lids. Is that what you were expecting?'

'Oh, that's OK, we know what to do with them. I assume you have a few other boxes for us,' Paddy said. 'They will contain everything we need.'

When the final boxes were brought in, Paddy opened them and inspected the contents. He nodded to the deliveryman. 'Yes, that's the lot.'

'Good. OK, you know the drill, everything goes back in the van and nothing will be left here. Don't forget the trolley and rubbish.' The courier handed the keys of the van to Michael. 'Right, that's it, my ride is round the corner, so I'll leave you to it. Good luck guys.'

He shook hands with Michael and Paddy, and without a further word he disappeared into the night.

Jacob receded into the shadows and sat back against the wall. He took a swig of whisky and considered the scene he had witnessed. Something about the manner of the men had reminded him of the Army, although he couldn't quite place it. Perhaps it was their military efficiency, or maybe their Irish accents simply took him back to his time in Northern Ireland. Just as likely, he considered, as he peered into the yawning void of his hiding place, he was jumping at shadows, as he often did in the dark with a bottle in his hand.

Once the deliveryman had departed, Paddy plugged in the two air conditioning units, one on either side of the lock-up, then sent Michael to buy dinner from the High Street. He felt refreshed after his sleep and rejuvenated by the arrival of the deadly consignment, the buzz of the imminent mission proving far more potent than any medicine.

He closed the door behind Michael and unwrapped the first tray of yoghurts. He then removed from the boxes the various tools and equipment they would use to modify the snacks and laid them out on the worktop next to the latex gloves and masks. They had all they needed to transform them into Blarney Yoghurts, and he smiled at the name the Brethren had chosen.

Paddy picked up his phone and sent a simple message:

Everything arrived, all set for the morning.

Paddy knew that he'd receive no acknowledgement. None was needed. With just seven words, he had confirmed that the strike would take place in only a few hours' time. He may not live long enough to see how it all panned out afterwards, but he didn't need to see it to know that London would never be the same again. This would change everything.

He heard footsteps outside and put away his phone. Michael stepped through the door with a carrier bag in one hand and two cups of tea in the other. When the smell of the pie and chips reached him, Paddy realised how ravenous he was, and he took his meal to the back of the lock-up, away from the cooling atmosphere of the air conditioning units.

'Good idea,' Michael said, following his partner. He raised his eyebrows at the array of equipment laid out for their night's work, but said nothing. He tucked into his chips and the two men ate in silence.

'Right, let's get to work,' Paddy said after they'd finished their supper, and he beckoned Michael to the worktops.

'The Brethren talked me through this and it sounds easy enough, but let's go through it together. There are hundreds of these pots, so it's going to be boring, but we can't afford to be careless.'

Paddy glanced at Michael, who was studying the items with a bemused expression, as if not knowing what to do. Paddy pre-empted his questions by grabbing a pair of the gloves and one of the masks.

'There are a couple of things I need to show you, so I'll start on the first tray. You can watch me and then we can split the rest between us.'

Paddy demonstrated the process to Michael and explained each step in turn. Within a few minutes, he had completed the first row of yoghurts on the tray, their new labels and lids in place and the old tops discarded to one side. When he had finished, he looked at Michael. 'Any questions?'

Paddy watched his comrade shake his head then slowly lift his gaze. Michael's bewilderment had gone and he stared at Paddy with undisguised glee.

'Wow, this is amazing. I had no idea. When did you know about all this?'

'Only when the Brethren described it to me a few days ago, and they told me to show you rather than tell you in advance. It's clever isn't it?'

'You bet it is,' Michael said with an air of satanic rapture. 'Just imagine how you'd feel if you ate one of these... you enjoy a free snack, escape the blast, then you find out later from the news how close you were to death.'

'And you'd been warned,' Paddy said, holding up a yoghurt and reading the label aloud. *'An explosion of flavour, a taste of Irish culture.'*

'Ha, that could really mess with your head afterwards.' Michael laughed. 'I guess it's what they meant when they said they wanted to send a message to the people of London.'

Paddy did some quick sums in his head. 'Judging from that row, I think it will take us three or four hours to do all of these yoghurts, so if you don't have any questions, we better get cracking. You'll still have enough time to wire up the explosives, which we'll do last as usual.'

The two men set to work. They split the different flavours between them and, as each tray was finished, they stacked them on the shelves next to one of the air conditioning units to keep them cool.

Jacob's curiosity had been piqued by the increase in activity below. However, from his partially obstructed vantage point, he couldn't see what the two men were doing, nor could he hear their conversation over the sound of the air conditioning units. But his interest waned when he saw the results of their labour, the growing stack of yoghurts now bearing bright green labels. He was impressed with their standards of hygiene, seeing their gloves and masks whenever they emerged into view, but there was little of interest to keep him away from his whisky. He grabbed his bottle, returned to his spot against the wall, and after a few more gulps he drifted off to sleep.

After about an hour's work, Michael and Paddy retreated to the back of the lock-up for a cigarette break. Michael wandered around the dingy space and his gaze fell upon the back door.

'Hey, Paddy, have you used this door at all? There's a key in the padlock, and I don't remember seeing it there before.'

'No, not me.' He joined Michael at the door. 'No one's been in here this afternoon, other than Maria. But she didn't use this door. The key must have been in there all along.'

'OK, if you're sure. It must be my memory playing tricks. But we shouldn't leave the keys lying around,' Michael said. He took the key from the lock and slipped the key ring into his pocket. 'No one's going to need this door anyway.'

'Right, back to work, no rest for the wicked,' Paddy said, with a sly grin.

***

They were nearly there and it felt good.

Donovan had watched the delivery from her room. She'd seen the courier walk away, followed a short time later by Michael, but she maintained her vigil, one hand on the curtain, watching, waiting. She needed to be sure. Only when Paddy's message arrived did she relax and breathe more freely, and she felt a huge burden fall from her shoulders when she stepped away from the window.

She had been concerned about the operation for a while, especially when Michael had recruited that girl to help them out with the cleaning. But everything was back on track and, as it turned out, he had made the right decision, as that young woman was now part of a grander plan. She would die in the morning, after helping them deliver the lethal cargo, and no one else knew they were here.

Donovan planned to stay until the two men left the lock-up in the morning and then her job would be done. She wouldn't follow them to Liverpool Street, not because she feared being recognised or caught, but because she wanted to be as far away from those carts as possible when the bomb went off. That was the beauty of City Airport. She could be on a plane within minutes of leaving Shoreditch, and with a bit of luck she would see the pall of smoke from the air, carrying death and destruction on the City breeze. *What a sight that will be.*

What could stop them now?

***

The men lay motionless as enemy fighters entered the building, the slightest movement almost certain to give away their position. Other than the faint glow of light from outside, which silhouetted each insurgent in the doorway, everything was in darkness. That is, until one of them struck a match and held it out in front of him, then slowly turned and watched the flickering shadows circle the room. Thankfully Jacob and his men were high up in the eaves and silent as the grave, and the glow of the match did not reach them.

By the light of the flame, Jacob counted a dozen fighters, far outnumbering the three Army men. The enemy also had the advantage of home territory and would know the layout of the building, its exits and vulnerabilities. Maybe more remained outside, so his men had no choice but to stay where they were, fighting their urges to move or sneeze, ignoring their pains and dismissing any thoughts of communication. It might not be possible for them to survive a whole night undetected, but time would tell.

The fighters below talked in whispers, but their words were indistinguishable from the incessant shuffling of their boots that accompanied their every movement. What were they doing down there, and why did it need to be done in the dark? Jacob strained to hear and see, but it was no use, they were deaf and blind.

Eventually the sounds faded and the fighters rested, the scraping and rustling replaced by snoring and heavy breathing. Occasionally another match would flare and then the tiny glow of a cigarette would last for a few minutes, but otherwise the men below slept.

Jacob's men couldn't risk sleep. The slightest snore or grunt threatened their lives, and they battled their craving for rest and struggled to remain alert and vigilant throughout the small hours. Every second was a torment, a potential moment of discovery and certain death, and the night dragged for an eternity.

At last, the faint gleam of day appeared in the doorway and the men below gathered together. Jacob saw by the dim light that they had unwrapped a deadly cargo, and each man slung several automatic rifles over his shoulders before heading out. He heard the rumble of a truck outside and then the men were gone, spectres of the night vanishing into the murderous morning sun.

It took Jacob and his men over quarter of an hour to rouse their aching limbs, frozen joints and tortured minds, before they could follow the enemy out to the battlefield.

***

Brandon had finished his whiteboard masterpiece, a work of genius in red and black, and he had tested his programs to exhaustion. He could do no more. He was ready, and in a few hours' time he would be pushing the button at Liverpool Street to release *Proximity*.

Brandon sat back on his sofa and admired his art. He was the grand master of a work that would live long in the memory, sketched on a glass canvas and perfected on his laptop screen with a few keystrokes. Anyone who owned a mobile phone would see it, even if they didn't appreciate its beauty or its genius. Like all bold, modern movements, it might take a while for cyber artistry to be taken seriously, but maybe in years to come, today would be remembered as the day when a new artform was created.

His stomach fluttered at his thoughts. The excitement and anticipation of the morning hit him, and he knew he could do with some rest. But he wouldn't be able to sleep. It wasn't just nervousness about his project, although that in itself was enough to make anyone an insomniac. It was also his disguise.

Brandon walked to the other sofa and looked into the bag he had dropped there earlier. It contained everything he needed to transform his appearance, but now that the time had come, he was in agonies. Had he made the right choice? He couldn't shake the thought that he was committing a supreme act of self-betrayal in the altered image he had chosen and, when he saw the clothes and make-up, he trembled at the visions conjured up in his troubled mind.

Brandon knew that he needed a convincing disguise. It was inevitable that the epicentre of the cyber-attack would be traced back to Liverpool Street, and even though Brandon thought it unlikely that it would be pinpointed to the exact spot where he'd be standing, he couldn't take the chance that he might be recognised if he was caught on camera using his laptop at the precise time the attack was launched.

Brandon went to the bathroom to start his transformation. First, he shaved his face as close as he could. It made his skin pink and itchy, but he knew that it would pass and he would apply make-up later to hide any residual redness. He then washed his hair, grabbed the bottle of hydrogen peroxide, and applied the solution over the sink. After a moment's hesitation, he then did the same to his eyebrows. Giving it time to soak in, he wrapped a towel around himself and wandered into his den to relax in front of the market news.

He wasn't usually awake to see the Far Eastern markets open, but despite the novelty of watching his screens at this time of day, Brandon couldn't concentrate on the numbers or the headlines. After half an hour he returned to the bathroom and, with a little trepidation, he rinsed the peroxide solution from his hair. He took a step back and reviewed the results in the cabinet mirror.

'Not bad,' he said to himself. 'Not exactly bleached blonde, but quite a bit lighter. It will do.'

The loft contained only one full-length mirror, mounted on the wall of the second bedroom. Like the window blinds in the living area, it had seemed a good idea at the time, for use by potential guests, but as with everything else in that bedroom it was redundant. Brandon never used the mirror, in part because he had little need to check what he looked like in his habitual attire of jeans, T-shirt and a hoodie. But the main reason he didn't use it was self-loathing. He despised his body, the shape and form of it, and in particular the reminder it gave him of his darkest days and nights.

But Brandon knew that he needed to examine his entire reflection tonight, unsullied by his memories and experiences, not just his face and hair. The power of his disguise depended on it. He took a last look at himself in the small bathroom mirror and sighed, then dragged himself into the bedroom wrapped only in his towel. For a couple of minutes he stood there, paralysed by doubt, inches from the mirror, and stared at his clean-shaven face and new hair colour. *Come on, I can do this. I must. It's too late to change my disguise now.*

He stepped back to see his full-length image, took two deep breaths, and let the towel drop.

Brandon placed his hands over his face, his forearms squeezed in to cover his chest, and he glimpsed himself between his fingers. His hands inched down to his chin and then his neck, and his elbows parted to reveal his breasts. His fingers continued their journey downwards over his nipples and he shivered. He paused at his belly button, then dropped his hands to his sides.

Brandon stared at his body in the mirror and recalled how Orla had described him earlier: 'I always said you were too pretty anyway, for a boy.'

'Well,' he whispered to himself with a wry smile, 'maybe I'll still pass for a girl then.'

The perfect disguise. One last time, Brandon would go out as a girl. Overcome with feelings of shame and duplicity at his choice, he sank to the towel in front of the mirror. He hugged his knees, and wept.

18

Jacob woke to the sound of a train clattering around his skull. He looked at the empty bottle beside him and hoped that the whisky had caused his pulsating headache, rather than Nathan's assault the day before.

He pushed himself up and winced at the pain in his chest and groin, although not loudly enough to be heard by the men below. He grabbed the bottle and filled it with the contents of his bladder, a quieter option than risking discovery by urinating in the corner of this elevated space, and somehow more satisfying. He screwed the lid back on.

After relieving himself, he felt more comfortable propped up against the wall, and after a few minutes his pains subsided. He heard the occasional murmur of voices over the hum of the air conditioning units, and shadows darted around the top of the walls. Intrigued by what they could still be doing at this time, Jacob crawled to the opening and looked down at the two men still at work. Instantly, his skin prickled with frost and his blood slowed to a glacial dribble, and he was glad he'd emptied his bladder.

Paddy was out of sight, but Michael sat at a table next to the carts, and in front of him were the unmistakable ingredients of a bomb. Jacob had seen countless different devices in his time, some more professional than others, and there was no doubt from the explosives, detonators and electrical equipment arranged on the table, that these men knew what they were doing.

He recalled the thoughts he'd had during the delivery, his impression of their military efficiency, and now the full force of it hit Jacob like a blow from a heavyweight boxer. They were paramilitary; organised and equipped, dedicated and murderous. From the amount of explosive on the table, they intended to inflict significant damage and bloodshed. What had he stumbled into, and what about Maria? She was an unwitting accomplice to their plan who would be shown no mercy. He had to do something.

He looked quickly around the lock-up and his eyes settled on two handguns at the far end of the table. Jacob was by nature a courageous man, but not a foolish one, and he knew that he couldn't risk trying to reach the guns while the two men were nearby. They would certainly get there first and would kill him instantly. There was no way out other than down the ladder, which was in full view of the men wherever they were in the lock-up. He was trapped.

Down below, Michael was oblivious to the troubled spectator above him. He concentrated on his hateful task and with a steady, practised hand, he assembled the weapon. Once satisfied, he placed the rigged devices into the base of the carts and called Paddy.

'See in here, Paddy, I've placed the explosives at the bottom of each cart, next to the cooling system. You were right, it's a great idea to use these things, as there is already a power supply right here for the fridge electrics, and no one will suspect anything if they see any wires.'

Michael pointed to the receivers. 'These have been set with different codes, so I can set them off one at a time from my phone. They can also be detonated manually from underneath, although of course that's not recommended!'

He laughed at his morbid joke and Paddy wheezed a weary chuckle in reply. Michael failed to notice his partner's discomfort and he grabbed a container from the table and placed it in its housing above the explosives in the nearest cart.

'The yoghurts sit on top. We can get four-to-five-hundred of them in each cart, which should guarantee a big crowd. When most of the yoghurts have gone, I'll detonate from my phone.' He took a slip of paper from his back pocket. 'But, just in case anything happens to me, I've written down the codes so you can do it. Make sure you put them in your phone in the right order.'

Michael passed the note to Paddy. 'So, all we now need to do is load in the yoghurts. Are they finished yet?'

Paddy nodded. 'Yes, I've just done the last row. Took a bit longer than I thought, but we got there in the end.'

'Great, let's fill the carts and then get them onto the van.' Michael looked at Paddy and appeared to notice his fatigue for the first time. 'On second thoughts, I can do that. You take a rest. It won't take me long.'

Paddy moved towards the door, but Michael called him back. 'Let's not forget these things, eh?' he said, and pointed to the guns on the table.

Twenty minutes later, the van was loaded with their unholy cargo and the two terrorists had a final smoke in silence while they waited for Maria. For men intent on massacre and destruction, they appeared surreally calm, absorbed in their own thoughts. Watching helplessly from the shadows above, Jacob shivered.

***

Maria reached the lock-up ten minutes early, humming to herself in good humour despite the early hour. She was keen to make a good impression and she stopped to adjust the sleeves and collar of her jacket before knocking on the door. She poked her head inside.

'Hi Martin, Peter. Everything OK?' She looked around the lock-up. There were no signs of the night's activity and no food products. She frowned.

'Yeah, all fine,' Michael said, putting Maria out of her misery. 'We're all loaded up and ready to go. You're a little early, so we'll just finish our fags and then we'll get going. The others are meeting us there.'

Relieved, Maria leaned against the table where an hour earlier Michael had assembled his murderous devices. From his hideout above, Jacob saw the excited smile that lit up her face, like a child about to enter Santa's grotto. He wanted to shout a warning, tell her to run and call the police, but he knew it would be futile. Maria would never escape the two men, even though the older one looked pale and drawn after his sleepless night, and Jacob himself couldn't escape. If they sacrificed themselves now, who would stop the death-carts in the back of the van? Jacob had no choice but to wait, and he prayed that he'd get another chance to stop these monsters.

The terrorists stubbed out their cigarettes and Paddy nodded to Michael. 'It's time.'

Maria didn't catch the tension in his voice. 'Watch out Liverpool Street, here we come,' she said and laughed, but neither of the men joined her. She couldn't help looking upwards, where she knew Jacob would be hiding, and she smiled into the void. But then she was gone, led out of the lock-up by Paddy.

'You shut the place up,' he said over his shoulder to Michael.

Michael made one final circuit of the lock-up, even though he knew everything was secure. At the back door he tugged at the bars, still bound together by the chain and padlock, and strode to the front door. He glanced up at the hatch and thought he saw a puff of dust swirl up in the dim light. His hand hovered over the light switch and he stared at the opening for a few moments.

'Rats,' he said under his breath. He hit the switch, slammed the door and slid the bolts. 'I hope you bloody die in there.'

Michael climbed into the driver's seat and reversed the van out of the parking bay, as a macabre joke occurred to him. 'So, this is it, strike day, eh?' He looked at Paddy and the two men howled with laughter.

Maria felt that she'd missed the joke, but said nothing.

***

Brandon wiped his eyes with a corner of the towel, buried his face into the soft cotton and inhaled through the fabric. It smelled fresh and calming, and he took a few powerful breaths to fill his lungs to the very bottom. Self-control, that's what he needed. He had to be strong and clear-headed today, focused solely on the task he'd worked so hard to achieve. He couldn't allow himself to wallow in self-pity. Too much was at stake.

Brandon picked up the towel and returned to the bathroom, without another look in the mirror, then stood for ages under the powerful stream of warm water washing away his tears and lingering doubts. He dried his hair, plucked his eyebrows and applied his make-up in front of the small cabinet mirror, taking his time to perfect the look. As he waited for his nail polish to dry, he told himself that, if this was the last time he would go out as a woman, he should do it well. He wanted to create a feminine appearance that wouldn't attract too much attention, and he smiled at the challenge of this concept in the male-dominated world of the City. But when he stepped back to review his work, he was happy with the understated elegance of the face looking back at him. *Just right.*

He picked up the dress, slipped it over his snugger-than-usual underwear and smoothed it down over his thighs. The fit was good and the end result was simple and comfortable. However, his final act was to camouflage his new look, as he wouldn't be able to pass the building's reception unnoticed wearing this outfit. He folded the hem of his dress back up over his thighs and eased his loosest pair of jogging bottoms over the dress. When he then put on his hoodie and pulled the hood forward over his head, careful not to disturb his make-up, like a chameleon he reverted to his usual appearance. Unless someone looked at him head on, they wouldn't notice his lighter colour hair or make-up. Perfect.

Brandon placed his laptop and a pair of low heels into his rucksack. Finally, he walked into his den to make sure that everything was set for his return, even though he'd already checked a couple of times. For once he had turned off his news feeds, and his screens were all locked into programs he would need as soon as he returned to the loft, once *Proximity* and *Replicant* had done their bit at Liverpool Street.

He was ready.

He took the lift to the ground floor and strode across the lobby without a glance towards the receptionist. Elwyn looked up from the book he was reading, saw Brandon's back as he disappeared through the door, but thought no more of it and returned to his novel.

Brandon's chosen route took him over the tracks at Worship Street and then down Bishopsgate. The morning was bright and clear and, despite the early morning rush hour traffic, the air felt clean and fresh. With the Gherkin straight ahead of him in the distance, he turned down a little-used path next to the 'Eye-I' abstract artwork. But before reaching Exchange Square, he stopped, checked that no one was coming, and then ducked into a recess that housed a couple of bicycles. He removed his hoodie and jogging bottoms, placed them into his rucksack, pulled down the hem of his dress and then headed up the stairs to the square.

In his female attire, Brandon suddenly felt conspicuous and self-conscious, and a little chilly. He hadn't thought about removing layers of clothing in the crisp morning air and had forgotten how that felt in a dress, and he hurried up the last few steps to the shelter of the covered walkway that ran alongside the station. With those negotiated, he removed his trainers and changed into his heels.

Brandon walked to the end of the passage and took the short escalator down to the station's Bishopsgate entrance. A rush of adrenaline hit him and he felt light-headed, and he paused to let it pass. *Breath, control yourself.* He took a few moments, pulled back his shoulders, then entered the terminus.

A magnificent bright and open space greeted him, and light streamed through the panes of the spectacular Victorian roof onto the modern concourse below. Even at this early hour, it was vibrant, full of life and vitality, the beating heart of the City.

He was here, it was actually happening, and all he had to do was choose the right moment. For cyber mayhem.

***

Pitch black.

The moment Michael closed the door, all light was extinguished from the lock-up, and to Jacob it felt darker and more suffocating than the deepest coal mine. He forced himself to wait until his eyes became accustomed to the lack of light, even though every second was a lost opportunity to stop an atrocity of devastating proportions. Slowly, a gossamer-thin filament of light appeared under the lock-up's door, giving Jacob a tiny beacon to reach the exit, and with it a flicker of hope that he could stop the terrorists.

On his hands and knees, he inched forward and felt for the opening, then climbed down the ladder. From hours of studying the activity below, he had memorised the position of the tables and shelves, and with only the feeble light below the door to guide him, with arms outstretched he navigated his way across the space. Almost there, he collided with one of the shelf units and pain shot through his injured chest, but then his hands touched the switch on the wall. He shielded his eyes as the lights blinked awake.

Jacob hurried to the back door. Relieved that he'd had the presence of mind to leave the keys in the padlock the previous evening, he should be out of the lock-up in no time. But expectation turned to frustration when he saw the empty lock, and then to despair when the keys were nowhere to be seen. He yanked at the padlock but it wouldn't release, and he rattled the bars as hard as he could.

'Get me out of here!' he shouted. 'Can anyone hear me out there?'

Jacob kicked the doors then shoulder-charged them with as much force as his injured chest allowed, and raised a din for several minutes, but the doors were unyielding and no one responded on the other side. This narrow side road was too distant from the High Street to be heard over the morning traffic, and Jacob imagined it would be deserted this time of the morning.

Jacob searched the lock-up for tools, anything that might enable him to break the chain, open the doors or remove them from their hinges. He tried using an old wrench to prise the steel bars away from the doors so that he could slide off the chains, but they held firm. It was no good, the back doors were too strong, even after all those years of neglect.

He darted to the front doors to see if they were any easier to open, but as soon as he got there he realised they were solid, locked and bolted from the outside. He punched them in anger. Even if he could raise someone's attention, they would still have the same problem; the doors seemed unbreakable. He slumped back against them, panting from his exertions, and tried to contain his rising panic. His hope of raising the alarm was ebbing away.

He looked upwards. Then it hit him. There might be a way out, just maybe.

He ran for the ladder and scrambled up, dismissing the pain in his ribs. What a fool he had been, the answer had been there all along. The railway track. Jacob recalled the faint breeze he had felt every time a train passed overhead, and he tore at the boxes piled in the corner. He uncovered two holes in the wall about two feet apart, each of them scarcely large enough for a small child to squeeze through, yet alone Jacob.

There was only one thing for it. He drove his boot at the edges of the holes, each kick jarring his ankles and knees. After a few furious blows Jacob was breathing hard and sweat broke out on his forehead, but he could feel some of the bricks starting to loosen and he kept going. A couple broke away. He sensed the weakness caused by years of decay and vibration from the trains, and he knew he was almost there. He aimed a final venomous kick at the wall and the remaining section between the two holes caved in.

Jacob peered through the new opening and, through the billowing dust, he spotted a faint glow of light to his left. With renewed hope, he squeezed through the gap.

He emerged into a narrow space between two tall brick walls. Judging from the countless cobwebs and vile odour of rats and excrement, this ancient passage hadn't been used for decades, and even to a man used to living on the streets, the smell was putrid and festering. But Jacob had no time for such sensibilities and he headed for the glimmer.

The light emanated from a hole above one side of the passageway, where the top of the wall had collapsed and sections of brickwork littered the floor. The passage was still passable, but when he looked up Jacob saw that the avalanche provided the perfect escape route. He pushed as much of the rubble against the wall as he could, and although bricks slipped from under him, he clambered up the rubble and surfaced between the two railway tracks. He gulped the cool breeze, the Shoreditch air providing blessed relief from the fetid atmosphere below.

Jacob looked both ways and dashed across to the side of the elevated track, hunting for a way down to the ground. Sheer drops of over twenty feet stretched in both directions. With no time to lose, he turned south, in the direction of Liverpool Street, and jogged as fast as the uneven ground would allow. He looked over the edge at regular intervals, and on reaching a spot where the track crossed a road below, Jacob saw a pitched roof above a single-storey building, erected against the side of the viaduct. Jacob could see no other way down and he was running out of time, so had to give it a go. He straddled the wall, gripped the top bricks and lowered himself as far down the wall as he could. He clung on and looked down at the roof below, braced himself, then let go.

Jacob's ankles buckled on impact. The angle of the roof and his momentum pitched him backwards, head first down the roof. He dug his fingers into the tiles but, although he slowed, he could not prevent himself from tumbling over the guttering and onto the tarmac below. He landed on his side, his right hip and leg taking the brunt of the impact with a sickening thud.

He lay still and groaned. He made no attempt to raise himself just yet, while he tried to assess the damage, although a voice inside implored him to get going again.

He heard a door slam and a blurred figure appeared in front of him. 'My God, mate, are you OK?'

Jacob felt a hand on his shoulder and he rolled over. His vision cleared and he saw a young, shaven-headed man looking down at him. 'Call the police,' Jacob said between gritted teeth.

'Police? I don't think so, you need an ambulance mate.'

'No, the police. There's going to be a bomb, at Liverpool Street.'

'What? You're talking gibberish. You must have bumped your head when you fell. Just lie there and I'll get an ambulance for you.'

Jacob summoned all his strength and grabbed the man by his jacket collar. 'No, the police, there's a bomb, I saw it.'

'Look, you're babbling nonsense.' The man shook his head. 'Let me help you up, mate, and then you can calm down. We don't need the cops around here.'

Jacob's head span again as he got up, and he clung to the man until he was leaning against the wall. 'Thanks, but we really need the police.'

'No way, sorry, you'll have to call them yourself.'

Jacob studied the man's expression and saw that he wasn't going to help, no matter how much he asked. His steadfast refusal was etched in his face and Jacob wondered what he was hiding. Whatever it was, he wasn't about to let Jacob use his phone, and he'd have to find another way. In a fitter and stronger condition, he'd have been able to force him, but in his current state he had no chance.

He steadied himself and stepped away from the wall. Everything hurt, and the pain in his knee was agonising, but to his amazement, other than the rib he had already injured, nothing else appeared to be broken. Jacob lurched forward and broke into a limping half-jog along the deserted backstreet, longing to find someone with a phone or an open shop or office from which to raise the alarm.

At Curtain Road there were no open businesses or stores. The street resembled a long gallery, with layers of graffiti scribbled on boarded-up buildings earmarked for demolition or redevelopment. He couldn't have chosen a more derelict street. However, the sight of the criss-crossed girders of Broadgate Tower on the horizon renewed Jacob's spirits, as it meant he was edging closer to Liverpool Street, and he increased his pace.

He called and waved to two cyclists as they approached, then stepped into the road to try to stop them, but they swerved round him and shouted insults in return. Exhausted, breathless, Jacob bent over with his hands on his knees. Then he saw it: his salvation. He raced over to the woman and grabbed the Boris Bike out of her grasp.

'What the hell are you doing?' The woman flailed for the bicycle but Jacob batted away her hands.

'Get away from me,' Jacob said through clenched teeth and glowered at the woman. She took a step back in fear as she realised she had more to lose than a bike she didn't own. The thought struck Jacob at the same time.

'Give me your phone.' Jacob stepped towards the woman and held out his hand. 'Now!'

The woman flinched and sprang back, ashen-faced, then span on the spot and fled. He knew it was pointless chasing her, as by the time he'd caught the woman, taken her phone and forced its code out of her, he could have reached his destination. He turned and threw his leg over the saddle. Intense pain shot all the way up his right side, but he pedalled as hard as he could. He would be there in a few minutes.

At the busy crossing on Great Eastern Street, Jacob barely noticed the traffic lights and he careered across the yellow box on the tarmac. Horns blared and curses filled the air, yet miraculously he managed to weave through the traffic. He heard a squeal of brakes and the sound of shattering glass, but he didn't look back.

Jacob disobeyed the no entry signs and rode against the flow of oncoming traffic. He flung his weight to the right, mounted the payment and turned into Luke Street, again ignoring the no entry sign and profanities aimed his way. Seconds later he slid to a halt outside the Refuge, dropped the bike on the street outside and charged through the entrance.

'Call the police, quick,' he shouted to an elderly woman he didn't recognise at the reception desk.

'What—' was all she managed to say. She recoiled and pushed back her chair, her face contorted with fear at this startling, violent apparition.

'The police, now. There's a bomb, at Liverpool Street. We must stop them.'

The sudden commotion brought Ginger out of his office. He rushed forward. 'Jacob, whatever is the matter? What's this about a bomb?'

'Call the police, tell them there's a bomb at Liverpool Street. It could go off any minute.' Then, as if he hadn't already provided enough motivation, he said, 'And they've got Maria. She's with those bastards.'

Ginger blanched, but he picked up the phone and dialled 999. He stared back at Jacob with a look of fear and anguish, then shivered when a further devastating realisation struck him.

'My God, I think they've got Orla too. She left a few minutes ago.'

Jacob reeled at the revelation, but his years of combat experience and training sent him into overdrive, and he recalled information he wasn't even aware he'd absorbed.

'Tell them about Orla and Maria, and ask for Harry Saunders,' he said as he backed towards the door. 'Tell Harry to meet me at the station, he'll recognise me. And tell them it's in the yoghurts, they must get everyone away from the yoghurts.'

Ginger was talking to the police operator, relaying the messages whilst trying to listen to Jacob. 'What's that about yoghurts? Jacob?'

But Jacob had gone. He jumped onto the bike and he rode, hard. Deep inside, he had known he would be there at the end as soon as he'd seen the explosives at the lock-up. All he could think of now was saving Orla and Maria; not the mass of faceless, nameless innocents on their way to Liverpool Street, but these two women. For Selma and Leila, he must save them.

Endorphins surged through his veins, numbing his pain and suffering. Jacob knew it was temporary and that he'd pay for it later.

If he survived.

Deliverance

The station stirred as the first trains of the day spilled their bleary-eyed travellers onto the platforms beneath the vast gothic cathedral of iron and glass.

Morning worshippers made their daily pilgrimage to the City altar, in search of fortune and glory, and today these early-risers would be well rewarded. With their lives. They wandered across the concourse ahead of the morning rush, blissfully unaware of the approaching evil, and only later in the day would they discover that, in the very places they now trod, others would pay the ultimate sacrifice for their devotion.

The commuters stepped out into the cool, crisp, early morning sunshine. There was no sign of the storm clouds that gathered around Liverpool Street, the two weather fronts that hurtled towards them on a collision course, or the raging tempest that would follow. It seemed just like any other day.

19

They arrived with plenty of time to spare, courtesy of lighter-than-expected traffic. Michael sat at a red light on Bishopsgate, waiting to turn into Primrose Street rather than the opposite way into their original target of Spitalfields, and he smiled at the irony that strike days were intended to make travel harder, yet had in practice eased their journey to much bigger prey. He couldn't remember ever being thankful for the trade unions, until today.

The van crossed the tracks and circled Broadgate before Michael pulled up at the pedestrian crossing in Eldon Street, where James stood on the pavement waiting for them. He beamed at Maria when she stepped from the van, and then helped Paddy unload the carts.

'You guys get everything out, and I'll go find the man with the list. We need to be ticked off,' Michael said, and he went in search of Bill.

He spotted the security guard waiting by the rusting steel girders for his second cash instalment. He was alone, although Michael had no doubt that his colleagues would be close by and would appear at the first sign of trouble. But he had no intention of causing Bill any problems right now. He would be in enough hot water later when his bosses found out what he'd done, which would wipe the irritating smirk off his face.

'Here's what I promised you,' Michael said and he pressed five fifties into Bill's palm. 'Once we've unloaded, we'll wheel the carts into the station, but if we need anything else we'll give you a shout. I have to pop away at some point, so if you can keep an eye on my friends, that would be appreciated. If they're looked after, there will be a little extra in it for you. Understood?'

Bill leaned out to look past Michael and his eyes moved up and down Maria. 'Yeah, that'll be fine, I'll keep a close eye on them.'

'Thanks, in that case I'll see you later,' Michael said and he turned away. He had no intention of paying any more money to Bill, he just wanted to keep him on side while they were in the station. Once he had 'popped away', he would detonate the bombs, leaving Bill to face the music. Or die.

When he returned to the group, the carts had been unloaded and Paddy was handing out green T-shirts to James and Maria.

'Corporate uniform,' he said. 'We've got a couple of sizes here so hopefully they'll fit well enough.'

Michael was impressed. The Brethren had thought of everything, down to the tiniest detail. When Maria and James slipped on their new shirts, he saw the now-familiar motif of Blarney Yoghurts on both sides, and realised how well the bright colours would stand out in the crowd. *Nice touch, very professional. Couldn't be better.*

'Hey Michael, over here,' a voice said from behind him. He turned and saw Jenny coming down the stairs from Broadgate Circle. When she reached him, she stood on tiptoes and gave him an affectionate peck on the cheek.

'Michael?' Maria said. 'I thought your name was Martin.'

Michael cursed himself for such a foolish mistake. He should have remembered that Maria knew him by a different name. He didn't know why he'd bothered, as neither name was his real one, but his spur-of-the-moment decision to enlist Maria had come back to haunt him again. But at least this would be the last time.

'Sorry Maria, that's my fault, I should have told you earlier. We were using false names because the promotion was so top secret. My real name is Michael, and Peter is really Paddy.'

Paddy glared at Michael.

'Oh, OK,' Maria said, and looked down at her hands. Michael could see that her earlier excitement had evaporated, but whether that was because she mistrusted him following the revelation about his name or because she had seen the kiss from Jenny, he couldn't tell. Not that he cared. Her day wasn't turning out as she had hoped, but then he'd always known it wasn't going to end well for her.

Orla walked past her employer's offices and kicked herself. Why hadn't she thought of it earlier? She'd need to make this journey numerous times today and it was only now, when she passed the entrance to her workplace, that she realised she could have brought a change of clothes with her and then gone straight to the crèche after this stunt for Michael. *Wise after the event.* Orla shook her head at the thought and wondered what else she might have missed. She dragged herself towards Liverpool Street.

From the top of the stairs leading down to the station, she saw a group of people in green T-shirts below her and she stopped abruptly, confused by what she was seeing. She had expected to see Michael down there, but whatever were Jenny and Maria doing here? Something wasn't right, and she vowed to find out what Michael was up to.

Michael saw Orla coming and could tell from her stony expression that she wasn't pleased. He had expected this to be a challenging moment and had prepared himself, although he was still surprised by her vehemence when she launched her salvo without any preamble.

'What the hell's going on, Michael? You didn't tell me that Maria and Jenny were coming. Why all the secrets?'

Michael figured that another bout of contrition would help calm Orla, and he put his hands up in a gesture of submission.

'Hey, hey, Orla, slow down. It was all a bit rushed, I told you that. I know I should have said something about the others, but it slipped my mind. I'm sorry, honestly I am.'

He stepped forward to put his arm around Orla, but she pushed him away. 'Get off me. You seem to be spending a lot of time apologising recently, and I'm not sure I know who you are anymore.'

'Let's not have this conversation here,' Michael said. 'Let's talk tonight and I'll explain everything.'

He glanced at Jenny, who was trying hard to conceal a smile, and then at Maria, who appeared shaken by Orla's arrival, and even more by her sudden aggression.

Orla followed Michael's eyes and looked around the group. Everyone stared back at her, waiting for her next move, and immediately she felt embarrassed at her outburst. Perhaps Michael was right. After all, he was doing this as a favour for someone else, so maybe he wasn't to blame. She closed her eyes and let out a long sigh.

'OK, OK, let's do it later. This isn't the time, you're right.'

Paddy had heard enough and he clapped his hands to attract everyone's attention.

'OK, we're all here now, so let's get going. This is how it's going to work.'

Michael and Paddy had rehearsed their instructions beforehand. Paddy gave them a two-minute briefing on the fictitious company behind Blarney Yoghurts, in case anyone asked when taking their snack. He then split them into two teams, pairing Orla with Maria and Jenny with James, and told them where they would be standing.

Then Michael gave Jenny and Orla one final instruction. 'When you get down to your last tray of yoghurts, call me. I will then get the van back here so that we can pack up as soon as we're done. I know you have other places to be afterwards.'

In reality, however, none of them would ever see the van again. The calls from Orla and Jenny would be the signal for Michael to detonate the bombs. They would be ringing their own death knell.

***

Timing is everything.

Brandon tapped his painted finger nails on the railing and waited for the crowds to arrive, for the right moment when the unwitting pawns in his game would be most vulnerable. He remembered the previous day's TV images and knew he would be able to judge when the throng on the concourse and the queues along the walkway were at their most concentrated. He watched commuters jostle by the closed shutters of the Underground entrance, as if hoping that the service would suddenly resume. He saw them congregate around two bright green carts that stood between the platforms and the station exits, grabbing a free snack on their journey to work. And he observed the looks of resignation on the faces of those who joined the long bus queues that snaked around the raised walkway and past the shops on the station's upper level. They queued, they ate their free snacks and they stared at their phones.

Brandon took his position on the raised walkway, immediately beneath the station's main departure board. He was only a few steps from the bus queue and he could almost touch the crowd on the concourse below. The ideal birthplace for *Proximity*. From here he could see hundreds of smartphone and tablet screens, and all were within reach of his creation. He was ready, his prey lay before him, it was now or never.

Brandon took his laptop from the rucksack and felt a tremor pass through his whole body. He imagined being seen, that somehow someone knew what he was about to do, and he looked both ways. But no one was paying him any attention. Everyone was engrossed in their own lives, troubles and concerns, so why would they look twice at just another businesswoman? He lowered his gaze and the *Proximity* icon glowered at him, urging him on. Everything had been pre-set.

He pressed the button.

For five or six seconds, nothing happened. No hits were registered and no pop-up messages appeared on the screens below. Brandon held his breath and looked down at the sea of people. Then suddenly, right in front of him, a bright purple flash filled a screen, then another, a few feet to the right of the first. He heard a faint ping. *Proximity* had contaminated its first victims with *Replicant.* The bug was in the open. Several more purple messages flashed, more pings and ringtones sounded, both below him and in the bus queue next to him, and his screen registered the hits. *These are just the first level infections. Now come on, replicate!* He closed his laptop and put it back in his rucksack.

All around, fingers prodded purple screens to dismiss the message that read:

HAVE YOU BEEN IN AN ACCIDENT IN THE PAST FIVE YEARS?

If there was one unsolicited question designed to annoy people, other than one about payment protection insurance, that was it, and Brandon knew it was the perfect bait. Everyone would close that screen, but hitting 'X' would only prompt a new pop-up, this time in orange rather than purple:

YOUR DEVICE IS BEING UPDATED. PLEASE WAIT AND DO NOT SWITCH OFF.

A frustrating screen for many gadget owners, but they had probably seen similar ones before and it shouldn't cause any alarm. Behind that message, though, all hell was breaking loose in their phones. Brandon watched purple screens turn orange, accompanied by further chimes and pings, and he waited for the next stage. For the replication, the ripple.

When it happened, it was far more startling than Brandon had ever imagined when he sat in his den writing the programs. A circle of purple screens suddenly surrounded the small group of orange ones, more pings, chimes and ring-tones sounded, and they soon turned orange accompanied by another chorus. Then a third circle of purple appeared, this time more quickly than the second. A fourth, a fifth and a sixth soon followed, each successive one faster than the last, and from above it looked like a purple ripple of water spreading out from a stone dropped into a pond, that filled with a pool of orange as each new purple ring changed colour. The momentum grew, the ripples became less distinct, blurred around the edges as people reacted at different times to the arrival of their pop-ups, and within a minute the concourse was an ocean of orange lights, with the occasional speck of purple.

Brandon stood transfixed by its beautiful progress, but it wasn't only the colour, the aura from the screens that hit him. It was the sound. What had started as an initial faint chime of half a dozen phones, built with each successive ripple into louder choruses of pings, jingles and old-fashioned rings. Like a hymn, where the organist starts with one quiet note and then introduces more and more until eventually every organ pipe vibrates at full volume, the glorious crescendo grew and filled the immense Liverpool Street nave, before flowing along its cloisters and out towards the open air.

Startled at first, then far more impressed than he had ever dreamt, Brandon was euphoric. The climax of pings, beeps and even the odd claxon transformed him into the character Jobe, and he longed to stand on the railing above the concourse and shout with all his energy, 'Lawnmower Man!' It would be a fitting tribute to his cyber success and the genesis of his idea for *Replicant*.

The atmosphere was electric. Everyone in the station looked around, wondering what had happened. For the first time in ages, if ever for some of them, commuters talked to the person next to them, then checked each other's devices to see if they had the same message or if their phone was working. They were excited, chatty, even friendly to their fellow travellers.

But the orange glow persisted and the devices remained in the 'updating' mode, and people returned to type. Excitement gave way to frustration and surly faces looked down at phone screens, all thoughts of chatter forgotten. A few people tried turning off their phones, but to their dismay discovered that they wouldn't react to the usual method of pressing and holding a button. Others removed the battery, only to find on placing it back into the device that it remained stuck on the orange screen, whereas many phone owners realised for the first time that the latest model they'd acquired no longer had an accessible battery. Their devices were unusable, and they experienced their first withdrawal symptoms.

Brandon smiled. *Replicant* had disabled the on/off function and was already onto its next task, the Denial of Service attack on their banks. He knew it may take a while for this to happen, as the bug needed to infect a lot more devices first. However, after seeing the rate at which *Replicant* had spread throughout the station, accelerating with each successive wave, he wanted to make sure that he didn't miss it, and he picked up his rucksack so that he could see it unfold from a better position.

He walked past the war memorial and the flower stall by the main entrance. He turned down the steps towards the concourse, but stopped on the landing halfway down, directly above a set of cash machines. He leaned on the hand rail, as if he hadn't a care in the world, and waited.

Since the Lawnmower Man moment, Brandon had sensed the mood change. Now, nearer the concourse, he could hear some of the commuters' conversations, and he recognised the new emotion that rose up at their continued inability to use their phones. Anger. Brandon was surprised at how quickly people became lost without their phones, how dependent they were. But then something else happened that changed the course of events that morning. They also lost access to their money.

Brandon knew that the banks' infrastructure would struggle in the face of a flood of internet traffic directed at their websites and mobile banking apps. Failure of their ATM networks was inevitable, and he witnessed the moment it happened at Liverpool Street.

First one young woman, then a middle-aged man, came away from the cash machines below him, both shaking their heads. The latter spoke to the next person in the queue behind him. 'Great morning this is turning out to be, eh? No tube, no phone and now no cash. Whatever next?' He sidled his way through the crowd without looking back.

Despite the warning, the next few people in the queue stepped up to the ATMs, only to be confronted with 'out of service' messages. Brandon had seen enough. He knew that *Replicant* was in full flow, infecting hundreds of new devices every second to harass the banks' computer systems. The deluge would increase over the next couple of hours and the banks would struggle to coordinate a rapid response with so many mobile phones disabled, and while they grappled with the onslaught and invoked their contingency plans, Brandon intended to reap the rewards.

He climbed back up the steps and walked past the bus queue. He heard the conversations, the urgent whispers and the consternation in people's voices. And then something else. Anger was turning to fear.

'I don't like this, first all that ringing, then the phones not working, now the cash machines.'

'Let's walk, I've got a bad feeling about this place.'

'This is really giving me the creeps, let's go.'

People started to leave Liverpool Street. Spooked by the symptoms of Brandon's viruses, a foreboding dread settled over the congregation and, first a trickle and then a stream, they headed for the exits. Brandon smiled. He didn't care if they left. They were infected and now they would spread the virus further and faster.

If *Replicant* had been less voracious or if it had taken longer to spread, if Brandon had admired his work and left ten minutes later, or if the yoghurts had been taken from the green and white carts much sooner, events that day would have turned out differently. As it was, he left behind hundreds of bruised and battered people, all praying that their day would get better. Like them, Brandon was unaware of the maelstrom only moments away.

Timing is everything.

20

Michael and Paddy left the teams in position and checked that they knew what to do, then strolled out of the station and into the sunshine of Broadgate Circle. After parking the van two blocks away and wandering back to the station, they sat at a café, drank coffee and smoked, like two friends without a care in the world. What more could two men want than the sun on their faces, in the company of a comrade, just minutes away from the greatest triumph of their lives?

From here it should be easy. They would let the crowds build, wait for the signal that the yoghurts had almost gone, and then walk back to the van before detonating the bombs. Until then, they wanted to stay close by in case of any last-minute hitches. But everything was in place and it was a simple matter of calling a number, so what could go wrong?

'Well, Michael, it's been great working with you again. This time tomorrow you'll be a hero of the Brethren, and in years to come they'll still be talking about this day.'

'You too, my friend,' Michael said between puffs. 'I'm just sorry that it will be our last operation together. We've had some good times, haven't we?'

'Yeah, not too shabby, but all good things come to an end.'

They sat in quiet contemplation and enjoyed their final moments together, while they each considered the magnitude of their murderous project. Their silence would have lasted a little longer, had Michael not sat up, suddenly alert, and cocked his head to one side.

'Do you hear that?' he asked.

'No, what?'

Michael looked around and noticed that one or two other people had turned towards the sound, which appeared to be coming from the station. 'I don't know, an odd sound, like a fairground ride. Ringing or music, something like that, and it's getting louder.'

Paddy had now heard it too and he nodded. Suddenly the volume increased and everyone in the café looked towards the station, and a cacophony of chimes burst out of Liverpool Street and rushed straight towards them.

'What the—?' Michael said, but before he could finish, his phone pinged and Brandon's message appeared on his screen. He looked down at it with wide eyes.

'My God, look at that. Bloody ambulance chasers, whatever will they think of next?' He prodded the 'X' button.

A moment later, Paddy received the same pop-up message and, like Michael and hundreds of others before him, he dismissed the message and his screen turned orange.

Michael stared at his screen. 'Updating?' He couldn't believe what he was seeing, and it couldn't have happened at a worse time.

Like his screen, his face had turned colour in an instant and was now a violent shade of red. He prayed that the phone update would be quick, otherwise their entire mission would be wrecked, but he had a bad feeling about it. The way the message had come at them like a wailing banshee was not a good omen.

He tried turning off his phone, but the button didn't respond as it usually did. He then inspected the back of the case and saw that there was no cover for the battery compartment.

'Damn, you know what this means, don't you Paddy? We can't send the codes. If this doesn't clear, the operation's over.'

The men leapt from their seats and strode towards the station entrance. They needed to know what was happening. The crowds would be almost at their peak and they couldn't miss their chance. Surely it wasn't going to end like this.

They stopped where the group had assembled earlier and stared down into Broadgate Arcade, from where the barrage of ringtones had come. Frozen by indecision, Michael's eyes flicked back and forth between the distant concourse and his screen, and he willed the orange message to disappear. Paddy's jaw was set in an expression of contempt, and his eyes burned with pure hatred as he thought of the unexploded bombs on the concourse.

And then the situation changed again. People started streaming out of Liverpool Street, some with fear on their faces, others chatting nervously with their companions. Both men knew what this meant. Their prey was escaping and they had very little time left if they wanted to cause maximum bloodshed. It was decision time.

Paddy grabbed Michael's arms and confronted him with a face of steely resolution. 'Run, Michael, run. Get away from here while you can. I'll set it off.'

'What? You can't do that, you'll go up with it. I can't let you do that,' Michael replied, his mind in turmoil. But he knew that he could. And he knew Paddy meant it.

'Don't be an idiot. What have I got to look forward to, eh? Better to go out this way, as a hero, than to end my days in disgrace and in pain. Remember, we were warned not to leave anything behind.' He let go of Michael and pushed him away. 'Now be off with you, before I blow you up too.'

Michael stepped back, but Paddy had a few last words.

'Good luck to you Michael, and remember what you said to me. God works in mysterious ways.' He turned and strode into the oncoming tide.

Michael span round and started jogging back towards the Circle, but then he saw a sight that stopped him in his tracks. Hurtling down the stairs into the auditorium was a shabby man on a Boris Bike. Although he'd never seen him before, Michael knew instantly who he was: that vagabond Jacob, Orla's homeless friend. What the hell was he doing here?

The two men locked eyes and Jacob threw down the bike. He rushed at Michael, his fists balled and his teeth clenched. But Michael was saved by the sound of a loud bellow, as Bill and his two colleagues dashed out from the shadows, jumped on Jacob and wrestled him to the ground. Commuters fleeing the station forgot their anxieties for a few seconds and stood transfixed by the spectacle of a wild homeless man being restrained. But not Michael. He ran up the steps and sprinted away down Eldon Street.

Jacob thrashed against the men. 'You bloody fools, stop him. He's got a bomb, in the yoghurt carts.'

At his words, Jacob felt Bill's grip loosen, and a mixture of fear and uncertainty crossed his face. Jacob sensed his chance and, using reserves of energy and strength he didn't know he possessed, he pushed Bill off him. He looked after Michael and knew he wouldn't catch him. In any case, the danger was in the opposite direction.

He grabbed the stricken Bill by his collar. 'Where's the other guy, the older one?'

Bill pointed down the Arcade towards the station. 'Over there, that way.' The ashen look on his face betrayed the chaos and confusion in his head.

Jacob saw the back of Paddy disappearing into the distance. 'Oh God, no, I'm too late.'

Jacob roared. Without any regard for his own safety or the pain that racked every bone in his body, he sprinted after Paddy. He had to catch him, had to warn everyone to get away. 'Stop him, he has a bomb. Someone stop him!'

His booming voice was amplified by the tunnel-like Arcade. At the sound of his words, Paddy turned and fired a shot at Jacob. He missed by quite a margin, but it had the desired effect. Pandemonium broke out. Already unnerved by Brandon's dramatic ring-tone opera and the failure of their phones and the cash machines, at the echoing report of the gunshot, the mass of people on the concourse surged towards the exits. Fear gave way to outright panic, and the sea of fleeing, screaming people parted in front of Paddy and he had a clear run at the first cart. Orla and Maria stood petrified with yoghurt pots still in their hands, but Maria threw hers down and pulled Orla away from the cart. At the sight of Paddy, her memories of the last two days came flooding back and she realised what she'd done.

The human tsunami swept up the stairs, out of the main station entrance and straight into the path of an armed counter terrorism response team, alerted by the Refuge's earlier call. Alongside them, Harry Saunders and other officers struggled against the tide of people streaming out of the station, but pushed their way through to confront the danger.

Harry leaned over the railing and saw Paddy closing in on the cart, now alone in the middle of the concourse as commuters scrambled and stumbled away. 'Shoot the lead man, not the guy following!' The marksmen took aim.

Below, Orla and Maria rushed past the oncoming terrorist straight towards Jacob. He knew he was too late to stop Paddy, and he grabbed the two women. He thrust them towards the exit by the Arcade, running behind them to shield them as they went.

Shots rang out from the balcony, but they thudded into the cart as Paddy slid behind it. He wasn't done yet. He was determined to finish the job and, sheltering behind the wagon from a barrage of further shots, he rolled it in the direction of the second cart, determined to leave no evidence behind. But moments later Paddy was hit in the shoulder by a round from above, and he slumped back against the compartment. Undaunted, despite the pain, he reached underneath and found what he wanted.

'Down, hit the deck!' Jacob pushed the women to the floor, glanced back at Paddy and saw the hateful look of triumph in his face.

The world turned upside down in a ferocious fireball of unbridled fury and savagery. The force of the blast cleaved through the Liverpool Street air and exploded upwards to the historic great roof and across the modern sweeping concourse. Glass from the roof, windows and shop-fronts shattered into millions of tiny projectiles, and steel and iron structures buckled. The shockwave ripped through the station, twisting platform barriers and obliterating merchandise in the shops. Worst of all, it lifted people from wherever they were cowering or fleeing and slammed them into walls and railings, killing and maiming indiscriminately.

The destruction continued for several seconds, although to anyone there it seemed to last a lifetime. For some, it did. But slowly the onslaught subsided, the deafening noise and the searing heat abated, and the echoes of the blast receded into the distance.

For a fleeting moment, there was silence, but for many of the outrage's witnesses, what replaced it would haunt them as much as the brutal power of the explosion. Shards of glass and metal came to rest, but beneath the rising smoke, the full horror of the carnage and butchery revealed itself, and the unbearable torrent of noise and heat unleashed by the terrorists' bomb was replaced by a torment of agony and despair.

Harry was one of the first to rise, his skin lacerated by fragments of glass and his ears pounded numb by the explosion. His first thought, that he was happy to be alive, turned to guilt when he surveyed his surroundings.

People were raising themselves up, others were moaning, but bodies also lay prostrate and lifeless just a few feet from where he had fallen. Death was random. The railings around the walkway had buckled and splintered from the raw power of the explosion, and none of the glass panes within those balustrades or the huge windows behind him had survived the blast. The war memorial just feet away was spattered with drops of blood, and petals from the flower stall fluttered down and settled onto the carpet of glass beneath it.

Yet despite all of the death, blood and devastation, Harry's enduring image of that day was the giant departure board, which still hung above the walkway where Brandon had stood earlier. Acrid smoke and dust swirled around it, but the sun shone through the shattered roof and bathed the board in light. Like St. Paul's in the Blitz, it appeared untouched as everything around it burned, except for one detail. Whether by fate or simple design, every service was now showing as cancelled.

Beneath Harry, in the dark, ruined carcass of Liverpool Street station, Jacob opened his eyes to a scene of unutterable horror.

21

On his way back to the loft, Brandon donned his jogging bottoms and hoodie and tripped along Worship Street. Moments away from his apartment, a loud echoing boom reverberated in the crisp morning air and the ground trembled. Some ravens took flight and Brandon looked up at the clear morning sky, but he dismissed the disturbance as noise from a local building site. He entered the building and thought nothing more of it.

Once in the loft, Brandon stripped off all of his clothes and slipped into his familiar garb of T-shirt and jeans. His hair and make-up would have to wait. Undistracted by any news or price feeds, he settled down in front of his screens and surveyed the progress of the programs he had left working. He was encouraged.

As he had anticipated, all of the major banks were suffering significant system issues. His *Surveillance* program showed that none of their online or mobile banking services were available, and each of their website homepages had a banner message warning of outages. All payment services were suspended, and even bank branches had no access to customer balances or transaction data. The financial system was in meltdown. Brandon had expected problems, but he was astonished that attacking the banks' personal and mobile banking interfaces had wrought such havoc in so short a time.

But the retail banks weren't Brandon's real target. He was only attacking them to weaken his true quarry, and he turned his attention to the next tab in *Surveillance*. He smiled at the results. The Bank of England's website was unavailable, even though it hadn't been subject to the cyber-attack. Unlike the high street banks, it didn't rely on retail or commercial banking business, so Brandon hadn't been able to destabilise it by forcing millions of customers to deluge its accounts. Instead, he had targeted the central bank as the custodian of UK financial market stability and, in particular, its role as banker to the banks it regulated.

As a result of the turmoil being faced by the UK's banks, Brandon knew that the central bank's crisis management team would have implemented various contingency plans. But this didn't mean better, safer markets. The recent surge in demand for mobile, on-the-go banking applications had resulted in the retail banks investing heavily in new electronic interfaces and tools for their customers, but these were little more than thin, digital veneers wrapped around their older legacy payment and accounting systems, which had received little new investment.

Faced with the onslaught of Brandon's Denial of Service attack, the banks would temporarily disable their new systems and would deploy older versions, ones that had supported the financial system in past times. They were considered a capable back-up when the latest generation of systems failed, in part because they were less woven into the fabric of today's mobile infrastructure, and they were kept in reserve for this scenario so that key market operations and payments could continue through the central bank. Brandon knew this was their drill, so this is what he was now attacking.

It was a one-sided contest.

Many of the back-up systems used archaic software, programs and codes, most of which hadn't been updated for years, and this twentieth century architecture was no match for the latest arsenal of computer hacking techniques. Brandon's *Old Lady* program had prodded and probed the central bank's firewalls since the release of *Replicant*, learning as it went which attacks were being repelled and which contained vulnerabilities.

Brandon looked at his screens. The eponymous program had broken into the Bank of England before he had returned to the loft. He now had access to all of its accounts and records, including the log-in credentials of the bank's senior management and supervisors in its settlement and technology sections. He could begin his task.

He sat in front of his screens and tapped out his commands. He overrode security protocols, he installed new codes that he had previously drafted, and he uploaded account and payment data into the bank's settlement systems. Brandon felt like a conductor in front of an orchestra, where each of the programs he commanded was a virtuoso whose skill and speed far surpassed his own, but which he directed with a flick of his wrist or a tap on his keyboard.

Brandon worked without rest, other than occasionally stepping up from his chair to stretch his limbs or top up his coffee. After four hours' effort, he sat back and surveyed his work. Was he done, had he set up everything? He had ticked each item off his list and felt he'd left nothing to chance, but the fruits of his labour wouldn't be known for another couple of hours, once he'd turned off *Replicant*. The banks would immediately regain control of their accounting and reporting systems and should be able to bring customer systems back online before the end of the day. But it would only be when the Bank of England's internal reporting systems were rebooted that the new transactions would become apparent. These irreversible, anonymous, encrypted trades had already taken place; the Governor just didn't know about them yet. But she soon would, and her log-in credentials had approved them.

It was time to retire *Proximity* and *Replicant*. The programs had delivered everything he had desired, and more, but he had no further need for them. He could send a kill broadcast at any time, and there was no point prolonging the misery. He hit the button.

Brandon exhaled and slumped back in his chair, exhausted now that all his efforts were over. He'd catch up on the news and markets later, but first he needed to wash away his disguise forever. Removing his make-up, restoring his hair colour and having a long, relaxing bath suddenly felt more important than the news. Wonders will never cease.

He flicked the switch to turn on his news and market feeds and headed for the bathroom. On his way out of the den, he heard a single line of the newsreader's main report.

'... and of course, dominating our headlines today is the terrorist attack on Liverpool Street during this morning's rush hour...'

Brandon knew that what he'd done could be described as a type of terrorism, although he didn't see it that way himself. He looked forward to hearing more about it later.

***

The sheaf of papers in his hand quivered like long grass in the autumn breeze, and Aubrey felt the chill. He closed his eyes and knocked on the Governor's door.

'Come in,' Governor Perkins called from behind her desk. She'd had her worst day in office since her surprise appointment less than three months earlier, and what could be wrong now? 'Oh, hello Aubrey, what is it? I hope it's better news. We could certainly do with it.'

'Ah, actually, no... not really Madam Governor.'

She sighed at Aubrey's use of the old-fashioned title but ignored it. 'Go on.'

'We have a problem,' he said, and passed her the report from the top of his pile. He waited for her to review the columns of data and then explained. 'The column you need to look at is the third-to-last one, before the totals. It's headed "BTC" ... which stands for Bitcoin.

'What? Bitcoin? But that's not a reserve currency, in fact it's not even a real currency at all.' The Governor knew that nit-picking wasn't going to change the fact that it was listed on the report as one of the Bank of England's international reserve currencies, but it didn't make sense. 'Why's it on this report?'

'That's the problem, Madam Governor, we don't know. But the thing is, we actually do own this Bitcoin, it's been checked out. We apparently bought a load of it during the outages this morning, and we're still trying to work out how.' He paused to let the news sink in before dropping the second bombshell. 'There are also Bitcoin balances in the reserve accounts we hold for each of the clearing banks, which you'll see on the next page, so we can't rely on these balances or our liquidity calculations at all.'

The Governor sat back and stared at the report. 'Aubrey, you're not making sense. We don't have authority to hold Bitcoin, even if we were mad enough to want to. Someone would need to authorise a transaction to buy some, including paying for it in another currency, presumably dollars or sterling, for which payment approvals are needed.'

She slapped the report on the desk in exasperation and Aubrey resisted the urge to speak further. He hadn't told her yet that their systems revealed her as authorising the trades, and he sensed it wasn't a good time to broach it.

'We don't have a Bitcoin account to settle the transactions,' Governor Perkins said, and Aubrey could see that she hadn't finished. 'Our systems wouldn't just invent this column on the report, it had to be done deliberately. So that's several reasons off the top of my head why this cannot happen and I'm sure there are more. Is this someone's idea of a joke, because if it is, it's the wrong day to play it, given what's happened in the City today?'

'No, Madam Governor, it's not a joke. The Bitcoin ledger confirms all of the transactions were authenticated, and we definitely own them.'

'OK, well let's just get them to reverse the trades, and then we need someone to look at what happened as a matter of urgency.'

Aubrey shook his head. 'That was our first thought too, but that cannot happen as Bitcoin trades cannot be reversed. New trades can be entered into, but the prior ones cannot be undone. It's all to do with the way the blockchain process works and how the register is verified. And to agree new trades, we'd need to know the identity of the other party... but we don't.'

'How's that possible? Surely with all of today's anti-money-laundering rules we must know who we're dealing with.'

'Not with Bitcoin. We could be dealing with Elvis Presley and not know it.' Aubrey instantly regretted his attempt at levity when he saw the Governor's scowl, and he rushed to explain. 'Bitcoin digital wallets don't need to be in your own name and you can have a different wallet for every transaction if you want. It's just how the system works.'

'My God, so we may be dealing with terrorists here? And do we know where the sterling or dollars were sent?'

'Yes, we know that bit,' Aubrey said, and he handed over several sheets of paper with a list of hundreds of names. He paused to allow the Governor to review the pages. 'This is where the money went, and it's weird. If we were dealing with terrorists, why would they do that?'

'Wow, you're right, this is weird. No, it's crazy.' The Governor collected her thoughts. 'OK, so in theory we could contact everyone on this list and ask for our money back, and give them back the Bitcoin?'

'In theory, yes. But there are two problems. The first is the obvious one of publicly asking all of them to send us back the money. The political fall-out could be huge.'

'Yes, you're right, and there's no way we could keep it quiet with so many people involved. And the other problem?'

'The second is that we rather overpaid for the Bitcoin.' Aubrey paused. This was the bit he most dreaded telling the Governor. 'We're not sure every name on that list owned the Bitcoin before today, or even if they know what Bitcoin is. The point is, according to all the records, they made a legitimate sale of Bitcoin to us, and we paid about a hundred times the current market rate.'

The Governor leaned forward and buried her head in her hands. She needed to consider all of the implications, including who else could be blamed. 'Surely there are controls to stop that happening. Why weren't our operations or settlements people alert to this?'

'They didn't know about it, as the trades took place when we were on contingency systems and only appeared in our accounts when we returned to regular operations. Bitcoin didn't even exist when some of these old systems were last used. But as far as the price is concerned, that's another issue with these cryptocurrencies. They are valued at whatever you pay for them, as the market price has no basis in reality. That's one reason why they're so volatile. As you said, they're not really currencies at all, not in the conventional sense, so normal rules don't apply.'

'So how much did we pay, exactly?' the Governor asked, although she knew that the answer was on the first page of the report and she thumbed back to it again. She slumped back in her chair and looked up at the ceiling as if in prayer. Her head was reeling. They were facing something new, untested and alien, and she would have a lot of explaining to do to Her Majesty's Treasury.

'Aubrey, call another crisis meeting, as if we hadn't had enough of those today. And then I think we better have a word with the Chancellor of the Exchequer. He's not going to like this.'

***

'Have they sent you here to interrogate me, Detective Constable Saunders?' Orla asked, propped up on the gurney in the overworked corridors of St. Bartholomew's Hospital.

'No, Orla,' he said with a tender smile. 'So you may call me Harry.'

Orla considered herself lucky. She had stitches in some gashes on her arms and head, now wrapped in bandages, and she was waiting for a couple of X-rays, but she was sure that everything would soon heal. The same could not be said for all of the explosion's victims, many of whom had suffered life-changing injuries, or worse.

'Do you know how Jacob and Maria are doing?' Orla looked at Harry, who glanced down the corridor before answering.

'Jacob's fine, although he's added a few more cuts and bruises to his collection. He looks like a prize-fighter after a street brawl and I'm sure he's had worse.'

'And Maria?'

'Not so good, I'm afraid. She's in intensive care and hasn't come round yet. But she's fighting, hanging in there.'

Tears welled up in Orla's eyes and Harry squeezed her hand. She couldn't remember much of what happened at Liverpool Street. Her last clear memory was running away from the cart with Maria and Jacob. She had a vague recollection of being lifted from the ground, but nothing more until she drifted back to consciousness to the sound of nearby wailing and moaning. Jacob had been there with her, but she couldn't recall seeing Maria.

'I'm sorry, Orla, but I'm sure she'll pull through.' Harry knew that his words were inadequate, but he still had one further message for her.

'Jacob is speaking to the counter terrorism team at the moment. They wasted no time getting here to interview key witnesses, even if they are injured, as it's vital they find out everything as soon as they can, in case there are any more devices. Possible booby-traps.'

Harry waited for the implications to sink in before continuing.

'You'll need to speak to them soon. You know Michael, and he's now on the run and we have no idea where he is. You may know something, anything, that will help. And you may need protection. You're the only one other than Jacob and Maria who knows anything about him. They're already checking out your flat.'

Orla looked up, her eyes wide with fear, although she didn't ask Harry the question he was expecting. 'What about Jenny and that barman James? They know Michael.'

Harry shook his head. 'I'm sorry, Orla, they didn't make it. They were in a group trying to get up the stairs. They were too close and never had a chance.'

Orla couldn't breathe. She gulped the air and tears immediately streamed down her cheeks. She put her face in her hands and turned towards the wall. 'No, no, no. I killed Jenny. If it hadn't been for me, with Michael, she would still be alive.'

Harry wrapped his arms around her shoulders. 'No, don't do that. You're not to blame. He was the murderer, not you. You had nothing to do with her death, or anyone else's.'

But Harry knew he had no proof of that. After all, what did he really know about her? He held Orla, but when he glanced to the side, he saw the counter terrorism team watching them. They certainly wouldn't give her the benefit of the doubt.

22

Brandon stood at his bathroom mirror and inspected his hair. He had picked a dark dye, although it hadn't taken as well as he'd wanted and his hair still wasn't his natural colour. But it was a step in the right direction and would be fine under his hood, for the time being at least, until it grew out or faded.

But he couldn't worry about that right now. It was time to catch up on the news. The main story was bound to be his morning's conquests, and he had a sudden urge to hear if any of his financial manoeuvres had been made public yet. He stepped into his den and was delighted by the opening line.

'And now we return to our on-the-scene reporter at Liverpool Street, Justin Entwistle, who will bring us up to date with the latest.'

Brandon bounded over to his chair, but then froze in his seat when the picture changed to a grim-faced reporter who stood at a cordoned-off street junction. Behind him were scores of vehicles from the emergency services, with blue lights flashing everywhere. *What the hell has happened? I can't have done that.* Brandon watched the screen open-mouthed.

'We understand from the City of London Police that the death toll now stands at thirty-seven, with hundreds more

seriously injured. Victims are being taken to several local hospitals including the Royal London, Barts, Mile End and various specialist burn and trauma units across London. Fire and ambulance crews are working to free people still trapped inside the station, with the structure having now been passed as safe following earlier concerns about falling debris from the roof.'

'And is there anything you can tell us about who is responsible for this atrocity?'

'The City Police and Counter Terrorism Command are remaining tight-lipped on that at the moment, and no established terrorist group has so far claimed responsibility. There appears to be some confusion about whether the bombs were detonated by the same people responsible for the earlier cyber-attack, one theory being that it was designed to knock out the City's telecommunications network, thereby hampering efforts to get help and assistance to the scene. If that is indeed the case, it sends out a very chilling message about the ruthlessness and capability of this terrorist group.'

Brandon shivered in his chair. He couldn't believe his eyes at the pictures of utter carnage, and the thought that *Replicant* may have somehow exacerbated the situation sent him into paroxysms of fear and guilt. But he kept watching, despite the torture. He wasn't looking for news of his financial crime anymore, that was all forgotten now. He was glued to the screen in growing fear about the role he may have played in a completely different act of terror.

'And the other result of knocking out smartphones is that there's no amateur footage of what happened this morning. Usually by now there would be numerous videos circulating on the internet or recordings would have been handed to the police, but this attack is characterised by a lack of information so far. Again, was that a deliberate ploy by the terrorists? That's something else we don't know at this moment.'

Brandon slumped in his chair. Why had he disabled everyone's devices? He hadn't needed to do that to establish the botnet, it was just the best way of stopping people from trying to reboot their phones or changing their settings.

'However, we have obtained eye witness accounts from survivors at the scene, and here are some of the things people have been telling us.'

The news channel showed a succession of short clips with survivors, whose reports varied according to their appearance and demeanour, ranging from the tattered, torn and emotional to the dishevelled and matter-of-fact.

'There was someone shouting about a bomb and that set everyone running. Many were screaming, it was complete panic.'

'It was terrifying. Even from where we were at the other end of the station, we were lifted off our feet and the heat and noise were unbearable. But we are so lucky to be alive.'

'A lot of people had already started to leave because of the phones not working and there was a bad vibe in the

station. Then two men ran in. The second one appeared
to be chasing the first, as he was yelling to stop him, that
he had a bomb. Everyone just ran for the exits.'

'We heard gunfire from the police on the upper level
and knew it was for real. I've never been so scared.'

'If it hadn't been for the man who was chasing, I think
more people would have died, as it was him that set
everyone running. He was so brave to do that, and he
pulled two girls away from the bomb. He looked like a
tramp.'

The news report then returned to the studio, where the
newsreader announced that they were switching to a live
press conference, convened by the City of London Police.

To a melee of clicking cameras and flashes, the
Assistant Commissioner laid out what they knew so far.
Brandon watched, mesmerised by the event and the
unfolding detail.

'In response to earlier rumours, I can confirm that
several people are helping us with our enquiries. In
particular, we are interviewing one of the people who had
been attending the cart that exploded, as well as the man
cited in many eye witness accounts who pursued the
bomber into the station. We have also detained a number
of security personnel from the Broadgate complex and
have taken scores of eye witness accounts. But our
enquiries are still at an early stage and we would urge
anyone with information to come forward as soon as
possible.'

To repeated questioning, the Assistant Commissioner refused to reveal the identity of any of the witnesses or speculate on their potential role in the attack, and he then moved on to further updates. He advised the watching media that counter terrorism units had raided two premises in the Shoreditch area, one a residential apartment building and the other a lock-up near Old Street. As a result, the authorities now believed that the bombing had been carried out by a two-man cell of an Irish extremist organisation, and that one of the men had set off the bombs at Liverpool Street and had died in the attack. The other was now on the run and was known under a number of aliases, most recently as Michael Sweeney. Members of the public were urged to contact the police if they had any further information on him or his whereabouts.

Finally, the briefing turned to the cyber-attack that had occurred before the explosions, where another officer read out a statement.

'At approximately seven-thirty this morning, a computer virus was released that targeted hand-held devices such as mobile phones and tablets. We believe that it originated in the Liverpool Street area, although we are continuing our investigations to pinpoint the exact location. The virus spread quickly around the mobile network, infecting millions of devices, which then prompted a concerted attack against the UK's banks in what is known as a Distributed Denial of Service attack. This temporarily disabled the banks' IT systems, leading to widespread disruption of banking services. However,

the situation is now under control and bank systems are slowly getting back to normal.

'A taskforce has now been established, led by the Bank of England and including representatives from the financial services regulator, the Financial Conduct Authority, Government departments, mobile phone manufacturers and all of the banks targeted today. This group will investigate the shortcomings in handset security and bank systems that allowed this to happen.

'We are continuing to look for the perpetrators of this distressing attack. We are keeping an open mind about whether it is linked to the bombing today at Liverpool Street, although at this stage we have reason to believe that the two are unconnected.'

Brandon had turned down all of his other news broadcasts so that he could concentrate on the statement and the subsequent barrage of questions from the impatient media. There wasn't a single indication that the police were close to identifying him, but perhaps he wouldn't know until his door was broken down.

***

Deep in thought at City Airport, Donovan was in a dilemma. She couldn't believe what had happened this morning; today of all days.

It had all started so well. She had watched Paddy, Michael and the girl leave the lock-up for Liverpool Street, on schedule, with the carts loaded in the back of the van.

There was no need for her to stay anymore and she was at the airport within half an hour, confident that she would be in the air by the time of the attack.

But soon after her arrival, all flights had been suspended. The airport authorities called it a computer glitch, although Donovan suspected that it was somehow linked to the strange problem with the phones. Like everyone else, her smartphone was stuck on an orange screen, *updating*, and there was no way of finding out what was going on with the operation. She had a feeling of dread that it had somehow back-fired, but she needed to know for sure, so she queued with a long line of other passengers at a public pay-phone, unaffected by the same issues as the mobile phones. She called it three times, but there was no answer from Paddy's number.

Then came the news of the bombing at Liverpool Street. All TVs in the terminal were now tuned into rolling live broadcasts of the aftermath, and while her fellow passengers reacted in shock to the news, Donovan relaxed. She was sure that everything must have gone to plan, and maybe she just couldn't reach Paddy because of the mobile phone outage, nothing more.

But the planes stayed on the ground and she was drawn to the screens as further details emerged, and it soon became clear that something wasn't quite right. From eye witness reports, it appeared that Paddy may have sacrificed himself in the explosion. But what had happened to Michael? If he was now on the run, he may need help, and there was a risk that he might give away valuable information if he was caught. And who was the vagrant who had chased Paddy and what did he know about the mission and the Brethren? He could still cause them problems if he knew too much.

Then the mobile phones started working again and Donovan sighed with relief. She should now be able to reach Michael, and maybe agree how to deal with their troublesome meddler. She sent her message:

What's happening? We need to deal with the tramp.

An hour later, Donovan's flight was ready, but she'd had no reply. The operation was still at a critical juncture and she wasn't sure if she should sort it out herself, or if she could rely on Michael. *Last Call.* She shook her head, made her decision, and joined the taxi queue to return to the City.

***

Jacob spent a weary couple of hours with the Counter Terrorism Command in their makeshift interview room at St. Bartholomew's Hospital. During his interrogation, he recounted several times what he'd seen and heard at the lock-up and gave his version of events at Liverpool Street. They also asked numerous questions about Orla and Maria, and from the tone of their questions it was clear to him that they were trying to ascertain if the women might have known about the bomb before it exploded or if they were innocent victims of the atrocity.

Eventually they finished their questioning and excused him, and Jacob found Harry waiting for him in the corridor. Unlike the first time they'd met at the Refuge's medical bay, there was no frostiness between them, bound as they now were by mutual trauma, and Harry gave Jacob an update on Orla and Maria.

'What you did this morning was heroic,' Harry said. 'You saved many people, including the lives of these two young women.'

'Nothing heroic about trying to save lives. Anyway, look about you, I didn't do a very good job, did I?' Jacob swept his arm around the scene of suffering in the hospital. 'And I even got you involved, lured you straight into the path of the bastards, could have killed you. How's that heroic?'

Harry knew that, despite saving possibly hundreds of people, Jacob would blame himself for not rescuing more. He would always ask himself if he could have reached Paddy, or shouted louder or run faster. Harry let it go.

'Well get some rest, anyway. The Refuge will give you a bed for a few days, which may keep you out of harm's way. And I'm not talking about terrorists this time, it's the media you want to keep away from. They seem to have latched onto your story and they will follow you anywhere, on or off the streets. Talking of which, I suggest you don't leave the hospital by the main entrance, as they're waiting for you there.'

Jacob looked at Harry with a bemused look. 'First you call me a hero, then tell me to act like a coward. I've faced worse than a mob of journalists.'

'Suit yourself, but don't say I didn't warn you.'

Harry's tone was light-hearted, quite an achievement in the circumstances, and he stretched out his hand. 'Good luck, and thank you. From everyone you did save this morning.'

The two men shook hands and Jacob sidled away past the gurneys lining the corridor.

***

Still glued to his screens, Brandon listened to the news while trying to watch the markets. It had been an eventful morning for equities and he was glad he'd had the sense not to take any large positions in anticipation of the fall-out from his virus attack. That would have raised a red flag to any regulator or investigator looking for unusual or suspicious activity, and he'd known he couldn't take that chance.

'Further details are emerging on the cyber-attack this morning. According to unnamed sources in the financial markets, during the attack there were a series of unusual payments linked to accounts controlled by the Bank of England. We understand that this included a number of transactions in Bitcoin, the fast-growing cryptocurrency known to be a favoured way of moving money around the criminal world, owing to its relative anonymity and lack of

government regulation. The Bank of England hasn't responded to our requests for comment, so we must emphasise that these are currently unsubstantiated rumours, but we will bring you more when we have it.'

Brandon was both unnerved and excited by this report. Although it proved his transactions had gone through, it also increased the chances of linking everything back to him. He was confident in the precautions he had taken, yet he couldn't help glancing at his front door.

'But now we are going back to today's main story, the bombing of Liverpool Street. We have a sensational update on the identity of the man who tried to thwart the attack by chasing the bomber into the station. A video has now been posted on various social media websites that is claimed to have been recorded on a camcorder by a tourist at the station. It appears to show the bomber running past the camera and then, seconds later, a man in pursuit. The pictures are grainy and slightly shaky, but it is the first video evidence we have of what happened this morning. Some viewers may find the scenes upsetting.'

Brandon watched, spellbound, as a man of around sixty years of age ran towards the camera, before passing within a few feet of the lens. Behind, another man was chasing him, but before he came into focus the camera swung round to follow the first. There was a clearly audible bellow of *'Stop him, he has a bomb. Someone stop him!'* and then, moments later, the cracking sound of a shot. Mayhem ensued, and just before the screen turned to the floor amid scenes of scrambling and screaming, the camera caught the profile of the pursuer the moment he passed.

The video was one of the most haunting recordings Brandon had ever seen. His stomach lurched and he retched, and he looked down at his feet and gasped for breath. He forced himself to look back up, at the still shot of the man's profile on screen, while the newsreader revealed the results of their channel's research.

'We have tracked down the man shown in this video and can reveal that he is an ex-British Army soldier now living on the streets of London. A short time ago, we caught up with him returning to a homeless shelter on the edge of the City, as these exclusive pictures show.'

Jacob's return to the Refuge was now on screen. A reporter shoved a microphone into Jacob's face and then tried to follow him into the lobby, but a stern-faced Ginger held up his hands and refused him entry. The reporter's pleas for comment went unheeded, but the triumph of his scoop was evident when he turned to the camera.

'That was our hero of Liverpool Street, arriving at the Refuge, a homeless shelter in the Shoreditch area. Our investigations reveal that he is a former Army officer, who once again today faced down his country's enemies. We understand that his name is Jacob Monk.'

The screen turned back to the profile picture of Jacob at Liverpool Street.

Brandon was suffocating. He was overwhelmed by the emotion of the day, the exhaustion of his endeavours and the raw tension and revelations of the past few hours' news. But more than all that, it was the still image he would always remember afterwards. He forced himself to breathe, put one hand to the screen, then whimpered one word:

'Dad…'

23

He had made up his mind; he would call Ginger.

After seeing Jacob's face on screen, Brandon sat for over an hour wrestling with his emotions. He hadn't seen his father for years and it would be easy to keep it that way, but Brandon had felt an intense yearning the moment his image appeared on TV. Perhaps it was the realisation that his father was homeless whereas Brandon lived a comfortable life, possibly it was watching replays of him almost losing his life, or maybe it was the simple fact that they were blood. Whatever the reason, Brandon was consumed by an urgent desire to see his father again.

As one of the Refuge's previous residents and, nowadays, its major benefactor, Brandon knew most of the shelter's administrative staff, and he had a high regard for their dedication, efficiency and, above all, their discretion. As a donor, they respected Brandon's request for anonymity and protected his identity well, and he knew that Ginger would appreciate the sensitivity of the current situation. Even though he would be surprised at his request, Brandon was sure he would accede once he understood the circumstances. The question was, would his father agree? There was only one way to find out.

Ginger listened in silence while Brandon revealed his familial relationship with Jacob and the events that led to their separation. He avoided the more graphic details of his painful and personal history, but even so, by the end of his narrative Brandon could hear the occasional sniff from Ginger's end of the phone. Brandon had guessed that he would be moved by the story, which would make him more amenable to his request.

'Ginger, if he's willing to see me, can you bring him to me, please? I know I'm asking a big favour, but I think it's best we meet here rather than at the Refuge. It's a lot more private, whereas judging from the earlier news report, I'm assuming you have quite an audience with all those reporters, and no doubt they will dig up the dirt on anyone who turns up right now.'

Brandon didn't tell Ginger his other motivation for not going to the Refuge, that he didn't want to be caught on camera because of his own activities earlier that day.

'I guess you're right. I think I can smuggle him out of one of the back exits as there aren't any reporters by them. That's one advantage I suppose of the way we have grown over the years.'

Brandon thanked Ginger and hung up. He couldn't sit still, nor could he concentrate on his screens, and he resorted to wandering around the loft, his phone in his hand, while he waited. Now that he'd made the call, he wasn't sure if he was doing the right thing. It had been eight years since they'd last met, and Brandon suspected he would be almost unrecognisable from the delinquent teenager his father had last seen. What would he remember of Brandon, especially given his own difficulties at the time? And how had he ended up on the streets too? Was it because of him, had Brandon pushed his father over the edge?

He was beginning to think that his father had declined the reunion, when the intercom buzzed. Brandon picked up the handset and heard the familiar, unhurried tones of Elwyn from reception, who announced that two gentlemen had arrived to see him.

'Thanks, Elwyn. Can you let them up to my floor please and I'll meet them at the lift?'

Less than a minute later, the bell chimed and Brandon saw his father, alone, rooted to the spot at the back of the lift. He made no attempt to move when Brandon took a hesitant step forward.

'Where's Ginger?' Brandon asked, as if meeting his father after so many years was of less consequence.

'He said we should be alone, he'd only get in the way.' Jacob stared at Brandon. 'Are you going to invite me in, or should we chat in the lift?'

Brandon stepped back. 'Of course, sorry,' he said, and held an outstretched arm towards his apartment door.

Jacob passed Brandon without a sideways glance and stepped into the apartment. He stopped after a few strides, surveyed the loft and then turned to look back at Brandon, who had closed the door behind them. Jacob's expression was one of confusion, as if he didn't know what to do next or what to say, whether to proceed further or wait until invited.

Brandon could bear it no longer. His emotional dam burst in a torrent of pent up sorrows. Despair, betrayal, loneliness and regret all cascaded down, and he threw himself into the arms of the only man he had ever loved.

'Dad, oh Dad,' he cried, and buried his face into Jacob's chest. He didn't smell the grime and sweat from Jacob's lowly existence, nor did he feel the debris and dried blood of Liverpool Street's darkest hour ingrained in his tattered clothes. Brandon was back in his childhood, and all he smelled was his father and all he felt was the tender, unsure hug of an embarrassed dad suddenly faced with a distraught child. Racked with sobs, he let it all flood out.

Taken aback by the force of Brandon's outpouring, at first Jacob placed his hands on his shoulders, not knowing what else to do. But when burning tears rolled down his own cheeks, he held the back of Brandon's head and buried his face into his hair, and succumbed to the emotion of the moment.

Brandon's sniffing eventually subsided and the two men parted. Jacob wiped his eyes with the back of his hand and turned away to hide his embarrassment. 'I could do with a drink,' he said.

'Of course,' Brandon said, and turned towards the kitchen, relieved at the distraction. 'Tea, coffee, juice?'

'I was thinking of a proper drink, you know, alcohol.'

'Sorry, I don't have any. I haven't had a drink since my time on the streets and I don't have many guests here. In fact, none. You're the first.'

'Tea then. Please.'

Jacob stepped further into the loft.

'Nice place,' he said, not with any malice or sarcasm but with a genuine appreciation of the space. He stopped in the middle of the wide living area and looked around, until his gaze rested on the windows.

'What's that? Modern art or a puzzle?' Jacob pointed at Brandon's diagram, scrawled over the glass with the blinds still drawn from the night before.

'Oh, nothing, just a few doodles, I'll wipe them off.' Brandon reached for a cloth.

But Jacob had already moved on and he stopped at the door of the den. He stared at the screens, each still showing market data or news.

'You're big news now, Dad. Everyone wants to know about you and your story.' Brandon lowered his head. 'So do I. We have a lot of catching up to do.'

'Yes, we certainly do, Leila, perhaps starting with why you left us.'

Jacob's tone was curt, almost accusing, and it took Brandon by surprise. He studied his father's face and wondered if he had used his former name as a taunt, or did he not realise who Brandon really was? It was too important to let go. If they didn't address this now, they would never be able to move on.

'Dad, you've just demonstrated one of the reasons. I'm not Leila anymore, I'm Brandon. You never understood how I felt growing up, trapped inside the wrong body.'

'You didn't give us a chance, you kept it to yourself. The first we knew that anything was wrong was trouble at school with bullying, then drink and drugs. Everyone told us it was due to moving schools frequently, or because of my work. It wasn't until just before you left that you told us you wanted to be a boy.'

'I didn't keep it to myself and Mum certainly knew. I tried to tell you, but you were never there, always away in some far-flung war zone helping other people.' Brandon sighed, but knew he had to press on. 'You have no idea how we struggled when you weren't there. When you left the Army, we were relieved as we thought you'd spend more time at home, but it wasn't any better. You started spending more time with your colleagues and clients, wining and dining, and hardly saw us.'

'Oh, so I'm to blame for everything am I? Well I've certainly paid for it since, in spades.' Jacob's expression was surly and his mood dark.

Brandon was conscious that he had opened the lid of a box full of potential incrimination, and the conversation wasn't going the way he wanted. He had to steer away from blaming his father and bring it back to less acrimonious topics.

'Dad, that's not what I meant. I know it was difficult for you, as it was for all of us. It's just that school was a bad time for me, as no one understood what I was struggling with, including me to be honest. I wasn't mature enough to deal with it, I felt all alone, and leaving home seemed the only way out. I was wrong, I know that now. I'm sorry.'

Jacob looked at Brandon, but in his own mind he still saw Leila, his daughter. Still gentle and vulnerable, still struggling to be heard and, after all these years, still damned right. He hadn't been there for Leila, but not because he hadn't wanted to be. Jacob had had his own demons to deal with, no less real to him just because they were in his head. That's why he had failed Leila, and afterwards Selma, but that was no reason to fail Brandon. He took a deep breath and tried to explain.

'Leila... sorry, I mean Brandon. I will try to get it right, honest, I just have to get it straight in my head. You're right, I never understood what you wanted and I wasn't able to see what you were going through. After you left, we looked for you, tried to find you, but you had done too good a job at disappearing, covering your tracks. Maybe you got that from me.'

Jacob smiled and was encouraged by Brandon's impish look in return. 'So, what happened to you, after you left us?'

Brandon wasn't ready to describe the full horror of his time on the streets, and might never be able to tell his father everything. But he gave Jacob an abridged account, how he had slept rough for a time before falling into the wrong company. That was when the abuse started; physical, sexual and psychological. He had been used as a prostitute, although he hadn't received any money, only a few scraps of food to survive in a squalid house north of the City. Through a haze of drugs, Brandon had somehow managed to escape and then forced himself by sheer willpower to walk for hours, before he eventually stumbled into the Refuge.

'That was the worst year of my life and I wouldn't wish it on anybody. Not even those murderers at Liverpool Street today.'

Jacob said nothing. He had heard similar stories during his time on the streets and he knew it was all true, but he couldn't think of any comforting words. Maybe there weren't any. He waited for Brandon to continue.

'The day I found the Refuge was the day my life changed for the better. I felt safe for the first time in years. They listened to me, looked after me and gave me chances I'd never had before. The biggest thing was the computer room. I'd been pretty good at school with that sort of thing, probably because I could do it alone and I'd always had a logical, mathematical mind, and I seemed to understand computers and their language the way I couldn't understand people.

'I was also intrigued by the City, which was right on our doorstep, and I spent almost all of my time at one of the Refuge's computers, researching the financial markets and writing programs to track market trends. Everyone at the Refuge encouraged me, and in fact one of the volunteers even gave me a little money to open a trading account. Incredible generosity. That tiny account soon grew, and by the time I was eighteen I'd made enough money to buy this place. Hard to believe, but true.'

Brandon paused and looked at his father's rapt expression. He realised that he'd done all the talking and had been in full flow. But he'd said everything he wanted to, for now, and the rest would come out in time.

'So, now you know about me. What about you and Mum, what happened to you? Is Mum OK, do you know?'

As soon as the words left his mouth, Brandon saw a change in his father and instantly knew the answer to his last question. When Jacob didn't answer, he tried again in a softer voice.

'Dad, how's Mum?'

Jacob rested his furrowed brow on his fingers as he struggled to find the words. Then, through bloodshot eyes and tears, he told Brandon what he'd already guessed.

'There's no easy way to say this. I'm sorry, Brandon, your Mum died. I thought you'd have known already, somehow...'

Jacob's voice trailed off and silence filled the void between them, punctuated only by a single high-pitched gulp when Brandon drew in air and fought to retain control of his emotions. But he didn't cry, not yet. That would come later. Instead, he sat in shock and watched his wretched father, the agony and guilt etched on his tear-soaked face, and wondered how often he relived this torture. Eventually Brandon asked the question, even though he wasn't sure he wanted the answer.

'How did it happen, Dad?'

'Overdose... sleeping pills. I came home from work one night, after wining and dining as you called it, and there she was, in our bed. Beautiful, even in death...'

Jacob took a moment to compose himself. 'The coroner ruled it accidental, but I don't think it was. The thing is, she never had any trouble sleeping, except when I woke her up with one of my nightmares. They were becoming more frequent, more violent, maybe because I was drinking too hard. The sleeping tablets were mine.'

Jacob let the words sink in before he added, in a voice so low it was barely audible, 'I killed her, as surely as if I'd fed her the pills myself.'

Brandon didn't know what to say, so he sat still and let Jacob gather his thoughts. He knew there was more to come. After a few moments, Jacob continued in a hoarse whisper.

'After she died, I tried to carry on without her, but it was no use. I was drinking heavily and my nightmares were getting worse. Every night I'd wake up drenched from a horror I couldn't really remember, just fading shapes and shadows. My demons. One day I drank too much and started a fight at a bank function, and I knew that was the end. I didn't even wait to be fired. That night I didn't make it home, I just drifted into the Barbican and found a bench to sleep on. I never went home again.'

They fell silent. Neither knew what else to say or how to console the other, and they reverted to their tried and tested method of handling their grief and sorrows, the way they had learned through thousands of nights in solitude and fear. They kept their thoughts to themselves and suffered alone.

Brandon was first to break the silence. He stood and reached for his hoodie.

'Where are you going?' Jacob asked, perplexed.

'I've changed my mind,' Brandon said, before giving a wan smile. 'We both need a drink. Wait here and I'll bring something back, I'll only be a few minutes.'

Jacob raised his eyebrows in surprise but said nothing.

'Make yourself at home and take a look around.' He pointed towards his spare bedroom. 'That's your room, that is, assuming you'll stay the night.'

When he returned clutching a couple of bottles, Brandon had half expected to find his apartment empty. But Jacob still sat in the same spot, lost in his melancholy thoughts and dark memories, as if oblivious to Brandon's short absence. But he looked up when Brandon placed the bottles on the table, and Brandon knew from his father's expression that he had made the right choice.

They drank together, cried and laughed together and, both exhausted, fell asleep on the sofas together.

He tipped his head forward and kissed Leila's hair, the smell of salt mingled with her own natural perfume as they sat on the sofa after spending the afternoon on the beach. She had fallen asleep in her father's arms to the sound of him reading one of her favourite stories, the Frog Prince, and was now curled up in the crook of his arm, which moved to the rhythm of her slow, deep breathing.

It had been one of those clear, bright early-autumn days where the cool breeze did its best to erase the final residue of summer, but the sun's rays were still strong enough to stay warm, just. They had all donned light jumpers and had wandered along the shingle beach, where Leila had collected shells in her bucket and chased seagulls. After turning back for home, Jacob hoisted Leila onto his shoulders and she squealed when the sea breeze blew her hair into her eyes and around her head. Selma clutched Leila's bucket in one hand and squeezed Jacob's free hand in the other.

They so rarely had time together. Even when Jacob was home from a tour he would be shattered, both mentally and physically. Afternoons like these were so few, so precious, and Jacob wanted to stay snuggled up on the sofa until Leila woke. But he glanced up and saw Selma looking at him, her contented smile full of love for them both, and he ached for her. Torn, he asked if he should carry Leila to her bed, but Selma shook her head, still smiling, and said, 'No, Jacob, stay with her, you don't have enough time together and she needs you.'

For once, Jacob wasn't jolted back to reality panic-stricken from a terrifying nightmare. Instead, he drifted into consciousness longing to return to his dream, where he could escape his miserable life. It took him a couple of seconds to remember where he was, and then his eyes settled on Brandon asleep on the other sofa. The lights were still on and half-drunk glasses of whisky sat on the table next to a near-empty bottle.

Jacob's head pounded when he stood to go to the lavatory, choosing the one in the room Brandon had indicated earlier. The bathroom was spotless and he instantly regretted drying his hands when he saw the vivid streaks across the towel afterwards. He felt grimy and worthless, and his reflection in the bedroom mirror on the way out didn't alter his opinion.

Jacob stared at Brandon for an age. He saw Leila, he couldn't help it, the beautiful, fine lines of her face and the small, turned up nose reminding him of Selma. She was his princess, a latter-day one who had turned adversity into triumph and risen above the harsh bullying of her youth to create her own version of a happy ending. Except that she wasn't happy, not yet, and wouldn't be until she'd completed her transformation into a prince. Whether that was enough, Jacob didn't know, but if he was going to be part of it, he had to banish his thoughts of Leila, his daughter, and devote himself to Brandon, his son.

If I'm going to be part of it. Jacob took the photograph of Selma and Leila from his pocket, the images worn and faded. It was time to let Leila go. Jacob knew that Brandon yearned for his love and respect, but first of all he needed his acceptance. But Jacob wasn't sure he was ready to live with him. Apart from his false pride in regarding Brandon's hospitality as charity, Jacob didn't think he was prepared to return to society. Just like the Refuge's itchy sheets had made him anxious to leave, so the elegant furnishings of Brandon's apartment made him feel uncomfortable. Too many clean towels.

Jacob needed time and space to think. He dropped the photo onto the table and picked up the bottle, and looked a final time at Brandon. He slipped out of the loft and back onto the cold, harsh, City streets.

24

He heard the latch of the door and woke up with a start. Brandon pushed himself up on his elbows and groaned. He struggled to open his eyes against the blaze of brilliant light that pierced his eyelids and ignited an inferno in his head. *Why are the lights still on, and why such a headache?* And then he remembered.

He squinted and saw that his father wasn't on the sofa, and even in his fragile state it didn't take long to search the loft and discover that Jacob had gone. On reflection, Brandon wasn't surprised. It was inevitable that he would feel stifled by the loft's atmosphere and events of yesterday, and hopefully he would be back later. He picked up the tattered photo, discarded by Jacob on his way out, and he ran his fingers gently over the paper. *I remember this, the beach*, and a tear ran down his cheek.

He knew that he wouldn't sleep again, so Brandon shuffled into his den and looked at how the Far Eastern markets were doing, already well into their trading day. He played with a few numbers, but his heart wasn't in it, and he flicked through the news channels. He watched a re-run of a statement from the Prime Minister, who referred to the atrocity as a 'crime against humanity and civilised society' and described the terrorists as having 'a warped ideology.' Brandon rolled his eyes at the language, which he'd never understood. Why did politicians insist on giving terrorists credibility and propaganda by saying their barbarous acts were inspired by an ideology? What was wrong with calling them what they were: murderers without a cause? It never occurred to Brandon that others might say something similar about his actions as a cyber-terrorist.

Then a new update interrupted his musings.

'Counter terrorism agencies now believe that the cyber-attack yesterday was not linked to the bombings, and that the timing and location were entirely coincidental. Sources close to the Government have revealed that the virus used in the attack may actually have impeded the bombing, as it prevented the terrorists from detonating their explosives remotely because of the loss of signal to the remote trigger. According to investigators, this explains why the perpetrators resorted to manually setting off the devices, as shown by those dramatic pictures of the chase across the station concourse yesterday. The cyber-attack is also reported to have prompted many people to leave the station in the minutes leading up to the bomb and, as a result, it is believed that the loss of life was significantly lower than it might otherwise have been, although that will be of no comfort to yesterday's victims.'

Brandon smiled at the conclusion, even though in his own mind he believed that his attack may have made things worse, if only because it hampered rescue efforts.

'And in another twist to this story, there have been numerous reports of unexpectedly large donations to

charities across the UK yesterday, which appear to have been made during the time when the banking system was subject to the Denial of Service attack. Some financial commentators have linked the donations to the spike in Bitcoin activity witnessed during the cyber-attack, with a growing body of evidence that the payments came from accounts at the Bank of England, although so far there has been no word from Threadneedle Street on these rumours. One financial security expert has now coined the phrase "the Robin Hood virus" to describe the infectious computer code used in yesterday's cyber-attack, as it appears to have been responsible for a redistribution of wealth to the charities sector.'

Brandon thought about the new name for his virus, which would no doubt stick in hacker folklore once the dust had settled. They were right, he had transferred money from the banks to the needy, not only the poor but also to the sick and vulnerable. It remained to be seen whether the funds were returned, or if they were considered proceeds of crime, but that would be up to the Bank of England and the Financial Conduct Authority. In any event, he decided that he liked *Robin Hood virus* better than *Replicant*.

Brandon let out a huge sigh. He knew he wasn't completely safe yet, as people cleverer than him and computers far more powerful than his would be combing through the detail of the attack, looking for errors, computer signatures or the tiniest clue that might lead them to Brandon's door. But he felt better about it now, despite his lingering doubts about how the phone outage may have hindered the response to the bombing. He had committed numerous serious crimes, but at least his motivation shouldn't be doubted.

Brandon looked over his shoulder at the door, although he wasn't anxious about discovery. He longed to hear a knock. From his father.

***

Jacob wandered the familiar streets. It was dark and quiet, before the first early-risers and zombeciles arrived at their City desks. But he knew one person who would be working.

He paused at the gates of the Honourable Artillery Company, unlike the last time when he'd hurried past. He would have to exorcise many of his demons if he was to make things work with Brandon and, although he knew he'd never erase the deep scars of his time in the Army, it was time to face the enemy head on.

He strode through the Beech Street car park entrance and chuckled when he heard Whoopi's shriek.

'Oh, my good sweet Jesus. Jacob! I knew it, I said you'd come back here soon. Now let me take a good look at our returning hero.'

Whoopi vacated her booth and rushed towards Jacob. She crushed him in a bear hug and he winced from the pain in his sore rib.

'Oh, I'm sorry, how could I forget that?'

'No need to apologise, Whoopi. I came to thank you for helping me the other night and getting me to the Refuge. I hadn't forgotten, I was just occupied with other things.'

'Yes, we know all about that,' she said in a quieter, sombre tone. 'It's been all over the news. Wasn't it terrible? And you were so brave, chasing that murderer across the station.'

'It's not bravery, it's what anyone would have done. And I didn't stop him. Many people died.'

'But no one else did do it, Jacob, only you. From what I saw, everybody else ran away.'

Jacob had no response, as what Whoopi said was true. But he still felt inadequate and awkward, no matter how often people called him a hero.

'Anyway, I told them you would come, and we have a little surprise for you. You'll see, just go straight to the entrance.'

Puzzled by her comments, Jacob opened his mouth to ask what she meant, but her waving hands shooed him away. 'Go on, away with you!'

Whoopi watched Jacob until he turned the corner to enter the labyrinth beneath the Barbican, then picked up the phone in her booth.

'Jacob's on his way to you now. I told you he'd come back.'

Phone in hand, for the first time since watching the terrorists arrive at Rivington Street, Donovan allowed herself a smile. *It's time to end this*, and she dialled the number.

***

Jacob scratched his head at the sight in front of him. He had retraced his steps from a few days earlier, to the foot of Shakespeare Tower, but now found a makeshift sign taped to the door:

JACOB, THIS WAY =>

He had no idea who had put it there, although he suspected Whoopi had something to do with it following her earlier abstract comments. He opened the door a few inches and peeked through the gap, wondering if it was a prank, but then he saw another sign taped to the doors of one of the tower's lifts:

JACOB, USE THE LIFT

He smiled. Not only had they known he was coming, but whoever had placed these signs on the doors also knew where he was going. The building staff must have known about his visits all along.

Jacob called the lift and pressed the button for the top floor. He ascended all the way without stopping and everything was quiet when he stepped out. He walked up the two flights of stairs to the roof's emergency exit but, on this occasion, there was no need for him to short-circuit it. The door was already wedged open and a third sign confronted him:

JACOB, THANK YOU
ENJOY THE VIEW

He wasn't sure what to make of this welcome. The last person he had seen was Whoopi, and yet the signs must only have been put in place, and the door opened, a few minutes before his arrival. He was surprised he hadn't seen or heard anyone else. But why was he was getting the red-carpet treatment? *Is it because of what happened at Liverpool Street?*

Jacob stepped onto the roof and then climbed up the steel ladder to the second level, skirted by railings. He gripped the top rail and savoured the tingling sensation of the metal on his fingers and palms, cold but reassuring, and looked towards the eastern horizon's kaleidoscope. He witnessed the subtle changes in light and hue in reverent silence and, as always in this moment, considered the contrasts in his life. He grieved for the people who had lost their lives the day before and agonised that he hadn't been able to save more. But he also rejoiced that, out of the darkness of that hour, he had found Brandon. He felt fresh hope, that life could be good again, a life reborn.

Jacob knew that behind him to the west were the darkness, death and desolation of the previous day. So he didn't turn, he stared into the distance at the majestic view of the sunrise as he felt the simple pleasure of the wind on his face. He waited until the last wisps of colour had disappeared and the sky was a clear, crisp blue, and then it was time to go back.

He whispered his usual parting words. 'Time to go.'

'Not so fast, soldier.' Jacob recognised the coarse, grating voice, and an icy numbness seized him.

'Turn around, very slowly, and keep your hands where I can see them.'

Jacob did as he was ordered and looked straight into the barrel of Michael's gun, and then beyond it, his contemptible, sneering face.

'Surprise, surprise,' he said with malevolent glee. 'I bet you didn't think you'd see me again. Everyone assumed I'd make a run for it and the last place they'll look for me is the City, so I thought I'd pay you a visit. Orla told me about your pointless little trips up here, so I figured it was just a matter of waiting for you to turn up. Thanks for not making me wait too long.'

Jacob had recovered from the shock of seeing Michael. 'Why would you bother? It's not as though I stopped Paddy. You got what you wanted. You've murdered dozens of people and ruined the lives of many more. What have you got to gain from killing me, just one more person?'

'Ah, but it's not just one more person, is it? You're a hero according to all the TV reports and newspapers, someone who fought for his country, including time fighting my people. You're a marked man now, a dead man walking.' Michael's hatred for Jacob was evident from his curled lip and spitting words.

'Yes, I read the reports, particularly the ones from those American newspapers who publish more than they should, like snippets that your stupid British intelligence have given them. So I know you were in the lock-up watching us and that you led the armed police to Liverpool Street. You know too much about me and what we did to let you live.'

Jacob scanned the roof for an opportunity to escape, but there were no weapons of any kind and no way out. He was trapped, but he edged backwards and kept Michael talking.

'But what do I know that everyone else doesn't? You bombed Liverpool Street and Paddy died so that you could murder almost forty people.'

Michael looked at Jacob with a puzzled expression and then a look of astonishment appeared on his face. 'Oh my God, you don't know, do you?'

He started to laugh and Jacob felt the hairs stand up on the back of his neck. Somehow, he had missed something and, judging from Michael's reaction, it was big. What on earth was he laughing at? Jacob didn't have to wait long to find out.

'You fool, you actually think Paddy sacrificed himself to kill forty people?'

Michael couldn't contain his surprise and delight at the revelation that Jacob didn't know the full details of their operation.

'So, our hero doesn't know, eh? Well, before you die, I'm going to let you in on it, and the full extent of your stupidity will be the last thing that goes through your head, other than a bullet that is.'

Jacob reached the railing and stopped. Was this going to be the end, listening to Michael's boasts before being executed in cold blood?

'Today you are a hero, but in a couple of days' time you will be the idiot who helped us to conceal our real weapon. You see, this wasn't about the bombs, it wasn't about killing people at the station.' Michael paused and sneered at Jacob. 'It was all about the yoghurts. Almost a thousand yoghurts, each containing two drops of a highly contagious, fatal bacterium. Just think of it, out there right now, infecting one of the most populated areas of Britain. That's what we were doing in the lock-up, didn't you see us? Surely you didn't think we were only changing the labels.'

Jacob closed his eyes and cast his mind back to the lock-up. The two men below him had been out of sight most of the time they were altering the yoghurts. He only saw the final product, not what they did, but Michael's description explained the gloves and masks. How could he have been so stupid to think that terrorists were concerned about hygiene? He opened his eyes and his look of fear and resignation told Michael everything he needed to know.

Michael turned the screw. 'Its symptoms won't be apparent yet, and when they are it will be too late for those infected. The powerful neurotoxins will overwhelm them all, by which time they will already have passed on the infection to their families and friends. You see, the bomb was a decoy, which had the added advantage of destroying the remaining evidence.'

Jacob's head was reeling at the vision Michael had painted and the abhorrence of mass murder being described as a decoy. More importantly, he knew he had only a few moments to act if he was to prevent an atrocity of even greater proportions.

'So, that leaves me with just one final act. You will die and you won't be remembered as a hero, but the man who was in the lock-up and failed to stop the bacterium.' Michael's voice was flint, no longer even a hint of mirth, as he assumed the role of executioner. 'So, kneel before me.'

Jacob put his left hand on his knee as if steadying himself to bend down. He raised his right foot and felt the heel of his boot rest against the lower steel rail behind him, and he put his right hand into his coat pocket. He prayed that Michael wouldn't be able to resist a few further words, or a final insult. People were always less observant and slower to react when speaking.

'Easy as that, no fight in you,' he said. 'I always knew you British soldiers—'

Jacob exploded away from the railings and launched himself with full force at Michael. His right foot drove hard against the bottom rail, like a sprinter leaving the blocks, and propelled him forward and upward. The bottle in his hand swung round in a wide arc towards Michael's head.

A shot tore through the morning air and Jacob's left shoulder erupted with searing pain, but he crunched into Michael before he could get a second shot away. The bottle glanced off Michael's arm and then shattered when the two men hit the ground hard, Jacob on top.

They wrestled, but it wasn't an even contest. Jacob screamed in agony at the bolts of pain that engulfed his shoulder and chest, and Michael pushed him away. But despite his injuries, Jacob used all of his might to launch himself again at Michael, and his flailing right hand caught his enemy across the face with the severed neck of the bottle, still in his grasp. A shriek of pain and fury followed and Jacob saw Michael lunge for his pistol, on the ground three or four feet to his right. With one final, extraordinary effort, Jacob threw himself at Michael, and his weapon skittered away across the concrete.

The two men toppled together through the railings, over the side of the upper tier, and landed in the narrow walkway next to the concrete wall below, the only thing saving them from a forty-storey plunge to the Barbican terraces. Michael saw his chance and shoved Jacob back towards a low opening in the wall, designed to allow window cleaners to scale down the side of the tower. Jacob registered too late that he was going through the gap, but his last desperate act was to grab Michael's jacket sleeve with his right hand as he tried to stop back-pedalling. If he was going over, so was Michael.

Their momentum took them both to the edge and Michael gave one last hard shove as Jacob's heels hit the dwarf wall and his knees buckled at the low railing above it. His body arched backwards over the edge and Jacob felt a surge of panic at the sight of windows tapering almost to nothing below. His left hand found the railing and his legs locked around it, and he slewed to the side.

The momentum of his tumble backwards and the vice-like grip of his right hand on Michael's jacket brought the terrorist teetering over the edge, and for a split-second Jacob thought Michael had stopped. But he hadn't. His toes thudded into the wall and Jacob's weight pulled him over the edge head first. With a scream that pierced the morning air, Michael somersaulted over.

Jacob felt a rush of excruciating pain through his injured shoulder and ribs, but his hand grasped the railing for dear life. His legs took most of his weight, although they were already starting to tremble as his muscles strained against their unnatural angle.

But his real problem was Michael. Whether by luck or through a strong instinct for self-preservation at the moment Jacob had pulled him over the edge, Michael had somehow gripped Jacob's wrist, so that Jacob was now bearing the weight of them both.

Jacob clung onto the railing with his weakening left hand. He looked down at Michael and saw that he was trying to find a foothold on the window ledge below, but couldn't quite reach. His frantic motions were making it harder for Jacob to hold on, and he knew he could continue for a couple of seconds at most.

Then he heard a sound, above him. Someone else was on the roof. Maybe, just maybe, he was going to get out of this alive. His ears strained, his muscles spasmed and he called out as loudly as he could for help. Then he saw the face of a smiling, serene, beautiful woman, dark haired and slender, right above him. She put her hand over his, as he clasped the railing, and spoke to him in a voice as soft as cotton wool. *Selma?*

'Jacob, let go. It's time. You've done all you can. Give it up.'

No, it couldn't be Selma. She'd gone, and she'd never ask him to give up, not now that he'd found Brandon. And then Jacob stared into her eyes. Softness turned to stone and tenderness became brutality, and he saw the emptiness and inhumanity in Donovan's soul.

He was completely lucid; his mind was clear and he accepted what he had to do. He thought of his life. His childhood and his parents, they flickered in front of him, then old friends from school and in the Army, forgotten for years until now, rushed past. Selma and Leila. Whoopi. Orla and Maria. Selma and Leila again. Brandon.

His life. Brandon.

He looked down into Michael's hateful, evil eyes, and saw the look of realisation dawn on him. 'You wouldn't dare,' he screamed, the fear of inevitable and imminent death in his voice.

'Time to go,' Jacob said.

Epilogue

Orla's phoned vibrated on her bedside table and she opened her eyes with a sigh. She hadn't been sleeping well since returning to her flat, and even the slightest sound would wake her, no matter what time, day or night. Considering what had happened to her, it was hardly surprising that she was still on edge when alone in this place, especially with memories of Michael still fresh in her mind.

She glanced at the clock; seven-thirty, not too early, and it was probably just Harry texting to let her know what time he'd be round later. She smiled, leaned over and picked up her mobile. But she raised her eyebrows when she saw the name next to the message.

Are you OK? A tough few days? Brandon

Why would Brandon be texting her now? They'd had no contact since bumping into each other the day before the bombing. Curious, she gave a guarded response:

Fine thanks. Everyone tells me time is a great healer.

Orla doubted her scars would heal any time soon. She hadn't returned to the crèche or the Refuge yet, but she did need to get back to normality soon, although in retrospect she struggled to see how her previous life could be described as normal. Her phone buzzed again:

Me too. That's why I need to speak to you. It's about Jacob. B

Orla stared at the screen, unable to work out what Brandon meant. Was this yet another example of how little she knew about people in her past life? It was time to find out:

What about Jacob?

I'll tell you in person. Can we meet for breakfast? B

OK, I can't sleep anyway. Where and when?

When Orla arrived, Brandon was at the same table he had occupied during his *Replicant* test. Was that really only a week ago? It seemed a lifetime, and so much had happened since then.

He half stood and waved, and Orla joined him at the table. She looked older than when he'd seen her outside the Refuge; drawn, pale and exhausted. It was no surprise after what she'd been through, but she managed a weak smile and gave her order to Gianluca.

'Twice in a week. We'll have to stop meeting like this or people will talk,' Orla said with an attempt at humour. 'Although to be honest that would be better than what they're saying about me right now.'

She was right. Social media had been awash with malicious and unfeeling comments about how Orla must have known that Michael was a terrorist or, if she hadn't, questioning what sort of woman she was. Very few said anything about her work at the Refuge and her history of kindness and sacrifices for the homeless, as that wouldn't be sensational enough to gain any attention for the authors, or 'likes'. Instead, the trolls did what they always do. In their ignorance, they hid behind the anonymity of the internet and spread lies and half-truths without any regard for the consequences of their spite and cruelty.

Tears rolled down Orla's face and Brandon squeezed her hand. His words of comfort were inadequate, clichéd, but he felt he had to say something.

'I know it doesn't feel like it, but it will get better. You couldn't have known about him, couldn't have stopped him. If it hadn't been you, it would have happened to someone else. Just thank God that you got away.'

'Unlike Jenny.' Orla wiped her tears away. 'But at least Maria is pulling through, and hopefully she'll be back at the Refuge in the next day or so. But it will take a long time for her psychological scars to heal, given how close she got to those bastards. Believe me, I know how that feels.'

Brandon let the anger of Orla's words subside before raising the subject he had come to discuss.

'I've never met Maria, but Jacob mentioned her to me, as well as you of course, on the night of the bombing. He also told me all about Michael and what he did in the lock-up, but he obviously didn't know about the bacterium or he would have mentioned that too.'

Orla looked at Brandon, puzzled. 'You saw him the night of the bombing, before he went to the tower the next morning?'

Brandon nodded, but said nothing.

'But how do you know Jacob? I thought you left the Refuge before he came to us.'

'That's what I wanted to tell you, before you heard it from anyone else. It's bound to come out sooner or later.' He braced himself and took a deep breath. 'Jacob's my father. I saw him that night for the first time in eight years.'

Orla sat in stunned silence, a look of bewilderment on her face. Brandon saw her study his features and then her eyes opened wide and she slowly shook her head.

'My God, I don't know why I didn't see it before. I knew some of your history and Jacob's, and now I can see the resemblance, but I never put two and two together. If I had, you could have been reunited so much earlier and maybe things would have turned out differently. I'm so sorry, Brandon.'

'That's not why I'm telling you, Orla. As you said, we weren't at the Refuge at the same time and there was no reason to make the connection.' He looked into her glistening eyes. 'Anyway, I don't think things would have turned out any better. Probably would have been worse, as I wasn't ready to see him. Maybe it was fate, as our lives would have been different and then he wouldn't have been in the lock-up or saved anyone at Liverpool Street. In a way, we should be happy that you never made the connection.'

Orla appreciated Brandon's effort to make her feel better, and she could see his point. Over the past couple of days, she had started to come to terms with it all, and she knew that Michael hadn't been stupid enough to give her any clues about his activities. But that didn't stop her replaying everything over and over again in her mind, and she doubted whether she'd ever fully forgive herself.

Orla had also received similar pep talks from Harry, who had visited her every day since the bombing. Although it made her feel guilty and a little embarrassed, Harry's attention had given her a boost when she needed it most, with hope for a brighter future. She could feel her optimism grow, little by little.

'I suppose you're right, and maybe we wouldn't have found out about the bacterium in time either. Talking of which, don't you find it amazing that most of the news reports have been more interested in how Jacob survived, and the gruesome details of Michael's death, than the thousands of people saved from the neurotoxin?'

'Nothing the media says surprises me anymore,' Brandon said, and then he grinned. 'But you must admit, my dad's survival was incredible, especially when you consider that he only lived because Michael's impaling slowed them both down. The media were bound to love him after that, so soon after the recording of him at Liverpool Street.'

'You're right,' said Orla, shivering at the memories of some of the more graphic images that had appeared in the press and on social media. 'But they've hardly given him any credit for what he revealed about the bacteria in the yoghurts. Quite frankly it's amazing he could say anything with his injuries, and as far as I'm aware it's all he's said so far. His will to save others must be so strong. But at least he appears to be off the critical list now.'

'When he's out of hospital, he'll stay with me until he's completely better, and I'll try to keep the vultures away from my door.'

Brandon shuddered at the thought of what the intrusive media might uncover about his history, once they knew Jacob was his father. He was surprised that they hadn't found out already. But he knew that looking after him was the only proper choice. It was a chance he had to take.

He held Orla's gaze. 'Look, Orla, everything I have is thanks to you. You believed in me, supported me and even gave what little you had to set up an account for me. Without you, I wouldn't have this chance with my father, and I can never thank you enough.'

Orla shook her head. 'No, Brandon, you've earned this yourself. If I helped in any way, I'm glad, but you both deserve it and I hope it works out for you. You have exciting times ahead.'

Brandon and Orla finished their breakfast, talking about old times and shared memories. They had endured severe hardships in their lives, but they had survived and now they both had the chance of a fresh start. At the door they had a long, tender hug. Neither of them felt at all confident about anything in their future, but they promised to stay in touch. They squeezed hands, then walked away in opposite directions.

Orla's phone pinged. She looked at it and stopped immediately. Her heart pounded at the bright purple screen with its simple message:

THANK YOU

She dismissed the message and her screen turned orange:

LET'S CALL IT INTEREST ON THE MONEY YOU LENT ME

Her trembling finger hovered over the 'X' button, then she closed the box. Her mobile banking app opened, with her bank account balance displayed on screen. Orla gasped.

She span on the spot and glimpsed Brandon's back, moments before he disappeared round the corner.

NO
REFUGE

Acknowledgements

I find myself writing something I never thought I would. It's not that I don't want to thank people for the help they've given me, it's the realisation that this is the last act before I finish *No Refuge*. Once this is done, there really is nothing to stop me from pushing the button to publish it. I feel a bit like Brandon, wondering whether I am doing the right thing unleashing my work on an unsuspecting public, praying for no unintended consequences and hoping that it will be worth it in the end.

When I set out to write *No Refuge*, I think anyone who knows me thought that I just needed to get it out of my system. They were probably right. The idea for this novel came to me as I walked across the concourse at Liverpool Street almost twenty years ago, so it has taken a long time to get this story into print. My demon, maybe? The central plot is the same as it was then, although the story I have told is not quite the one I originally imagined, partly because the world is so different now, but also because I changed course several times whilst writing it. This meandering was usually the result of conversations with family and friends, and some of the elements I introduced were ones I knew little about but which I hoped would fit in.

It may seem an odd choice to many people, but I decided not to research these new subjects, as I wanted to avoid entangling myself in technical areas that I would probably never fully understand. As the saying goes, a little knowledge is a dangerous thing. However, my self-imposed ignorance gave me an excuse to employ a little artistic licence in certain areas, for example to distort how Bitcoin works or to exaggerate the ability of hackers to commandeer your phone. This is fiction, after all, not a tutorial on the complexities of our technology-obsessed world.

So, to the acknowledgements. First of all, I will thank everyone I know from the Emerald Isle, for forgiving me that I portrayed the terrorists as Irish. Some of the loveliest and most welcoming people I know are from Ireland, but it just seemed to work best with Jacob's history to create the Brethren, a dissident organisation with its roots in the troubles. If there really is such an organisation, or if the characters are in any way similar to real people, that is entirely coincidental.

Whilst on the subject of factual inaccuracies and coincidences, I should say that many of the places in *No Refuge* actually do exist. The majority of the street names and major places such as the Barbican and Liverpool Street are clearly real, but the businesses, shops, pubs, brands and the like are mostly made up, with one or two exceptions. The Refuge isn't based on anywhere in particular, nor as far as I'm aware did St Michael's church establish a homeless shelter (the actual church exists, but when I last checked it was occupied by an architectural ironmonger). In Rivington Street, there was once a comedy club near the railway arches, but it has since been demolished to make way for another social venue. That just goes to show that the gradual redevelopment and renovation of Shoreditch highlighted in the book is happening, whatever you think of it, just not exactly as I described.

I owe a huge debt to my friend, Rob Kaczmarek, for offering to read my first draft at the end of 2017. At that time, I thought I'd nailed it after only a few months, but sadly that was not the case. I took Rob's scholarly feedback on board, swallowed my pride and produced my second draft, and from there I started the long process of editing and re-editing my novel. I don't know how many drafts I've discarded since then, but I think the end result is as close to the finished article it can be without starting again from scratch. That's not something I have contemplated. As I write today, this version of *No Refuge* is quite different to the one Rob saw, so any technical errors, character inconsistencies, daft plots or typos are fully down to me. I don't even have anyone else to blame for the cover artwork, as that is also all me. Literally. That's me in the hoodie, although I doubt anyone recognises me after the heavy doctoring of the selfie. I sincerely hope not.

Supporting me lovingly and putting up with my cursing have been my darling wife Elaine and our three beautiful girls. They will probably never realise how much their chatter around the dinner table influenced this book, which they may find surprising given it is a novel about terrorists. I've given up calling it a terrorist thriller, as I believe there is now more to it than that, with the twists and turns the book took during editing. Also, when you've read a passage dozens of times, it tends to lose its thrill. I hope you find it otherwise.

My final acknowledgement is reserved for the characters, in particular the residents and helpers at the Refuge, and those like them all over the UK. This book may be fiction, but the world of homelessness is only too appallingly real, despite the efforts of many to get people like Jacob off the streets. I hope that in reading this book you feel compelled to help in some way, by volunteering like Orla or donating like Brandon. Please just don't rob the Bank of England to do it.

Author's Note

Thank you for buying this book. The net royalties I receive from *No Refuge* sales (whether paperback or e-book) will be donated to charities related to its characters, primarily those that help the homeless or members of our armed forces and their families. Like Brandon, I think this is the best way for me to support their cause. If you enjoyed reading *No Refuge*, please consider leaving a review on Amazon. It takes just a few moments and a good review may encourage others to buy the book, thereby swelling the royalty pot for these causes.

You may hold me to my promise to donate, from which I will seek *No Refuge*. Thank you.

Printed in Great
Britain
by Amazon